NEVER DATE YOUR EX

NEVER DATE YOUR EX

USA TODAY BESTSELLING AUTHOR

JULES BARNARD

Prologue

Mira

I turn in time to see the biggest girl in my junior high school grab my backpack and swing it in a wide loop—with me attached.

I lose my balance and land hard on the ground.

"What do you want, Britney?" I say, annoyed, my knee throbbing where it hit the concrete.

Britney's bangs are cut short and blunt across her forehead, giving her the caveman look when she glares. "Isn't your mom a hooker? I heard she sold you to the Sallees."

Her lisp is so heavy it takes me a second to figure out who she's referring to. And then my face heats at the crude reference to the family I live with.

Kids give Britney a wide berth, including the three girls on either side of her, but I'm not like other kids.

I lunge and shove her. Only I'm small for my age, so she barely budges.

Britney catches my shoulders with her long octopus arms, the other girls laughing behind her. "Do you let their

1

son Lewis *kiss* you? *Eww,* Mira. Are you going to be a hooker like your mom?"

I hate it when kids spread rumors about my mom.

I swing out my leg and try to nail Britney in the shin, but I miss.

"Who will you live with once Lewis doesn't want you anymore?"

For some reason, that sentence isn't jumbled by her speech. It comes out loud and clear.

The fight drains from my body and my arms drop to my sides.

I'm used to being picked on for my size, for where I came from, for the stories about my mom. None of it matters. But Britney said the one thing that does.

Lewis and his family told me they'd take care of me, but everyone leaves eventually.

Britney shoves my shoulders, sending me flying off balance.

My palms slam onto the pavement, and I stare at the grainy surface, the heat from the cement coating my skin.

My brain races a million miles an hour, and goes nowhere. Where would I go if the Sallees didn't want me anymore?

I don't know how long I kneel on all fours, but the sound of feet skittering catches my attention. I brush dark strands of hair off my face and look up...into pale blue eyes glowing with concern.

"You okay?"

The boy standing over me has high cheekbones and slightly hollow cheeks. He is tall, but skinny. I like his face. He has kind eyes.

He glances past me, sending an angry glare over my shoulder. "Leave her alone from now on," he calls.

I look around to see that the mean girls have taken off and are halfway across the empty parking lot.

The boy gives me a quick survey, then grabs my backpack. "Come on. I'll walk you home."

I sit on my butt and pull my knees to my chin, brushing gravel and dirt from my hands. "I'm riding the bus."

He swings my backpack over the shoulder that's not occupied by his large pack. "I'll walk you there."

For all his height, the two backpacks look like they might knock him over, but they don't. He's strong.

We make the trip in silence, and I wonder if he will leave me once we get to the bus stop. I want him to stay. Which is weird. Aside from the Sallees, who took me in when I was three, I'm not comfortable around people.

"I'm Tyler," he says, as we approach the pickup spot. His gaze flickers to me, but he doesn't stare.

I mumble my name and Tyler hangs out with me until the long yellow bus pulls up.

The driver opens the pivoting door and Tyler hands me my backpack. His mouth presses together in a serious look I've only seen adults use. "You okay?"

I nod and climb the steps to the aisle between the seats. I watch Tyler through the windows as the driver pulls away. He walks in the opposite direction, staring ahead, his wiry arm bent where he shoved his hand into his jeans pocket.

I sit in the rear of the bus and hug my backpack to my chest, a smile on my face.

I should be upset that the girls picked on me—but I'm not. If they hadn't, Tyler might not have shown up.

And I like Tyler.

Chapter One

Mira

Three years later

My fears have always gotten in the way of what I want. But not tonight.

Alicia Keys's "No One" blares through the custom sound system of Holly Walker's living room, her house packed with faces I recognize from the hallways of our high school.

The reason I'm here, when I normally avoid these parties like the plague, is because Tyler Morgan said he was coming.

I rode with Zach, a good friend from the Dresslerville Washoe reservation, who attends high school with me and my foster brother, Lewis.

Lewis is a study-o-holic. He doesn't come to these things, but Zach makes it to all the parties. He's currently homing in on Ella or Bella—some girl from my English class whose name ends with an *a*, like those of all the popular girls.

Technically mine does too, but if people know me, it's for the wrong reasons. *Bitch* and *trash* have been linked to *my* name.

"Zach, you look like you're ready to pounce," I say. "There is such a thing as finesse. You could chat with the girl. Get to know her."

Zach cocks his chiseled jaw to the side. "Why would I want to do that? Ruins the mystique."

For as long as I've known him, Zach has kept girls at arm's length. Emotionally, *not* physically. The guy gets around. I can't fault him. I do the same thing—the emotional distancing, not the hookups. That rumor is false.

He tips his chin up. "You okay here? I'm about to get my swerve on." He flexes his chest. "How are the pecs? Lookin' good?"

I shake my head. "You're lame."

He hugs me in a friendly headlock. "Love ya, Mir. Go hook up or something. It does a body good."

My shoulders stiffen. He has no idea how close he is to the truth.

Zach gives me a little shake. "Loosen up, girl. You got all tense."

I share everything with Zach and Lewis. Except my love life. That would just be weird.

Zach's manwhoring provides hours of banter, but it's a different story to talk about me and boys. That's where having guy friends who are like brothers gets iffy.

"Would ya leave already?" His lingering is making me nervous, and I've got enough on my mind.

Zach kisses his biceps and winks before striding off, angling his wide shoulders past the bodies crowding the living room.

I peer out, searching for my own quarry.

Since Tyler arrived an hour ago, I've been watching him like a stalker chick. Not really my style, but I'm running out of time. He's leaving in a few weeks for college, and if I don't make a move now, I'm afraid I'll lose my chance.

I run a shaky hand through my long, dark hair, and pull a wavy handful over my shoulder, the ends brushing my upper waist. Out of the corner of my eye, I catch the guy next to me checking me out.

I have no interest in other guys. Only one person holds my attention, and he's the one I walk toward.

I'm like Zach tonight, in hot pursuit.

Normally, I let men come to me. I may not be popular with the girls, but with boys it's different.

Lewis and Zach treat me like a sister, but with other guys... Well, they want *something*. Not that I put out. Despite what some people say, I've only kissed a few guys, fooled around with a couple of them, but never given it up.

I'm not sure why I've held on to my V-card. No one expects it of me, and I don't feel pure. It's possible that living with Lewis and his family has rubbed off on me. That I've grown standards without realizing it. But I think I haven't had sex when the opportunity arose for a different reason.

There's only one person I want to be with.

My advisor paired me with Tyler as a math tutor over a year ago. I *might* have requested him when I found out he was looking for students to assist.

The kindness behind Tyler's clear blue eyes when he scared away the group of mean girls in junior high left a lasting impression. I've never forgotten him.

I'm pretty sure he doesn't remember that day. He's never mentioned it, and I didn't remind him during our numerous study sessions together.

I watch as Tyler checks the downstairs bathroom just off Holly Walker's living room. He's bulked up since junior high—become broader in the shoulder and filled out in the chest. He's taller than most of the guys at our high school. Handsome too, but that's not why I like him.

There's something about Tyler that's different from other guys. I'm aware of his every move, the way he smells like peppermint and bike oil from the mountain biking he does, mixed with his laundry detergent. He's laid-back, but attentive, and I like hanging out with him as much as I do with my friends. More so.

When Tyler shows me equations while we study together, I want to smooth my finger over the calluses on his thumb where he holds his pencil too tightly.

Sometimes, when he's not looking, I'll stare at the dark stubble on his chin that shines reddish in the light, and wonder what it would feel like to rub my lips against that stubble and kiss his neck.

It's distracting.

Tyler will leave town soon. I should wait it out and ignore my feelings.

But I won't.

I'm going to do something I've never done before, and open up. Long enough to lose my virginity to the boy I like.

After trying the downstairs bathroom and finding it locked, Tyler shoves a large hand in his jeans pocket and makes his way to the second floor.

I glance around to make sure no one's paying attention, and follow him up the stairs.

Tyler is a year older than me, but two grades higher, because he's super smart and skipped freshman year. Holly's party may be the last chance I have to make a move before he graduates in a few weeks.

The second floor is crowded as well. Tyler moves up another flight, and I stay back until he reaches the landing.

There are four levels to Holly's house. Her parents are loaded, their home equipped with an indoor hot tub and an elevator. A gazillion bedrooms litter the upper levels. It can't be too difficult to get Tyler alone.

He knocks on a third-floor bathroom and enters, closing the door behind him. Most of the party is on the lower floors. Few people wander the top two, so there's privacy up here.

I walk quickly to the end of the hall and peek inside one of the darkened bedrooms. It's empty, so I lean in and set my crossbody purse next to the door, closing it behind me.

My chest is pounding. I press my hand to it and breathe deeply, trying to get calm.

I've sensed something between me and Tyler. I don't think he'll reject what I have to offer, but it will be a challenge to make myself vulnerable around someone other than Lewis or Zach.

I tend to push people away. But Tyler teases me. He doesn't take me too seriously, the way most guys do. Somehow that makes the idea of opening up easier. I wish I could have more with Tyler before he leaves, but I'll settle for this.

Sex...with Tyler.

There goes my heart, racing again.

I swallow and try to compose my face, if not the vital organ ricocheting inside my chest. I walk down the hall and lurk outside the bathroom Tyler entered, psyching myself up for what I'm about to do.

A few seconds pass before Tyler exits with his head tilted down.

Now or never. I step in his path, bumping lightly into him.

"Tyler," I say, feigning surprise. He grabs my arms to steady us, his face inches away. I smile coyly. "If you wanted to touch me, all you had to do was ask."

Wow—lame. I need to work on my pickup lines.

His expression is blank, and for a moment, I wonder if I've botched it. This whole sexual aggression thing is harder than it looks.

"Mira." His gaze softens, settling warmly on my eyes. "I thought I saw you downstairs." He grins—which gets my heart beating faster than ever.

Most people think Tyler's eyes are his best feature. They *are* devastatingly beautiful, but I have to go with his smile. It snares the deepest part of me, rendering me light-headed and dumb.

That smile is a menace. And I can't get enough of it.

My chest does a clench-flutter thing, my mouth twitching into what I hope resembles a happy expression. "How's it going?" I say, as if this is the first I've seen of him tonight, though I've stalked him like a panther.

"Good. You been here long?"

"For a little while." I grab his hand and tug him down the hallway, keeping my shaky grin in place. "Do you mind helping me with something? It's just back here."

His brow furrows in concern. "Sure, anything."

Yet another reason Tyler is perfect. He spent ridiculous amounts of time helping me with math, until I didn't just improve my grade, I aced the class.

Me? An *A* in math? It's all because Tyler cares when few people have. As though he sees potential in me that most people think doesn't exist.

I open the bedroom door and walk inside. "It's just this way."

Tyler chuckles nervously, but he steps into the room behind me. The light from the hallway frames his tall, athletic build. He plucks at his T-shirt and peers around. "So—what'd you need?"

I reach behind him and shut the door, bathing the room in pitch. I press my chest to his and wrap my arms around his neck.

"Just this." I kiss him.

His lips are still at first, his body tense. Then his mouth melts. Enflames. A kiss that sends a shiver through my belly.

His tongue teases mine, hands tightening on my waist...

My breath hitches. This is a mistake. I should have picked a different guy. One who doesn't affect me so much. I like Tyler, and when he leaves...

I pull away.

Tyler's hands slide to my hips, without letting go. "Mira, what's going on? I mean, I'm not complaining..."

What am I doing? I'm ruining it. This is what I've wanted for so long and I'm screwing it up.

Of course he's wondering why his aloof tutoring student is hitting on him. I thought he liked me, but I wasn't a hundred percent sure. Based on the intensity of that kiss, I think we're good in the attraction department. I need to stop freaking out, and go with it.

"Is this okay?" My eyes have adjusted to the dark. I stand on tiptoe and kiss his strong jaw, trailing my lips down his throat, my hands wandering across his wide shoulders and chest to a narrow, flat stomach.

His breath catches and he pulls me closer. "Are you sure? I mean—I didn't know."

I silence that thought with another kiss, my mouth parting and taking whatever he's willing to give.

Tyler is over six feet tall and I have to reach to meet his mouth, but he's holding me firmly, his lips moving eagerly with mine, sending more flutters through my belly, loosening my body along with my nerves.

The more his kiss gives, the farther those flutters spread and migrate, running out of control. He tastes like breath mints, his lips soft and warm, caressing in a way that has my hands shaking against his chest.

Normally, I'd let the guy take control and stop him when he wanted to go too far. But despite Tyler's eager mouth, his hands haven't left my hips.

He's a nice guy; what did I think would happen?

Obviously, I'm going to have to make the next move too.

I run my fingers beneath his shirt, against his warm, smooth skin, touching the contours of a toned chest, built from hours of after-school sports.

I'm just getting into fascinating chest terrain when Tyler pulls away. My fingers freeze and I look into his eyes, their brightness all but gone. In this light they are dark and murky with startling depths.

"Mira, what about downstairs? The party…"

No thinking.

In answer to his question, I raise the hem of his black T-shirt. His arms go up automatically, allowing me to pull the soft cotton over his head. I drop it to the ground, the dark fabric disappearing in the shadows.

Reaching behind him, I fumble for the door and lock it. I grab his hand and lead him to the bed. "It's okay. No one will come in." I sit on the edge of the mattress and gently pull him down.

He doesn't say anything at first. It might have something

to do with the fact that I slipped my top off. I'm bared from the waist up, with the exception of a pretty black bra I splurged and bought on sale from Victoria's Secret.

Tyler touches my naked shoulder. "Ahhh...?" His eyes remain on my breasts for a second, then flutter to my face and lock on my eyes. "I like you. We don't have to do this tonight."

For over a year, I've daydreamed about what it would be like to be Tyler's girlfriend. If he'd take me to the movies, or if we'd hang out at his house with his mom and the sister he's told me about. But that's a fantasy.

Tyler would never want me if he knew where I came from and how messed up my past is. We can never be more than we are, except in this one way.

At least by sharing this, I'll have a piece of him. This moment.

"I'm sure. I want you."

Chapter Two

Tyler

I *want you.*

That was it—the moment I lost my grasp on rational thought and gave in to what I've secretly dreamt of.

I've been in love with Mira Frasier for years, and she wants *me* in a way I only imagined in my fantasies.

I made sure our tutoring sessions ran over when we worked together. She needed help in algebra, but I dragged that shit out, creating any excuse to spend time with her.

I tutored her in math this year as well, though the advisor said it wasn't necessary. Didn't seem prudent to fill Mira in on that point. She could have cancelled our sessions at any time, but I wasn't going to be the one to suggest it.

Mira unbuttons the fly of her jeans, and I help her peel them off along with her shoes. We kiss and touch, and all I can think is, *How the fuck did I get so lucky?*

She reaches behind to unhook the clasp of her bra, and I put my hand over hers. "I got it."

I may have been too chicken to ask her out over the last

year and a half, but I'm not inexperienced. Well, not entirely.

I deftly unhook the clasp and pull the silky fabric away, trying not to stare at her breasts. I lean over her until she's sprawled on the mattress, my body covering hers.

Jesus, am I crushing her?

I brace myself higher. I could stare at Mira's beautiful, tanned curves all night, but I'd rather feel her in my arms beneath me—or above me. I'm not picky. As long as we're together.

Mira is the most beautiful girl I've ever seen, but that's not why she takes my breath away.

I teased her one day. It was out of nowhere. I'm not sure why I did it. She had taped her broken cell phone cover, going so far as to cut out thin strips around the charger outlet. It was cute. I couldn't help myself.

"Duct tape iPhones? Is that all the rage?" I said.

Mira isn't poor. She lives with that rich kid, Lewis, but after the words left my mouth I wondered if she'd deck me. Mira isn't the kind of girl you joke around with. She is tough and beautiful. I've seen her cut down guys twice her size.

But Mira didn't hit me, she laughed. The sound was light, full of life—the kind of laugh I'd raze mountains to hear.

From that day on, my goal was to get Mira to smile. If I managed a grin, my chest puffed up. If I pulled a full belly laugh out of her, I was riding somewhere in the clouds. But the half-smile—a curve of her lips that hinted at naughtiness—Jesus fucking Christ. The half-smiles heated me from the inside out.

Those half-smiles are mischievous and sexy as hell, and I've never seen her look at anyone else that way. It's as though she reserves them just for me. My own secret smile.

I run my lips over her stomach, grazing her upper thigh with my chin and mouth.

God, her skin is soft. And the way she smells, like vanilla and some underlying floral scent, along with something else I can't pinpoint but it has me wanting to plaster my nose to her flesh because I can't fucking get enough. She's perfect.

I have a raging hard-on, but if she wants to stop, I will happily live with blue balls for the rest of my life. As long as I can be close to her.

My lips brush the inside of her thigh, and her mouth parts, a light, breathy sound escaping.

Interesting...

I do it again, this time allowing my lips to linger on her delicate skin.

She releases another, more guttural moan, sending a blast of heat to my groin.

I press my dick into the mattress, stifling the need to explode.

It's torture, these little needy sounds she's giving me, but nothing can stop me from doing whatever it takes to make her feel good.

I move up her body, kissing her above her panties, my arms shaking at the sides of her hips at the restraint it takes not to remove that last bit of fabric and get closer.

"Tyler..." she says.

I suck in a breath at the surge of adrenaline the want in her voice drives through me. The need to be inside her is the most intense rush, my heart pounding, every instinct heightened.

Instead of launching on her the way I'm coiled to do, I slip a finger under the edge of her panties and pause, gauging her reaction.

She lifts for me and I slowly peel them off. And catch myself staring.

There is nothing more beautiful than Mira naked.

I blink and swallow the nerves that have suddenly balled in my throat. I need to at least *look* like I know what I'm doing.

Shaking the haze of lust and awe from my brain, I run my palms up her waist to her breasts, where I kiss and lick. If this is all we share, I'll die a happy man.

Mira shifts and her legs fall to either side of my waist, cradling my erection through my jeans.

All thoughts are blotted from existence, except for the need to be as close as humanly possible to her.

I rub against her center, clenching my teeth at the agonizing warmth and friction. It would feel amazing skin-to-skin...

Can't allow my thoughts to drift there. I'll explode.

She grabs my head and kisses me. "Take off your pants," she breathes near my ear.

Oh God. She's going to kill me.

Is this really happening? Seriously, what is going on? I'm not this lucky.

Despite my hesitation, I do as she says, because I'm not stupid. Dreamland or not, I'm not missing the opportunity to be with this girl.

I remove the rest of my clothes and sit on the edge of the bed, watching as she leans over the mattress and pulls a condom out of the back pocket of her jeans. At least one of us knows what they're doing.

A spark of irritation flares as I consider that thought. Has she done this with other guys? Recently? She lives with Lewis. And there are rumors about them being together...

I don't like thinking about Mira with other guys.

Caveman of me, but still. I want to be the only person she gives the half-smile to, or shares her body with.

She passes me the condom, and there's a slight tremor in her hands. Is she nervous?

Maybe she's not as experienced as she appears. But if she's not, why initiate at a party with a hundred people downstairs?

This isn't how I want our first time to be, but if I walk away, I'll have to kill myself later.

I slide on the condom, acting like I've done it a million times—or at least *once* before—and move back to where I was. Because lying on top of Mira, her light-brown eyes gazing at me like I'm her hero, is the only place I want to be.

The shaking of her hands against my shoulders brings back doubts. "Mira, I—"

She scoots down, and the head of my dick slips inside her an inch. I groan and instinctively rock forward.

She squirms.

Fuck, am I doing it wrong?

I inch back, and she clutches me. "Don't stop."

Taking a deep breath to calm down, I move forward—slower this time.

The sensation of her body tightening around me as I ease in and out, deeper with each push, is driving me wild.

I'm not going to last. Feels so good...*"God, Mira."* I love this girl. Love her...

Unable to wrap my head around what's happening, I don't even try. I go by instinct and kiss her mouth, her neck, then pull back and sink all the way until there's nothing separating us.

I pause as the most intense sensation sweeps me. The sense of being so totally connected to another human being that nothing will ever be the same.

Her breath catches and her arms band around me. "More," she says.

I kiss her lips, show her with my mouth and hands how much she means to me. Mira's arms loosen and her breaths increase, a dazed expression crossing her eyes as I lower my head, grazing my lips over her ear and sucking the flesh below it. All the while, my body moves in an instinctive rhythm that has us both panting.

I'm trying to keep things slow, keep it together, but the need for release is building. Stopping doesn't seem like a good idea. Not when Mira is making those little noises.

Our mouths and breaths mingle. Before I know it, the most intense orgasm roils through me, my body locked in waves of pleasure and trembling.

I brace myself above her for several seconds, gathering air, forcing my mind to work again.

Mira lies still beneath me. Too still. I kiss her forehead and roll to the side, taking her with me, unable to let her go. She feels so good in my arms. I hold on to her while my heart rate slows to something resembling normal. "You okay?"

She nods, but her eyes glisten.

I sit up on one elbow. "Mira?" After that experience, I'm damn near tears. But I don't think hers are the same kind. "Are you—"

She kisses me hard and pulls away, collecting her clothes from the floor. "We better get back."

I scramble unsteadily to my feet and wad up the condom in a tissue from the nightstand. I toss it in the trashcan by the bed, and feel around for my pants, which I can't find because the carpet is dark and I can't see in this light.

I glance nervously at her shadowed figure as she

dresses faster than I'm able to after what we just did. She seems upset, and that's not right. I want her to feel as good as I do.

"Wait—Mira—"

She grabs something near the door and lurches outside.

"*Fuck.*" I finally find my pants under the bed and throw on the rest of my clothes.

I search for Mira everywhere in the crowded house. I can't find her. She is gone and no one has seen her.

It's as if she never existed.

As if what happened *was* a dream.

Only I've never felt horrible after my dreams of Mira.

* * *

I TRIED CALLING Mira after she darted out of the house party. She was never home and didn't return my calls. I proceeded to freak the fuck out.

My only option was to go to her house like a stalker. The thought crossed my mind multiple times, but I couldn't do it. I didn't want to make her uncomfortable, but I *need* to talk to her.

Did I hurt her? People say sex comes naturally, but I doubt everything right now.

It's Monday, and I've never been so relieved to return to school. As long as Mira doesn't call in sick, I should be able to track her down. School isn't the ideal location for this conversation, but I'm getting desperate.

I arrive early and wait at her locker. Fifteen minutes pass before Mira rounds the corner to the hallway.

The pressure weighing on me these last two days lifts at the sight of her. I want to grab her and press her to my chest, but then she sees me and my nerves return.

Mira walks up to her locker. Her gaze cuts briefly to me, shyly touching on my face. "Hi."

I had a pretty good idea something was wrong after she left me in the bedroom with my pants down. Now I can't deny it. It's written all over her face.

Making love to Mira was my first time. I don't feel like it went badly. Yes, she seemed nervous, but the sounds coming from her when I kissed and touched her indicated she was into it. And when we were actually...Well, she had this dazed, sexy-as-hell look on her face, like she really enjoyed that part.

And believe me, I was paying attention.

But I wanted her to feel amazing. I wanted our first time to be perfect.

"Hey," I say gently. "I tried to call you a bunch of times. Is everything okay? Because the other night—"

Her face softens as she looks at me, then Holly Walker steps up out of nowhere and squeezes my arm.

I look back at Mira, but her face is no longer soft and open, and she's staring at Holly's hand on me. If it wasn't so rude, I'd shake off Holly's grasp. Holly is pretty and popular, and she's been driving hard to the hoop all year. I'm not into her at all. I made that clear, but she won't give up.

The only girl I've thought about for the last year and a half is the one standing in front of me with her hands shaking as she switches out books from her locker.

"So, Mira," Holly says. "You and Tyler?"

As far as I know, Holly has never spoken to Mira. Holly keeps to her pack of Tahoe beach club kids. Everyone was at her party Friday night; I wasn't surprised Mira went too. But Holly approaching Mira at school *is* a surprise.

"Heard you walked out of a guest bedroom Friday night with just-fucked hair. Isn't Lewis your boyfriend? Or are you hooking up with both of them? *Oh shit*—did you mess around behind Lewis's back?"

Mira's body tenses, the apples of her cheeks going rosy.

I'm momentarily too startled by Holly's ugly suggestion to react.

One of the reasons I never acted on my attraction to Mira is because I was never sure what was going on with her and the guy she lives with. Lewis is a senior like me. Quiet, but always with Mira—when I'm not tutoring her. Mira is friends with Zach too, but Zach gets around. I don't think Mira has anything other than friendship with Zach. It's never been clear what she shares with Lewis.

Mira's eyes harden as she glares at Holly. "What's it to you?"

"Settle down, I'm just curious. The two hottest guys in school? Damn greedy if you ask me. If Tyler was only a hookup, I want to know. I have plans for him."

Mira's eyes dart to me.

But I'm too busy mentally rehashing everything I've ever heard about Mira and Lewis. And thinking about the other night...Mira came on to me out of nowhere, and darted out of the room...Is Holly right?

Mira didn't return my calls. Why the fuck didn't she call me back? Is she brushing me off? *Was* she trying to keep what happened a secret?

There's a flash of vulnerability on Mira's face as she searches my eyes. Her head eases back as if she doesn't like what she sees. She looks away and swings her backpack over her shoulder, closing her locker door. "I wouldn't know if Tyler's available. I'm not his keeper. Ask him."

Only Holly doesn't. For some reason, she is determined to corner Mira. "So it was a hookup?"

Holly is putting Mira on the spot. I should do something, say something, but doubt fills me.

"He can see whoever he wants," Mira says.

Her words are like a punch to the gut.

"Awesome." Holly turns to me. "So what do you think, Tyler? Want to go to prom?"

Mira storms off.

What is Holly's problem? How many times does a guy have to say no? I sweep past Holly and grab Mira's backpack gently. She stops in the middle of the crowded hallway and turns to me.

"Looks like you have a prom date," she says, glancing over my shoulder. "Better not leave her waiting. Answer the poor girl."

"Is it true?" I tug at the T-shirt I'm wearing that suddenly feels too tight, too hot. "Was it a hookup you don't want anyone knowing about?"

She swallows, the pulse at her throat hammering. Her eyes go soft again. "I—"

"'Sup, Mira?" Chad from my varsity soccer team nods to Mira in passing, checking out her ass.

I'd like to punch him in the face. What's with the possessive look he's giving her?

"Are you sleeping with him too?" I whisper harshly, regretting my words the moment they're out of my mouth.

Mira's jaw drops. She slams it shut and breathes in deep, holding it.

Fuck. I let Holly mess with my head. "Mira, I didn't mean—"

She turns and smiles at Chad.

My smile.

The secret, sexy smile she reserves for *me*. It doesn't last the way it does when it's aimed at me, but it's enough of a flash to make my stomach pitch.

"Hey, Chad. Wait up?" she says. "I want to ask you a question about prom."

Chad stops a few feet away, his brow rising in interest. I glare at him.

"He's all yours, Holly," Mira calls down the hall, her voice shaky, eyes avoiding mine. She turns and loops her arm through Chad's.

My head pulses, ready to explode. I watch Mira walk away with Chad, her shoulders strangely curled in, and I can't move my legs. I don't know what just happened, if I ruined everything, or if the path was already set.

Someone slaps me on the back.

"Rough one, dude," Jake from my team says, and I stare at his back as he keeps going down the hall.

Does everybody but me know about Mira and other guys?

I should say something, do something, but the message is clear. What Mira and I had meant nothing to her.

I'm the idiot who thought there was more between us.

Chapter Three

Mira

Present day

A light breeze whips a lock of dark hair straight into my eye, because that's how my day is going.

I rub the sting and glance with my uninjured eye at the trees on the right, then the ones on the left.

Am I lost? The trunks all look the same. Your basic Tahoe forest range: miles of tall, straight pines, the reddish-brown bark, fissured like puzzle pieces, nearly black in the twilight. It's getting dark and the overgrown road is sketchy under the best of conditions.

The cabin my mom lives in is located in the densest forest that's relatively easy to get to. Which means I have to abandon my beater mini-truck and hike for forty-five minutes along a paved road too overgrown to navigate with a car.

So tired of this. I should listen to Lewis and stop helping my mom, but I haven't wanted to lose the last shred of family I have. Now that I'm out here on another fool's errand to give her money for what I fear might be drugs—though she says no—I regret not doing something sooner about the situation.

I flick off a bright green worm that landed on my jacket and rub my temples. My mom has done this before—squatting while she "picks up her life." She never remains clean for long. I'm aware of it, but it's difficult to let go. Lewis is pulling away now that he has a girlfriend, which is what I feared and why I've held on so tightly. I lose everyone eventually.

My mom abandoned me a long time ago. I don't know why I see space from her and the dangerous lifestyle she lives as another loss. You can't lose the same person twice, can you?

Glancing around, I recognize a tree split down the middle. It's supposed to be way off to the right. Definitely should have turned left back there. This would go more smoothly if I didn't get lost.

I joke with Lewis and Zach that I know the Tahoe Basin like the back of my hand, given I'm full-blooded Washoe while they're only half, but I totally don't. Our native knowledge died a few generations ago when burly frontiersmen kicked us off our land. It doesn't stop me from rubbing it in that both my parents are Washoe.

And that's all I have to brag about when it comes to my parents. I never knew my dad, and the Sallees took me in after Lewis and his father found me by myself at the age of three, living off stale cereal and water in my mom's cinderblock house on the reservation.

I sigh loudly. If I cut through the bushes to the left, it should get me back to that fork.

I walk around a boulder and squeeze through the bushes, but since this is a fool's errand and I've messed it up thus far, I immediately trip over a random root and catch myself before I faceplant.

I dust off the pant knee that sports a new dime-sized hole.

Dammit, these were my good jeans. Pines have deep roots. This one—the one in the middle of my path—decides to reach for the stars? It belongs in the ground.

A whistle sounds in the distance.

What the hell is going on around here? I'm lost. I nearly ate it over a tree root. And now someone's whistling in an isolated forest?

Long ago, my mom used to call me in from playing in the yard by whistling. It's one of the few memories I have of living with her as a young child.

Am I closer to her cabin than I thought? Is she worried about me? My mother's more focused on getting her money than anything else these days, but I was supposed to be there an hour ago...

Huh, maybe she is concerned. She said she was off drugs. And it's not like cell phones work in the woods, even if she owned one.

Strange warmth blooms in my chest. I shouldn't get my hopes up. Shouldn't still want my mother's love. And yet I jog to make up the lost time.

Another whistle sounds, halting me in my tracks.

Okay, both whistles can't be from her. They came from opposite directions.

A cold sensation sweeps my spine. It's getting darker and I've never come across anyone out here.

Well—except for *him*.

Of course I ran into Tyler Morgan in the middle of nowhere. As if everything weren't going downhill in my life, I run into the one guy I never got over. Just to spear the knife in my chest a little deeper, and wiggle it around for good measure.

I didn't intend to have a relationship with Tyler after Holly's party, but leaving him that night was torture. For a few days, I imagined we could make it work. Even after I returned home from the party, and Lewis's parents told me my mother was in the hospital with a cocaine overdose.

I lived in a nice house with Lewis and his parents, but my mom and the druggie friends she treated like family were a part of my life too. I didn't call Tyler back that weekend because I was afraid he'd learn the truth. I couldn't handle the rejection. Not from him.

When Tyler showed up at my locker that Monday, he looked so hopeful. For a moment, my hope grew too. But then Holly showed up and Tyler believed her lies. I allowed him to think I had slept around, because it was easier than watching him leave me.

I thought I'd never see Tyler after he moved away to attend some fancy college. He should be off earning his white-collar salary and settling down with the girl who would someday give him two-point-three kids. Only there he was a couple of weeks ago, riding his mountain bike through the woods past my mom's squatter's cabin, while I sat on the porch, my mouth open so wide I'm surprised a fly didn't take up residence.

I convinced myself I was holding on to something by leaving Tyler first, but I was wrong. I simply lost one more person I cared about.

A branch snaps in front of me. A tall, wide man in a denim jacket steps out from behind one of the trees, startling me.

Where the hell did this guy come from? He looks like he walked in off the street.

Fear lances through me, my heart racing. I'm mixed up with shady people right now. Maybe I shouldn't be here either.

I speed-walk in the opposite direction toward my truck, looking over my shoulder every few seconds. The man watches me wordlessly, but he doesn't follow.

I'm outta here. I'll return later. Or I'll make my mom come to me if she needs something so desperately.

Another man rises from behind the thicket in front of me. My footsteps falter, skidding in the dirt. Was he crouched? Waiting?

I sprint in a wide loop toward the road I came in on, praying my sense of direction is better on the way back. Terror courses through me, making my mouth dry, my mind racing as fast as my feet. I have no weapons. There's no one out here besides me and these men. How could I be so stupid? I should have been more careful.

I'm dodging trees, darting in front of thick trunks to hide my retreat. No shouts for me to stop come from behind. The only noise louder than my heartbeat is my feet crunching through the brush.

My legs burn as I stumble over logs, scraping my jacket on prickly bushes. The sun has set and it's getting darker. Maybe I'm wrong. Maybe they're not here for me—

Branches snap behind me and an enormous weight slams into my back, knocking me off my feet. My hands and elbows scrape across the brittle forest floor as I'm pinned to the ground, whatever breath I have left rushing from my lungs.

I gasp for air, the scent of pine needles and dirt filling my nose. I buck to free myself, fear gripping me so tight no sound escapes, not even to scream.

I am unceremoniously rolled over, the guy in the denim

jacket who appeared from behind the tree leering down.

I thrust my hand up to shove his face away, scratch, claw—whatever—to get him the hell off me. He catches my wrist and binds both my arms to my sides.

"Let me go." My voice comes out high and panicked. I hate showing fear. But sometimes the emotion chokes, oozes, from pores, until the body rattles with the force of it.

The second man slows to a stop a couple of feet away. "You owe our boss money, little girl."

The guy pinning me scoots further up my body, his hip digging into my thigh. I groan at the sharp pain. I have the cash I brought for my mom, but it's a drop in the bucket compared to what I owe. He shifts and grips both my wrists with one hand, raising them above my head—a biting hold I can't break, no matter how hard I pull.

He runs a callused finger over my cheekbone, down my throat, snagging my top and lowering it to the edge of my bra. "She's not like the others. Pretty," he says absently, his dark, heavy-lidded gaze moving to my face.

My throat dries to a sticky consistency, sweat beading between my shoulder blades. Would he hurt me—*like that*—because I'm late on my payments to his boss?

"I think we need to teach her a lesson in responsibility," the one above says, his features shadowed.

"Help me! Someone help me!" I scream, squirming to get free, my voice going hoarse from the strain.

The guy in the denim jacket has a biggish nose, black eyes. He's all bulbous features, an image straight from the funhouse wavy mirror. "We could teach her a thing or two." He cups my breast. "What's your name, beautiful?"

My heart is racing, I can't breathe, can't move. "Get off me, get off me..." I screech.

Denim Jacket leans down. "Mira, is it?"

I wiggle my arm loose and grab the first object I find, a rock no bigger than my hand. I slam it into his head, but my angle is off and I barely catch the back of his skull.

He stabs my arm with his elbow, digging in the muscle until I drop the rock. I cry out in pain. "Bitch—" His meaty hand cracks across my face.

Stars flitter in my vision. I moan, rolling my head to the side.

Hot fetid breaths steam my ear. "Got a message for you, *Mira*. Pay. Up." He shoves my chin, the hulking burden suddenly lifting.

I move to turn over, but the tip of a boot strikes my middle and knocks the air from my lungs. I cradle my stomach, gasping, curling into a protective ball. Another blow lands on my thigh and I cry out.

The tempo of kicks comes faster. I can't catch my breath. A booted foot hammers my back as though stomping out a fire. A final crack to the side of my head makes what's left of the evening light wink out. For a second, I can't see anything, not even shapes.

"That's enough," one of them says. "Let's go."

My body is patted down, the envelope with the two hundred dollars—the only cash I have—torn from my jacket pocket.

The men's footfalls recede and fade. My head and the rest of my body intermittently burn and pulse in pain.

I allowed my mom to manipulate me. I borrowed money for her. That was my decision, and now these men are after me.

I'm no stargazing tree root with dreams of reaching the sky. I belong right where I am, in the dirt like the rest of my family.

I should have known I'd end up here.

Chapter Four

Tyler

I should have known Mira would cause trouble.

Goddamn. I stop pedaling my Diamondback and glance down the wooded mountainside to the obsidian lake reflecting the moonlight. What the hell am I doing out here?

I was at my sister's place, where I've been crashing all summer, when I heard Mira had gone missing today. I didn't realize it until I arrived in town, but my sister's best friend Gen is dating Lewis, Mira's best friend. Supposedly, Mira has been causing trouble for Lewis and Gen.

Mira is heartless. This is probably some ploy to get Lewis's attention. Nothing has changed. I'm an idiot for biking out here, in the fucking black of night, to a secluded cabin, searching for the girl I said I'd never go near again.

I shouldn't even know about this place, but as fate is a brutal bitch that enjoys batting me around, I happened to run into the one person in town I had every intention of avoiding. During a bike ride from hell, in which I attempted to exorcise my Colorado demons through physical torture, I managed to get into off-road terrain I probably would have thought twice about had I been in my right mind. I found a cabin, with Mira, of all people, sitting on the front stoop.

It was like a black omen.

I have no idea what Mira was doing out here in the middle of nowhere. It's none of my business, but I decided to eliminate this location from the possibilities while the others search town. It would have been a challenge to direct anyone to this spot, and on the off chance she really is in trouble, someone should check it out.

I've run into Mira twice now since I returned home. The first time at this cabin a couple of weeks ago, the second time a few days later at a party I went to with my sister and her friends. Let's just say, I didn't stay long at that party. Before those two incidents, the last time I saw Mira was my final week of high school.

Mira never went to prom with Chad. In fact, I never noticed her with him again after that encounter in the hallway, and I never discovered who she was or wasn't sleeping with. I didn't want to know. I'd forgotten all of it, including how terrible I'd felt for weeks afterward. Until the day I ran into Mira in this forest. Then it all came rushing back.

I push off a boulder and grind the pedals, shifting to a lower gear over the thick, barely rideable underbrush. I'm roughly where I spotted Mira out here, give or take.

After a few minutes, I catch the silhouette of the cabin in the distance. I get off my bike and cross on foot.

Approaching the cabin, I cup my hand to the glass and peer inside a faintly illuminated window. Twin cots rest beside an empty fireplace. The place is nearly barren, but not uninhabited. A woman sits at a spindly table. She's the same woman who craned her head out the front door as I passed by on my bike a couple of weeks ago, while Mira swallowed her surprise from the porch, her gaze wide and clinging to me.

A man sits at the table along with the woman. They're huddled beneath blankets, playing cards by the light of a camping lantern. Beer cans litter the floor. And Mira is nowhere in sight.

She isn't here. I've done what I could for my sister and her friends. It was a waste of time, but hey, I'd rather someone else find Mira anyway.

Just to be certain I haven't missed anything, I walk around the cabin and glance inside another set of windows.

Nothing. And the place is too small to miss her. Mira is definitely not here, but where could she be? She rarely strays from Lewis's side. Though from what Cali has said, all that's changed now that Lewis is dating Gen.

Well, I'm not going to worry about it.

Not my problem.

I make it back to my bike and climb on, taking in the cold and dark around me. It's the end of summer, and the night air has a nip to it. I press the side of my watch, lighting up the face to check the built-in compass. The return trip to my truck would go faster since it's downhill, but the dark makes speed impossible without risking impalement on a low branch.

I ride blind, relying on my watch compass to get me southeast to the start of the road.

Partway down the hill, I stop to confirm my coordinates and make sure I'm headed in the right direction. A whimper sounds nearby.

My pulse kicks up, an eerie sensation feathering the back of my neck. Gotta be an injured animal. I hold my breath and listen for more.

The noise comes again. Only this time, it sounds like a

moan...the kind of noise a woman might make if she were in pain.

My gut knots, images of Mira flashing through my mind.

Can't be her. It's an animal. I should keep a safe distance. But just in case...

I prop my bike against a tree and rush in the direction of the noise, my heart pounding. Up ahead, a patch of light-colored fabric moves, revealing a face that catches my breath.

I run over, kneeling beside her, my hands shaking as I touch her neck, her wrist. "Mira?"

Where the fuck is her pulse?

Her eyes flutter open, beautiful golden-brown irises shining, even in this dull light. Normally her eyes are nearly the same color as her tanned skin—only now her skin appears pale.

I scan her body: a gash on the side of her head, mottled skin along her cheekbone, torn fabric in her sleeves and jeans.

She opens her mouth to say something, closes it, and swallows. "Tyler?" Her voice sounds bewildered and scratchy.

"It's me," I say, my tone gruff, a burning in my chest. For some reason, seeing Mira like this leaves me raw. "What happened?"

Her eyes flicker closed. She bites her bottom lip.

Mira's no wilting flower. She rarely shows emotion, and to see what I suspect is pain and fear on her face? It's too much.

I gently reach under her to help her up—carry her if I have to. "Come on. Let's get you to the cabin. It's not far."

She shakes her head and winces. Her hand flutters to the side of her scalp. The section that's matted and wet.

"Can't go to my mom's. Someplace else. Could you—could you help me to my car?"

A small, battered truck was the only other vehicle parked on the road I entered from. Either way—"You could have a concussion. You're not driving anywhere. We need to get you to the cabin. It's the closest place, unless..."

My shoulders tense. I look in the direction I came from. "Was it them, the woman and that man at the cabin? Did they do this to you?"

"No. It wasn't them."

But her omission implies it *was* someone. She didn't just fall. "Then let's go there. The nearest road is a mile and a half away."

"My mom—she won't...Forget it." Mira shifts from me and rolls to her knees. "I'll walk back." She stands upright, swaying like a boat on the ocean.

I grab her elbow. "Mira, you can barely stand."

I could ignore her protests and take her to the cabin, but she needs medical attention, and I doubt that cabin has anything in the way of an emergency kit.

Fine, we'll do things Mira's way. For now.

I place my arms beneath her back and knees and pick her up. Her eyes widen, her gaze running up my neck toward my mouth, where it lingers for an instant.

Which is long enough to scatter my senses.

Jesus, how can this girl still affect me? I'm over her. Was over her years ago.

She focuses on my eyes. "Now what?"

I haven't moved. I'm holding Mira in my arms, convincing myself that what I once felt for her is gone.

I really should have chosen a different town to hunker

down in for a few months. This place brings back too many unwanted memories.

I step forward, feigning confidence I don't have. "We get on my bike and ride to my car."

Her eyes search for my Diamondback, propped against the tree. "Both of us?"

I glare down to snap a retort about our options, because I'm in a piss-poor mood, but I lock on her beautiful face and lose focus. She's injured, and I'm mad for reasons I can't explain and worried about her at the same time, when I should feel nothing but eager to get her back to her friends.

I give my head a mental shake. "Why don't you stop talking, conserve your energy?"

Her mouth pinches as if she sees through to the insult. "Set me down, Tyler. I don't want you holding me." Her pale cheeks, which are normally a golden brown, darken even in this light.

"Nope." I hike her higher.

My demeanor is cool, as though I have everything under control, but I'm concerned about how this will work. Riding two-man goes more smoothly when one of the individuals isn't incapacitated.

I reach for the bike while balancing her in my arms. "Can you hold on to the back of my neck?"

She peers at me skeptically.

"Mira, I'm trying to help you. Throw me a bone so I can dump your ass—I mean—deposit you with Lewis."

She rolls her eyes, but her arms go up past my shoulders, gripping me surprisingly tightly given her condition. She rests her head below my chin and her mouth brushes the skin of my neck in what feels like a light nuzzle...

I nearly lose my grip on the bike.

"Mouth off." I'm not sure if the lip graze was intentional

or not, but I don't goddamn care. I can't do this if she puts her lips on me. My head is messed up enough without Mira screwing with it.

A heavy sigh warms the flesh her lips taunt. She lifts her head and tilts it back, her caramel eyes melting my rage a degree. "You can stop hating me, Tyler."

I don't answer. I have nothing to say.

"I didn't mean to hurt you," she says. "And you—"

"If this is about things that happened back in high school, I barely remember it. Spare me your apology and remain still so I can get us out of here."

She huffs out an annoyed sigh.

Still sassy. Nothing's changed. That's the problem. Too many things are the same.

I shift her in my arms and sit on my bike, supporting her weight with one arm and holding on to the handlebar with the other.

Progress is slow, but we make it to my Land Cruiser without me dropping her or crashing into a tree. Mira is slender, but my arms burn after navigating the bike through a mile and a half of bumpy terrain.

I ease her off my lap and steady her on her feet. She wobbles, and I'm concerned about the head wound. I help her to the car and open the passenger door.

The interior light reveals a red and purple smudge on her cheek—featuring a distinct handprint.

I grip the doorframe, a rush of heat rising from my chest, flaming my face. Mira definitely didn't fall in the woods. And for some reason, the thought of someone hurting her makes me extremely angry. "You wanna tell me about it?" I gesture to her face and the cut on her head.

She scoots onto the cracked seat cushions I've never paid attention to until now. The jagged edges of the upholstery scrape the exposed flesh where her jacket is torn. She tilts her head against the headrest, her gaze flickering to me, then out the window. She doesn't say anything.

I was a dick earlier. Of course she's not going to tell me what happened. I lean in and click the belt across her lap. I shut the passenger door and round the front of the Cruiser. I shoot a text to Lewis that I've found her, then climb in the driver's side.

"Sorry about back there," I say, squeezing the steering wheel. "And what I said. It was a long time ago. I'm just— I'm in a bad mood. Don't mind me." I insert the key and start the engine. "I'll get you someplace safe. You can tell Lewis what happened. He's really worried."

"But not you," she says to the window in a voice I can't read. Her stoic expression gives nothing away. No more high emotion from Mira. That moment has passed.

I stare at the side of her smooth cheekbone, the curve of her full lips. Mira is both classically beautiful and exotic-looking. Add long, dark-brown hair, beautiful eyes, and creamy skin, and the girl makes an entrance. But that's not what drew me years ago.

Well, okay, of course it did. But if that were all, I'd have been fine to love her and leave her. No matter what I tell myself, it hurt to discover I meant nothing to her. Because at the time, she meant everything to me.

Mira is wrong. I *am* worried. I'll always worry about her, no matter how many years pass.

It's my curse.

Chapter Five

Mira

Tyler pulls up to a small cabin a few blocks off of Stateline Boulevard, near the lake. I've been here before with Lewis, and today, several cars line the driveway.

Great. Just what I need, an audience to witness the hell that is my life.

I cradle my ribs, unlatch the seatbelt, and reach for the door handle, battening down the cracks that running into Tyler have made in my emotional armor.

I don't know how he found me, but seeing his pale blue eyes peering down was like being thrown a lifeline. A *déjà vu* of the hero from my past.

All the feelings for Tyler that I keep locked away crept to the surface. He smelled so good, and his arms around me were like coming home. I couldn't help myself. I pressed my nose to the crook of his neck to get closer.

And he snapped at me.

He thinks I didn't care about him in high school, and

that I used him. I didn't, but like he said, it was a long time ago, and the past has a way of shaping people.

"This is my sister's place," he says, and wraps his large hand around my upper arm as we make our way to the front door. "We were hanging out when Lewis got the call from his dad that you were missing. We split up to search for you. I texted Lewis that I found you and would bring you here."

I was supposed to swing by Lewis's parents' house after I got off work early tonight, but I received an emergency call from my mom. She sounded frantic and asked me to meet her at the cabin with cash. She wouldn't explain to me over the phone why she needed it, but the last time this happened, her life was in danger. I couldn't risk it. I went to her.

I thought I could make a quick trip to my mom's, drop off the cash, and be back in time to meet Lewis's parents. A tad late, but not never-show-up late. Lewis's parents would have worried when I didn't arrive. I've gotten into a few scrapes over the years because of my mom. If I don't show up after a couple of hours, John and Becky send out the search dogs.

I've been telling myself that this is it, no more money for my mom, but I haven't stuck to that decision. After tonight, I can't risk it anymore. One more scrape like the one in the woods, and...I don't want to think about how bad things could have been.

Tyler pauses at the front door, his strong hand moving from my arm to my lower back. He's been kind for someone who owes me nothing, and likes me even less. He turns the knob and nudges the sticky front door open with his shoulder.

Lewis is pacing the tiny living room like a restless bear. He stops as we enter.

"Mira." He takes two long strides and embraces me in a hug that squeezes my sore ribs.

"Ouch," I mumble into his ginormous chest.

Tyler is a tall, athletic guy, but Lewis—and Cali's boyfriend, Jaeger, who's a part of my audience tonight—is supersized.

Lewis looks down and gently brushes aside the hair at my temple, examining the bruise on my face, then the cut on my head and ear. His mouth compresses. "What happened? Where have you been?"

Everyone's watching, waiting for my answer. Tyler, his sister Cali and her boyfriend, Lewis's girlfriend Gen. I don't want to discuss my personal life around all of them, but I have to say something. "A couple of men jumped me."

Lewis's eyes darken, more than they already are, turning the deep brown raven.

"Probably has something to do with—you know—that problem," I murmur.

I hate lying to Lewis, but if he knew I owe the money because of my mom, I'm not sure what he'd do. The life my mom leads drags both of us down. Lewis has been pushing me to sever the tie with her. I don't like the stuff my mom pulls, but she's my mom. Lewis wants me healthy, but he's scaring me with his conditions, driving every anxiety over abandonment I possess to the surface.

One of my worst fears is that Lewis will leave me if I can't walk away from my mom. He's been my family for years, but insecurities run deep. Which is why I haven't told Lewis the real reason I owe the money.

The Sallees held an intervention and insisted I see a therapist when I told them I'd gambled away months of rent and borrowed from a loan shark. Not the most ideal of excuses, considering I work in a casino, but it was the best

I could come up with at the time. I visit a therapist regularly per the Sallees' request, but the therapist knows the real reason I'm in debt. She's helping me with my mom issues.

The Sallees wanted me to quit my job at the casino, which is understandable, but it's been my livelihood since I graduated. It's all I know. I promised to work through my problems with the therapist and never gamble again. I also promised I'd stop going to my mom's place because the people she hangs with aren't safe.

Tyler caught me red-handed, on my way to my mom's. Pretty soon, he'll tell Lewis where I was, and Lewis will know I broke one of my promises.

Gen grabs my hand, and I start. Her brow furrows in concern, but she doesn't let go. "It's okay, Mira. I just want to look at your wounds."

Gen and Cali lead me into the bathroom, and Cali locks the door behind us.

One person inside their closet of a bathroom barely fits. Three people leaves Cali straddling the edge of the tub, and me forced to sit on the toilet lid to make space.

Cali reaches across to the medicine cabinet—at the same time Gen rises from below the sink, knocking into her arm. "Quit it, Cali. I'm trying to get a towel."

"Well, I'm trying to grab the first-aid kit," Cali says.

They swat at each other for a second. Then Cali elbows Gen. Gen fakes a move, and reaches around Cali for the cabinet.

I've never had a sister, or close female friends. Watching Gen and Cali is like seeing inside a mysterious club. I've also never had friends, besides Lewis and Zach, worry over me.

There's that warmth inside my chest again, like in the

woods, when I thought my mom was calling for me. I press my arm to my ribs. All this therapy is making me soft.

"Got 'em," Gen says triumphantly, holding up the first-aid kit along with the towel.

"Maybe we should take her to the ER, or Urgent Care?" Cali says, scanning me from head to toe.

Gen sets the towel across my lap and looks me over. "She's moving okay, but yeah, the blood on her head doesn't look good. What if her brain is swelling?"

My what?

"We'll clean her up," Cali says, "then get her to a doctor. I'll grab clothes. Unless you think we should call nine-one-one? Should she stay in her clothes for the police? Do they need that for evidence?"

Okay, maybe these girls are insane. Funny, but insane. I'm beginning to feel sympathy for Lewis.

A knock sounds at the bathroom door.

"Just a minute," Cali and Gen shout at the same time.

"No," I answer their earlier question. "No nine-one-one. I'll be fine. I don't need a doctor."

They exchange a look. "Clothes, then ER," Cali says, and stumbles out the door, slamming it shut behind her. But not before heated voices from the other room drift in.

The guys are arguing?

Gen pulls out antiseptic and gently wipes the cuts on my palms, drawing my gaze from the door to the burning in my hands, which took a beating when the man tackled me to the ground.

I close my eyes against the frightening memory, sensing a tug as Gen eases off my jacket and lifts my shirt. She touches my ribs.

"Um, oww?"

"You were cradling your side a moment ago. This hurts?" She touches the spot again, more gently.

I nod. It hurts, but I was cradling my chest in part because of the warmth of their kindness.

Cali bursts into the bathroom, slamming the door against Gen's back.

"Son of a bitch, Cali." Gen glances over her shoulder, her face scrunched in annoyance.

"What?" Cali shrugs. "Sorry."

Gen lowers my shirt. "Her ribs look bruised. She might have broken one."

"And there's a footprint on her back," Cali adds dryly from her angle near the door.

Gen shakes her head, her lips compressed as she lets out a pained sigh through her nose. "Mira, who did this to you?"

I slip on my torn jacket and pull it around me. "I told you. Probably the man I owe money to."

"For the gambling?"

I nod, hesitantly. I don't like lying. It makes me feel dirty. Low. I don't want to be that person.

Gen has been kind since I showed up tonight. Kinder than I deserve after I snarled at her the first couple of weeks she dated Lewis. It was a jerk thing to do and I'm ashamed of it. Lying to her makes me feel worse.

After I reluctantly agree to remove my jacket and shirt, Cali and Gen wipe more grime from my face and arms. Cali helps me pull on the clean sweatshirt she retrieved, because raising my arms is tantamount to torture with my ribs hurting the way they do. She bundles my torn clothes in a bag.

The next knock that comes is more insistent. "Mira? You okay?" Lewis asks, his voice gruff.

"I'm fine," I call out.

"We'd better get her to the doctor," Cali says, and opens the door.

"I don't need a doctor," I reply as we emerge into the living room. The guys' heated voices die. Everyone's attention turns to me.

Except for Tyler. He's seated with his forehead propped on clasped hands, his gaze focused on the ground.

I swallow, my throat burning.

Tyler will never look at me the way he did before I ruined our friendship.

Here I am, my life dissolving before my eyes, proof that he and I come from two different worlds and were never meant to be together. That moment we shared six years ago, I stole out of selfishness because I wanted him. Now I'm paying the price for taking what was never meant to be mine.

Because the way I still feel for him and the way his eyes avoid me hurts worse than any physical injuries I suffered tonight.

Chapter Six

Tyler

"Why would she return to that place?" Lewis shakes his head. "Her mother—" He utters an oath and growls in frustration. "Never mind. I can't get Mira to see reason where her mom is concerned."

Lewis takes two steps, then turns and strides in the opposite direction.

Cali's chalet, as she refers to her dinky cabin rental, isn't ideal for pacing. Not for a guy Lewis's size. I'm larger than average at six foot two, but Gen's new boyfriend and my buddy Jaeg are so tall, they make me look like a little guy.

"How did you know where to find her?"

I'm sitting on the edge of the recliner, my hands dangling between my knees as Jaeg and Lewis discuss the situation. They seem surprised Mira is in trouble, but either Lewis isn't very bright—which I know isn't true, since he was valedictorian the year we graduated from high school—or Mira has him fooled. It takes a minute to realize Lewis addressed me.

I clear my throat. "I saw her. A couple of weeks ago. I was riding on an isolated trail and found a cabin that looked like it had been abandoned. Mira was sitting on the porch."

"Her mother was there?" Lewis asks.

I nod. "Mira said it was her mom's cabin. I saw a woman there tonight along with some guy. Not sure if Mira made it to the place, or if she was on her way back when..." I unclench the hands I'm fisting. "I don't know what happened, man. Mira wouldn't talk to me."

Nothing has changed between Mira and me. Our relationship was reduced to avoidance those last few weeks before I graduated. I burned up the trails on my bike until I could leave Lake Tahoe and forget about Mira Frasier. But not before I took Holly Walker up on her offer.

I went to prom with Holly and slept with her. I was so drunk I barely remember it. It was one of the worst nights of my life. I puked my guts out the next day from the alcohol—and from what I'd done.

"That'll teach you to drink, son. Good lesson for ya," my mom had said when she found me hugging the porcelain.

My mom was right, and she was wrong. I didn't hit the keg as hard as some of the kids I went to college with, but that didn't mean I was an angel. I was indiscriminate and gratuitous with my hookups. And I never let anyone in the way I did with Mira.

I shake my head, willing those memories gone, along with the fucked-up emotions they induce. I don't need this right now. I've got enough history I'm trying to work through.

"The hospital isn't necessary," Mira says a little while later, after exiting the bathroom with Cali and Gen.

"We're going." Lewis grabs his keys and gently urges Mira to the door.

She glances up before she walks out, and our eyes clash for an instant. Vulnerability and something else flashes in hers.

The urge to go with her burns through me.

I make myself stay.

No matter what we had or didn't have in the past, I'll never want anything bad to happen to Mira. Finding her in the woods hurt and alone fucked with my head. I feel connected to her again.

I squeeze the tops of my thighs, a pulse pounding at my temple. I don't want to see Mira in pain, but I also don't want her in my life. I've moved on from all that.

After they leave, Cali sits on the couch across from me while Jaeger rustles around in the fridge. "So what do you think?"

She must have said something, but I'm spacing. "About what?"

"What's wrong with you? You've been acting strange ever since Lewis got the call that Mira was missing. How well do you know Mira? Is there something going on between you two?"

"Fuck no." Her brows rise. Whoa. I need to tone down the angst. Unfortunately, running into Mira isn't the only thing that has me on edge. "There's nothing going on. I barely know her."

Mostly true, if you ignore carnal knowledge.

"*Oka-ay*. Well then, what do you think?"

Seriously, what is she talking about? "Cali, it's been a crazy night. I'm tired. Get to the point."

Her mouth compresses. "Your attitude sucks, Tyler. You've been an ass ever since you returned. And on that note, why *did* you come back? You still haven't said. I thought you loved Boulder."

I quit my job as a biology teacher in Colorado and returned to Lake Tahoe. It's not really home anymore, since our mom moved to Carson City a couple of months ago. But Tahoe is the place I associate with home.

My mom isn't pleased that I have no prospects...and leech off my sister. Put that way, it sounds bad. I just couldn't remain in Colorado. Not after things happened with Anna.

I envy my sister. She went through heavy stuff recently, but she's put her life to rights. Meanwhile, my head's so fucked up with guilt and anger, I can't see straight. That's why I returned. Not that I'm explaining any of this to my sister.

"I missed you. Isn't that enough?" I say, feigning sincerity.

Her eyes narrow. "Fine. Don't tell me. Just make sure you keep your drinking in check. Don't think I haven't noticed how many beers you're going through and how often you've come home hammered—when you're not being antisocial on your computer."

Christ, I gotta get my own place. So I've been going out, and burying myself in a writing project to keep my mind off things. I don't need my baby sister mothering me.

After Mira, I resolved never to get screwed over by a girl. *I* did the screwing. That's the problem. I was blind, insensitive. I ended up hurting someone I cared about. Anna deserved so much better than me.

Cali punches me on the arm.

"Hey." I rub my shoulder. Jesus, she's feisty. "Was that necessary?"

"Get your head out of your ass. Jaeger and I talked. We think Mira should move in for a little while. It's not safe for her alone in her apartment after what happened."

Correction. Make that new living space an emergency.

No way am I sticking around if Mira moves in. That's the last thing I need. But Cali's right, Mira shouldn't live on her own. It's not safe. Lewis's place is out. Gen moved in with him recently, and from what I understand, his place is small. That could get awkward. Cali says Lewis's relationship with Gen put a strain on his friendship with Mira.

Not that I care. Why am I even thinking about this? I've been around my sister too long. I'm getting dragged into chick drama.

"Yeah, sure. It's your place. Do what you want. I'll stay with a buddy. Mira can have the loft."

Gen and Cali rented a one-bedroom with a low loft above the kitchen. They shared the bedroom, until Gen moved in with Lewis a couple of weeks ago.

Cali sighs, exasperated. "That's what I'm talking about. If you were listening, you would know this. I'll stay with Jaeger so Mira can have my bedroom. You don't need to move out."

Whoa, what? "You want me to live here? With Mira?"

Hell no.

"Yes, jackass. Someone needs to look out for her. Gen and Lewis are finally getting some much-needed space from Mira. If we don't set something up so Lewis is convinced Mira is safe, he'll move her in with him and Gen."

"And I should care about this why?"

Cali throws up her hands, her face turning a bright shade of pink to match her strawberry blonde hair. Cali missed out on our mom's bright red crop, but only just. "Because you've been living here *rent free* for weeks, hogging the remote and behaving like an overall ass."

"You can stop busting my balls any time now, Calzone. This isn't my problem. It's yours. You fix it."

51

"Oh, my fucking..." Cali lets out a frustrated screech.

She hates it when I call her Calzone, but I have a feeling she's more angry I've put a wrench in her plans to save Mira.

Jaeger enters the living room. "Dude, help your sister out."

I glare at Jaeg. "What happened to bros coming first?"

He shakes his head as if I've missed something crucial. "Not with Cali, man. She comes first."

Fuck. I can't argue that logic. Cali is a pain in the ass, but she is my sister.

Still, this is Mira we're talking about. No way can I do what Cali asks. I spent a couple of hours in Mira's presence tonight and already I'm feeling things I don't want to.

"Why doesn't she move in with Lewis's parents?" I suggest.

Cali shrugs. "Mira won't move home. I'm not sure why."

And here we go again. Mira causing trouble. I escaped this; I won't step back into the fire.

"Sorry, Cali. No can do."

"Why not? What did Mira ever do to you?"

"She's done enough."

Chapter Seven

Mira

Lewis opens the passenger door of the Jeep for me. Gen tries to take the backseat and I wave her off, gingerly easing in back. The doctor said I don't have a concussion. Bruises, including a couple of bruised ribs, and a cut on my head the nurse cleaned and sewed with three stitches, but nothing that won't soon heal.

The police took a statement. I gave them the best description I could of the men who attacked me, and left out the part about owing a loan shark. It might not help my case, but I'm already in trouble and I don't need more. If I can't shovel myself out of this mess, I'll tell them. For now, I don't want to draw more attention.

As long as I stay out of dark, deserted places, I can earn back the money and be done with this. I'll have to stop giving my mom cash, no matter what she says. And no more visiting her in shanty homes. Too dangerous. I've gotta be smart from here on out.

"Mira," Gen says with a bright smile I'm certain is

genuine. Which is strange. All the pretty girls in high school were eager to elevate themselves by putting me down. "I just got a text from Cali. She offered you her place until the police find the guys who did this."

For a moment, I don't know how to respond. I'm not used to receiving help from anyone other than Lewis and his family. "Thanks—but she doesn't have to do that. I'll be fine at my place."

"No, Mira." Lewis shakes his head, glancing at me in the rearview mirror. "You either stay at Cali's, or with me, but you are not returning to your place. You could always crash with my parents—"

"No way," I cut him off. "That might put them in danger."

Lewis sighs. "Mira, they're your parents too. They love you and want to protect you."

John and Rebecca aren't my parents. They're kind, loving people I owe a debt of gratitude to for rescuing me when I was a kid. The last thing I will do to repay their kindness is draw thugs to their house. I'm not thrilled with the idea of drawing thugs to Cali's house either.

Lewis stares at me in the mirror again. "It isn't safe for you to live on your own. Not after what happened." Gen nudges him in the side and his lips clamp together.

"Mira." Gen twists around from the front seat. "Lewis won't be able to sleep if he doesn't know you're okay. You know how he is. He'll show up at your place every hour to check in. He'll call until your phone explodes."

Lewis is protective. He's always been that way. I love that about him, but I know what Gen is getting at. Lewis deserves a life, which he can't have if he's worried about me and putting everything aside to make sure I'm okay. It will be safer at Cali's than alone. At least for tonight. Those men abandoned me in the woods. I'm pretty sure they don't know where I am right now, but I won't risk them discovering it. I'll figure something else out tomorrow, but for tonight, no one knows I'm at Cali's, including my mom. And I just got done telling myself to be careful.

"So what exactly did Cali say?" I ask hesitantly. "She really doesn't mind me staying there?"

Gen snorts. "No. She's happy to have an excuse to live with Jaeger in his swank house on the lake. Believe me, it's no hardship for her."

"Okay, I appreciate it. I'll stay at Cali's for the night."

Gen smiles at Lewis and he grins at her, the moonlight providing just enough illumination to catch the warmth in his adoring gaze.

I look away.

I felt terrified, then numb, after the men beat me. Not even the pain of my injuries rattled my nerves. But this—this loving display of my best friend with the woman he wants enough that he's willing to build walls between us—it's too much. I know it's not quite like that. My therapist says my relationship with Lewis hasn't been healthy and that we need boundaries, but it feels like I'm alone.

I hate alone.

I have bad memories of alone.

Lewis pulls into the driveway of Cali's cabin. Jaeger walks out just as we exit the Jeep. It's late and dark, but the porch provides enough light to show Jaeger lifting luggage into the back of his truck. Cali walks out and smiles when she sees us.

I trusted what Gen said about it being okay for me to stay here, but it's good to see Cali's happy expression.

"We're all set," Cali says cheerily. "I've moved my

clothes out of the bedroom, Mira, and I left the essentials in the bathroom."

That sounds like a lot of effort for one night. I hate that she went to the trouble.

Tyler steps outside, a duffel bag slung over his shoulder. My face heats and the punch of emotion I get around him starts coursing through me.

Tyler's eyes narrow on the suitcase in the back of Jaeger's truck. "I thought we talked about this," he says to Cali in a low tone. "I'm not staying here. You'll have to keep an eye on her."

Tyler's living with Cali and Gen?

Well, that's not gonna work.

"No one needs to stay with me," I interrupt.

No way will I become a bigger charity case than I already am. I don't need to be watched over. I just need a place to crash until I figure out a new plan. It made sense to stay at Cali's for the night, but not with Tyler.

Tyler frowns. "You can't stay by yourself, Mira."

I understand he found me in the woods and felt some obligation to help, but why the concern now? He made it clear he doesn't like me or want to be around me.

"Of course I can. No one will know I'm here. I'll be fine. It's just for one night."

"Mira," Cali says, "you can stay at my cabin indefinitely. Tyler will look out for you." She shoots a glare at her brother.

Tyler shifts his shoulder and plucks the front of his T-shirt.

God—that tic. He used to do it when he was nervous, or agitated, I'm not exactly sure which.

I used to try and provoke Tyler into making his tic when we studied together. I'd *accidentally* brush my long hair

56

over his shoulder while leaning down to look at an equation, or graze his outer thigh with my arm when I bent to grab a pencil from my backpack.

The corner of my mouth twitches. There was always something about ruffling Tyler's easygoing exterior that made my heart race. Maybe that's why I pressed my mouth to his neck after he lifted me in the woods. Despite everything, that spark is still there, and I'm still addicted to it. Only Tyler's edgier these days. It doesn't take much to annoy him, and not in the fun, good ways. Living together, even for a short while, would be an utter disaster.

Tyler doesn't project the sweet, boy-next-door attitude he did years ago when he tutored me. I'm not sure what caused the change, but I always knew he had depths he never showed. The tic used to hint at the real Tyler. He was so in control around everyone else, he rarely showed the heated, provoke-able part of himself. But I glimpsed it when we studied, and especially the night we slept together.

I pinch my eyelids closed and take a deep breath. I can't think about that night when I'm around him. It reminds me of all the things I've lost.

Tyler drops his duffel on the porch's cement pad and glares at his sister. "Cali, you can't offer Mira your place to keep her safe, then take off. Someone needs to look after her. You and Jaeg have to stick around."

Cali's jaw sets. "Jaeger works in his woodshop, located at *his house,* Tyler. He'll be gone most of the time, and for that matter, so will I. I work during the day and take classes in the evening. That leaves one person who has nothing else to do at the moment."

Tyler lets out a growl.

I'm so caught up in the sibling angst I've forgotten this is about me. And damn, it's humiliating. I don't need a babysitter.

"Hold on a minute," I break in, but Cali and Tyler are having none of it. Their eyes don't even flicker toward me. They continue to glare at each other.

Tyler picks up his duffel and stalks back inside the cabin.

Cali claps her hands. "I'm glad that's all settled."

"What's settled?" I have this sinking feeling in my stomach, and it has nothing to do with residual nausea from those bastards' boots striking my abdomen.

Cali turns to me. "Tyler will stay with you, Mira. To protect you."

Oh, shit.

This might be the worst possible scenario, and I can't come up with an alternative. My mind is in freak-out mode.

Everyone busies around me, collecting items and stowing them in their respective cars, while I stand in shock, at first on the porch, then in the center of the living room after Cali ushers me inside.

Lewis hugs my stiff shoulders. "I'll check back in the morning. We'll get your truck and pack some things from your apartment." I cling a little too long, and he squeezes me again. "You'll be safe here, Mira."

What he doesn't realize is that I'm not afraid of those jerks returning. It's unlikely they'd find me at Cali's tonight. I don't want to be left alone with *Tyler*.

Misreading my hesitation, Lewis and Gen take off, assuming I'm safe now. Cali and Jaeger leave shortly thereafter. I'm still in the middle of the living room several minutes later, sifting through my muddled brain as to how it came down to this. Me and Tyler, alone. Living together. I wouldn't want those guys finding me here with Cali, drawing danger to her. But if Tyler is here with me, it isn't safe for my emotional stability.

Tyler kicks his duffel behind the recliner and strides into the kitchen. He shoves items around in the refrigerator, glass scraping on metal racks, bottles clanging together, ignoring me. I remain helpless as he pulls out a Sierra Nevada and pops the top with a bottle opener.

The brisk, yet controlled anger and the beer in his hand are a haunting reminder of a past life. Only then it was my mom or some guy she was dating, drinking and belligerent.

This is all wrong. I cradle my ill stomach, and sink onto the couch. "You can't stay here, Tyler."

"Tell me about it," he mumbles.

I look up as he walks into the living room. "No, really. Go to a friend's place. No one needs to know you aren't around."

His eyes narrow on my face. He takes another swig, gaze unwavering as he studies me. "First of all, they'd know. And second, you can't stay here alone. Cali's right. I'm the best person to look out for you."

"You're the *worst* person."

Tyler stomps over and slams his bottle on the end table beside the couch. I flinch, despite the solid nerves I pride myself on. It must be this night. The beating, seeing Tyler again—I'm off my game.

He looms over me. "Let's get one thing straight. *You* fucked *me* over, not that I minded the way you used me." He sneers, and I hold his gaze.

Anger I can relate to—a little piece of home. "If that's how you feel, then why are you helping?"

He leans closer, as if to spew more venom my way, only something happens. We're too close. The scent of him hits me, a hint of beer, but also bike oil and laundry detergent, and *him,* the scent that's all Tyler and smells so good.

I don't know if my expression changes, or if he senses it too—the spark that's always between us—but his eyes go dark. He slowly eases back and swipes his beer from the table, his gaze cutting away. "Stay out of my business, Mira, and I'll stay out of yours."

Tyler strides to the back door and slams it shut behind him. I sit there without moving, because I can't. Not after that.

Chapter Eight

Tyler

I slept like crap last night. I felt bad after I took out my frustrations on Mira. I shouldn't have gotten in her face like that. But fuck. Me and Mira living together? That's messed-up.

There's no question Mira is in danger. What I want to know is why. She owes money, so sayeth Lewis. I don't get it. Mira has Lewis's rich parents to help her out. It doesn't make sense that she'd turn to a loan shark instead of his family.

I rub my eyes and blink at the ceiling. There's gotta be a way to fix this. If I can fix it, I can get Mira out of Cali's place and return my life to normal. My new normal isn't exactly a peaceful existence—there's none of that after Colorado—but it's an escape. Cali's home has become my safe house, and Mira's presence has destroyed that.

Cali is right about my drinking, and I've been trying to ease up on it lately, but that went out the window last night.

I didn't drink as much as I have been, but I still downed four beers on the back patio before my mind calmed enough for me to drag my ass upstairs and crash.

Everything about Mira has me at peak anxiety, like I could punch a hole in the wall or kick down a door. The kind of pent-up agitation that needs an outlet.

Living with her is going to put me in an early grave. "Christ."

"You say something, Tyler?" Mira's lilting voice drifts up from below my loft.

Like I said, no peace.

"Nothing," I grumble, and sit up, pinching the bridge of my nose.

I put up with my sister and Gen's crap reality shows, the hogging of the bathroom, but living with Mira is—goddamn, how did I get here?

There was a time when my life was good; not great, but decent. Now...Now I don't think good is on the horizon.

The scent of spice fills the air, like cinnamon and licorice. I swing my legs to the floor of the loft, my knees near my shoulders since the mattress is on the ground. I reach for a pair of jeans and my gaze lands on the rumpled T-shirt I wore yesterday. Normally, I don't wear a shirt in the morning.

Fuck it. I'm not changing my ways. If I didn't change for my fiancée, I'm not changing for Mira.

Cali's right—I am an asshole. But I already knew that. It became apparent after everything went down in Colorado. I can never fix things with Anna. She's lost to me forever. But I can get my life together and be a better person than I have been.

I press the heel of my hand to my forehead, fighting a

headache that's building with every heartbeat, and glance around. It's not much up here—a mattress on the floor with a couple of bookshelves built into the wall on either side, my clothes scattered about—but I've come to like this place. It's cramped, and it reminds me I don't need a lot to survive.

I pull on my jeans and climb down the ladder. I should start paying my sister rent. As a dealer at Blue, she pulled in sweet tips, but all that's changed. Cali isn't making as much as she used to, and she and Gen are barely living here anymore. I enjoy irritating them both, but I'm not that big a mooch. I'll pitch in. I have money saved. A lot, actually. I just didn't want to be alone. Makes me sound like a pussy, but I needed to return to my roots and regroup after Colorado. There's something about Lake Tahoe. It's my hometown, and maybe that's it.

At the bottom of the ladder, I turn around to find Mira standing in the center of the living room, pulling her long, dark hair into a ponytail.

Her hands pause as she takes me in. She looks away, but not before her gaze trails my bare shoulders to the waistband of my jeans hanging low.

Movement down below has me fighting an adjustment. *Fuck.*

Maybe walking around without a shirt first thing in the morning isn't such a great idea. Mira is still a beautiful woman, and that little eye linger sent the wrong signals to my body—which is primed for release this morning, thanks to the anxiety I'm bottling.

Mira brushes past me into the kitchen, dragging a chair with her. She climbs on the bottom rung that supports the legs, and opens one of the upper cabinets, the chair creaking and wobbling beneath her.

Great. She's going to kill herself all on her own.

"What are you doing, Mira?" My voice comes out irritated. The view she's flashing me in her pajama shorts is adding to my annoyance.

I drag my gaze from her smooth, shapely legs to the cuts on her arms, the bandages on her head and the tip of her ear. She's injured, fragile. Only she's not acting like an invalid. She's moving around spryly for first thing in the morning. She seems normal, and the male parts of me, fully awake at this hour, agree. It doesn't matter that I tell myself she's off limits, the worst possible choice. My body has tuned out that voice.

Fucking biology. How can I possibly still have a physical attraction to this girl?

The black widow occasionally chews off her mate's head. How's that for postcoital thanks? Why the hell do we males put up with this? And yet, I'll need to remind myself continually what Mira was like in high school, because my dick has a mind of its own.

Mira reaches for the top shelf, her shorts riding up higher. The curve of her ass is on full display, her long legs narrowing to delicate ankles. I look up, and she's glaring at me. "You could help, you know."

This living together is the worst physical and mental torture I could imagine. "With?"

She points to the top shelf. "I need that mug."

Cali's place houses every coffee mug in existence. Cali and Gen have their favorites, and it seems Mira has picked out hers as well. Must be a chick thing.

I walk over and move right up behind her, resting my hands on the countertop on either side of her body, until my chest is touching her back.

"Which one?" I say near her ear.

She swallows. "That one." She points again.

Keeping one hand on the counter, I reach for the "Dear Karma, I Have a List of People You Missed" mug, and hand it to her.

"Thanks," she says, remaining very still.

It's not wise, but I'm a guy and she's beautiful, so I breathe in her scent. It's vanilla and floral, like last night, along with the intangible something I still gravitate to. The cells of my body are saying, *Her, her. Now.*

I'm telling them to shut the fuck up.

It's always been this way with Mira. From the first time we sat near each other during our tutoring sessions, she smelled so good to me. I couldn't stop myself from breathing her in then. I can't stop myself now.

But I *will* keep my hands off her.

It's sheer cruelty. Thanks to nature, my prehistoric pheromones recognize this girl's scent and form, out of all the other beautiful women out there, as the most attractive imaginable.

Mira pushes back, her ass against my lower abdomen, a not-so-subtle indicator that she wants me to move. And not at all helping my body's inconvenient physical response to her.

Her face is close—inches away—close enough that the glisten on her full bottom lip where she wets it with her tongue captures my attention. That, and her smell. Combine it with her slender body pressed to my chest and other areas, and a series of memories fire through my mind... Mira naked with me above her, my lips skimming the inside of her thigh...

Heat spikes down my groin, turning me rock hard, tension rolling off my back.

"Hold up." I move my hand from the counter to just

above her ass, keeping her still while I reach for another cup.

She scans my selection. A mug with the words "Morning Wood" scrawled below an image of a stack of lumber.

Those full lips twist into a smirk. "Classy," she says, heavy on the sarcasm. My hand and body continue to press into hers, and her breaths turn hitchy. Not so unaffected.

I have no doubt she can feel my want.

She clears her throat. "I'd like to get my tea now."

I back away, holding my hands out in surrender, the Wood mug in one of them. "Have at it."

I flip the switch on the coffeemaker I filled the night before, and stealthily make an adjustment to my jeans. How am I going to stay away from her when she smells the way she does? No one should smell that good first thing in the morning. Then she has to look at me all pissy and hot-tempered. Why is that such a turn-on? Was it always? I don't recall being drawn to bitchy chicks, but Mira's always had the sauce. At one point, I thought she had a sweet hidden core, but I was wrong. So wrong.

I push off the counter, away from the kitchen, away from her amazing scent.

Space. That's what I need. Space and distance.

Mira walks out of the kitchen with her cup of tea, and sits on the couch in the living room.

God. She's a tea drinker on top of it all. Out of every reason we're not compatible, that one settles it. I can't live with a tea drinker.

"How long do you think you'll stay here?" Not subtle, but whatever.

She stops in the act of raising the Karma mug to her

wine-tinted lips, and shrugs. "I had planned to only stay the night when I thought I'd be with Cali, but now I'm not sure. It's not ideal, but..." She takes in my tense features and lets out a huff, daggering me with a glare. "Lewis is right. I can't go home, Tyler."

At my blank stare, she sets her tea on the end table. "Jesus," she says, and stands forcefully. "I don't like this any more than you do." She storms out of the living room and into the bedroom.

A moment later, Mira returns with the clothes she wore yesterday in her arms, and slams the bathroom door behind her.

Humph. A little more sensitive than I remember.

I boot up my laptop, the squeak of the shower starting coming from behind the bathroom door, the pipes rumbling below the house.

I'm well into my edits by the time I register Mira emerging from the bathroom, her long, slightly wavy hair wet and hanging in thick strands down her back, making her beautiful face all the more pronounced.

My fingers pause above the keyboard, my breath catching in my throat. She removed the bandage on her ear, and the cut seems to be healing a little. The sweatshirt she borrowed yesterday hides the curves I know exist. Doesn't stop my gaze from searching them out before she disappears into the bedroom.

I grab a random textbook from the piles I keep stacked along the wall of the dining area and thumb through *The Neurobiology of Olfaction,* trying to focus on the words instead of the girl behind the bedroom door. A red Jeep pulls up.

Lewis's car.

He honks, and Mira exits the bedroom, whipping out the front door and slamming it shut faster than I can blink.

I slump in my chair, my head tipped to the ceiling. I breathe in deeply for the first time since I found Mira in the woods last night.

This will never work.

Chapter Nine

Mira

"I can't live with him, Lewis."

Lewis frowns at the road as he drives to my studio apartment. "Why? Tyler's a good guy."

And here's where it gets tricky. Tyler is a good guy, even though he's trying hard to be a royal ass.

What Tyler doesn't realize is that I know his game. I play it every day. I can tell the bad seeds from the good. Tyler doesn't make the cut. He's complex for sure, and something happened to give him an edge, but he's not what he's making himself out to be. For one, he didn't need to stay with me last night. If he were a true jerk, he would have left me on my own like any self-respecting asshole.

No, Tyler's a mix of good guy and fire. That fire was there all those years ago, but hidden, and never more evident than the night we were together at Holly Walker's house party. I wasn't ready for it then. I'm not ready for it now.

"It isn't a good idea for me and Tyler to live together. We didn't really get along in high school."

Lewis glances at me, his brow furrowed in confusion. "Wasn't he your tutor for two years? I thought you guys got along fine. Not that you needed his help. I still don't understand why you didn't let me tutor you."

Lewis was one of the best students in school, but I had my sights on Tyler, so...

I rub a smudge of dirt off the door that I've brought in with my shoes, feigning nonchalance. "He helped me for a year and a half. And I didn't want to bother you with tutoring. You spent all your time studying; you didn't need another reason to have your nose in a book. Studying with Tyler worked out for a while, but then we had a falling out. It happened right before you guys graduated. He pretty much hates me now."

Lewis's gaze flickers over, his expression contemplative. "I don't think he hates you, Mira. Give the guy a chance. Cali's is the safest place for you right now. You said so yourself—no one knows you're there. Tyler is taking time off work and he's around. He's the best person to keep an eye on you."

I could grumble about not needing anyone to look out for me, but even I have to admit that I'm in deeper than I thought. I woke up this morning in a cold sweat from a nightmare involving the men from the woods. In my dream, they didn't stop at a beating. I woke before the guy choked me to death with his hands.

"Yeah, okay."

"Good, now tell me about last night. I took it you didn't want to talk in front of everyone, or even the police, but I need to know the details. In fact, we should give the police the full story and how we paid off that man a few weeks back. The loan shark shouldn't be involved in this, but you never know."

I'd gotten so behind when I told Lewis and his parents about the money. Lewis insisted we pay the guy off. It sickened me to borrow from them, but there was no way I could get out of it without help. I asked for just enough to get the loan shark off my back.

"I owe more," I say.

"Mira," Lewis growls, which isn't like Lewis at all. I've really pissed him off. "What do you mean you owe more?"

"About twice what I told you."

"Twice the amount?" His gaze darts from me to the road and back again as he angles the Jeep down the street to my apartment and pulls into the driveway beneath the carport. He shuts the engine off and turns to me. "How did this get so out of control? Have you been gambling since?"

"No."

He sighs. "Well, that's one good thing. Your therapist is getting through to you?"

"Yeah, she is. She's helping me with my problems." Which is true. I see my therapist every week, and we go over all my mom trauma.

"Exactly how much more do you owe?"

"Another twelve. I didn't want to worry you," I say in a rush. "I thought if I told you the full amount, you'd freak out. I gave the man half, thinking that would get him off my back until I saved up the rest."

"You owe a hitman another *twelve grand?* What the hell, Mira? What were you thinking, spending that kind of money at the casinos?" He grabs the back of his neck.

I lean my head against the glass, staring at the dumpster beside the carport. "Loan shark. And yes, I've stopped." *No way can I give my mom any more money.*

"So the men who hurt you were sent by that man? Why didn't you tell me the truth? Do you realize how dangerous this is? My parents and I would have paid it off, Mira. We need to tell the police. And I'm giving you the rest of the money."

"Lewis, stop. You need to give me a chance. I have a plan on how to pay the rest back."

Well, the seed of a plan, anyway.

He stares at me. "You don't get it, Mira. You could have *died* last night."

I close my eyes for a beat, because he's right. That doesn't mean I can keep depending on Lewis to fix my problems. Yes, I'm making changes when it comes to my mom, but I'm also working on not relying on Lewis and his family for everything.

"Just give me a couple of weeks to look into some things. A job opportunity just opened up. I've wanted a normal schedule for a while. This position pays better and it's a total nine-to-fiver. If I cut down on expenses and find a better job, I know I can get these guys off my back. I don't need much, and I'm good at saving money."

"When you're not gambling," he grumbles. "You're frugal as hell. Which is why this entire thing makes no sense." He looks at me. *Really* looks at me, and I wonder if he sees the truth.

I avoid his eyes.

"In fact," he continues, "you hardly have any expenses as it is. I don't know how you think you can cut back."

I open the door and step out, meeting Lewis at the back of his car. "The guy I owe is an ass, but he takes installments. He charges insane interest, but it's worth it. I got behind last time, but I can fix this. I know I can. You can't bail me out of everything. Even my therapist says I need to stop depending on you."

Resignation crosses his face. My words hit their mark. Lewis has been asking me to listen to my therapist for weeks. He can't turn around and tell me not to now.

He rubs the back of his neck again and stretches it, as if our conversation has given him a neck cramp. It isn't easy for Lewis to allow me to take care of myself. The dependency goes both ways.

He drops his arm stiffly to his side. "Two weeks, Mira. I'll give you two weeks to come up with a plan." We start walking toward my apartment building. "*If* you live at Cali's, and stay away from your mom, and stick by Tyler's side. I'll cover the rent at your studio."

"You don't—"

"That's it. No exceptions." We climb the stairs to my second-floor apartment, and I pull out the keys. "You won't have to pay Cali for the cabin. Tyler texted Jaeger he'll pay the rent while Cali is away. This is what I'm proposing. Otherwise, I pay off that man, and you're going into a treatment center—for *gambling*."

Huge emphasis on the last word.

Lewis is no dummy. I'm sure he suspects my mom is behind this somehow, but if he isn't bringing it up, neither am I. Maybe he's giving me the benefit of the doubt. Or maybe he doesn't want to deal with the consequences of the truth.

I open the door to my apartment and we walk inside. It's not much. A love seat and end table. A small bookshelf with more knickknacks than books—a vase that held flowers from my high-school graduation, a small Washoe woven basket my mom gave me before she lost her home.

I turn to him. "But living with Tyler..."

73

Lewis shrugs. "Your choice. Those are my conditions."

I'm not sure how he thinks he can throw me in a treatment center without my consent, given I'm an adult, but I can tell he's at least trying to give me space to do the right thing. It goes against Lewis's instincts not to bail me out.

"Okay, agreed."

He looks around. "Where's your suitcase?"

I point to the closet by my bed, and Lewis pulls my suitcase from the top shelf while I grab clothes out of a drawer.

He stares at the broken handle and wheel, and shakes his head. "Frugal girl...You need a new one of these."

I dump the clothes on my bed. "It's fine."

Lewis unzips the suitcase. "Why *were* you in the woods? Tyler mentioned he found you near a cabin your mom is living in." He raises his eyebrow. "You said you wouldn't go to her place anymore."

I knew this was coming. "I was on my way to visit her," I say reluctantly, leaving out the part about how I was going to give her cash. That was so stupid. I can't keep giving her money and still be able to pay off my debt.

He groans. "We talked about this. She'll hurt you and keep hurting you. She's selfish."

He's right, but I don't want to be a crap daughter because I have a crap mom. That doesn't mean I'm risking my life again. I've been enabling, as my therapist puts it. It's a fine balance.

"It's not as easy as you think. If Becky made a mistake, could you walk away and never look back?"

His mouth compresses. "You know that's not the same."

Lewis's mom is amazing. She's loving, supportive without overdoing it. She's shown me the kind of woman I want to be.

"My mom is as fallible as anyone else." He grabs a stack

of clothes to toss in the suitcase, his gaze narrowing on the lacy underwear in his hands. He drops them like they're hot coal. "I think I'll wait in the kitchen while you pack."

Lewis moves away from the dangerous lingerie and heads out of the bedroom, but he pauses at the door. "The point I was going to make is that my mom tries to be a good parent. In her case, she succeeds most of the time. Your mother has never put you first. Her only concern is for herself, and she'll drag you down if you let her. Have you talked about your mom with your therapist?"

"Of course." I pull out jeans and a few tops and add them to the pile in the suitcase.

"What does she say?"

I avoid his gaze, hesitating.

"Mira?"

"Same stuff you do. That it's not a healthy relationship. That even though my mom may not intentionally hurt me, her actions do, and I need to make decisions that are best for me."

"You should listen to your therapist."

I roll my eyes. "You're saying that because she echoes you."

"That's not true. I want what's best for you."

"I know you do. I'll try. But I can't just cut her out of my life."

"Maybe"—he squeezes the back of his neck—"just work on distancing yourself. Your mom expects too much."

He has no idea.

* * *

Tyler

Minutes after Mira runs out to Lewis's Jeep, a knock sounds at the door. I climb halfway up the loft ladder and grab my T-shirt from the floor, pulling it over my head before jerking the sticky front door open.

A woman with graying black hair and tanned, wrinkled skin stands on the other side. Despite the prematurely aged look, the woman might have been attractive at one point. Bright eyes, high, full cheekbones.

I'm not surprised. It's Mira's mom, after all—the person I saw inside the cabin last night.

The woman's gaze darts past me into the cabin. "Mira stayin' here?" Her voice is slightly hoarse, a bit slurred.

Nice manners.

"Sorry, who are you?"

I know who she is, but I want her on the defensive. With Mira's tight-assed responses, I'm not opposed to maneuvering around her to figure out what's going on. I'd bet my right nut this woman knows.

The woman looks me up and down, as if I'm the one with unwashed clothes and sour breath. "I'm looking for my daughter. She living here? Girl never showed last night. Was supposed to bring me somethin'."

"Why don't you tell me what she was supposed to bring you, and I'll make sure she gets the message."

The woman's eyes narrow. "Jus' tell her I came by. And that I'm not happy." She punctuates the last part with an angry glare and turns around.

"Mira was attacked on her way to see you," I say.

The lady stops and looks over her shoulder.

"Your daughter didn't show up because she'd been beaten."

A flicker of something crosses her eyes. Or it could have been light shifting through the trees. "Who did it?"

I shrug as if it's no concern of mine, but I care. I'd feel bad for any girl who'd been hurt like that. Nothing to do with Mira.

"Yeah, well, she should have come when I asked her to. If she hadn't been running late, maybe it wouldn't have happened."

My jaw tightens. Her mom makes it sound like Mira deserved the beating. It pisses me off that this woman acts like she doesn't care about her daughter.

"I *said* she was hurt. Badly."

The woman squirms and looks away. "Well, she's alive, ain't she?"

I shake my head. *Fucking unbelievable.* "Whatever, lady. I'll tell her you came by."

I go to shut the door, but Mira's mom moves quickly, considering her disheveled look, and shoves her scuffed white sneaker against the jamb, holding it open. "Tell Mira not to wait too long."

I study her face. "How'd you know where to find her?"

Her eyes dart away. "I waited near that Lewis fellow's place and followed him."

And she didn't see Mira leave here with him?

It would depend how far back Mira's mom trailed Lewis. Mira left pretty quickly...to get away from me. Maybe Mira's mom only saw Lewis's truck pull away from Cali's cabin and thought to check out the place? Cover all her bases. She's dirty, likely drunk or high, but not stupid.

"You should call Mira if you need her so urgently. I don't know when she's returning."

Or *if* she's returning. Mira might decide to stay somewhere else, now that she knows we'll be living together.

"Can't. Don't have a phone." The woman turns and walks down the drive toward a beat-up, mammoth sedan.

"Jus' tell her I came by. She'll know what to do," she says without looking back.

If Mira hadn't been on her way to see her mother, those men wouldn't have cornered her alone. What does Mira's mom need so desperately she's willing to put her daughter in danger? And what kind of mother does that?

Fuck. I knew this would happen. It's why I can't live with Mira. I don't want to worry about what goes on in her life.

But if I discover the truth and a solution to Mira's problem, maybe I can put a stop to this mess. Mira will be safe and can move out, and life will be good.

Well, not good, but my new normal.

Chapter Ten

Mira

I drag my trashed suitcase on its single roller the last few feet to Cali's closet, then peek out into the living room. Tyler doesn't look up from his laptop at the dining table. I quietly close the door and press my forehead against the cool wood. I have a feeling I'll be spending a lot of time alone in this room, avoiding Tyler.

I grabbed a few things from my place and I have my truck, but I don't feel settled. Those men in the forest scared the hell out of me. I'm not sure where living with Tyler falls on the list, but it's up there under *undesirable situations*. I'm safer with Tyler than by myself, but I don't like it.

I told Lewis I had a plan, but now that I'm sitting on the bed in Cali's room, attempting to come up with said plan, my hands are shaking. I clasp them together, squeezing out the nervous energy, and grab my phone to search for jobs. The first one I apply for is the one I mentioned to Lewis. I fill out several more applications for positions that seem likely to pay more, assuming someone exaggerates my skill set for me to qualify.

An hour passes and I decide to give myself a break from my self-imposed isolation. I filled out ten online applications with my iPhone (a pain in the ass without a computer), which is a solid start. Plus, I'm hungry.

I open the bedroom door, expecting to see Tyler sitting at the dining table with his laptop, ignoring me.

He's not.

He's sitting on the couch, one arm across the back cushion, staring straight ahead. He doesn't look at me, but I get the feeling he's been waiting.

This does not bode well. The best way for us to live together is to avoid each other.

I stride past Tyler to fix myself a sandwich and then return to my isolation room when his words freeze me in place.

"Your mom stopped by."

I sense Tyler's hard gaze. When I look up, a smug look rests on his face. He shocked the hell out of me, and even I'm not that good an actress. How did my mom figure out where I'm living? She's crafty when she wants something, and she hasn't gotten her money, so...

My thoughts must be transparent, because Tyler adds, "She followed Lewis, and came looking for you."

Wow. She's tracking me now?

"Did she say what she wanted?" I know. It's the money —always money—but I want to see if *Tyler* knows.

"She says you have something for her. She's not happy you didn't show up last night." He spreads his feet in front of the couch and leans on his forearms, staring at me. "I told her what happened and why you didn't show."

Great. I don't like my mom knowing my business. It tends to make matters worse. "And?"

"And nothing. She wants whatever it is you have for her. That's all." There's a hint of concern in his eyes.

I take a deep breath, shift uncomfortably. I know that look. Sympathy. Because I have a mom who doesn't care like normal moms do. I understand that the sentiment comes from the right place, but it always manages to make me feel worse. I don't want pity, especially not from Tyler.

"Anything else?" I reply coldly.

"Yeah." He stands and looks down at me, his pale eyes dark. "What the hell is going on?"

The intensity behind his eyes leaves me stunned—until I regain my senses and storm past him into the kitchen. I fling open the refrigerator door, blindly grabbing bread, lunch meat, and any other items I can find for a sandwich I suddenly have no stomach for. Why does he have to be perceptive *now*?

"Nothing's going on. Just stay out of it, Tyler," I say without looking at the man whose gaze is burning a hole in my back.

"You're lying."

I look over my shoulder. "You don't know me."

"Wrong." He leans forward. "I know you *intimately,* if you recall."

The air I gasp stings my lungs, which are overheated like the rest of me. I can't believe he brought *that* up.

He shrugs. "Granted, there's probably a long line of men you've been with." I swallow, my throat tight, anger making my chest even warmer. "And unless you've hooked up with some of your friends too...Lewis, perhaps?" He raises an eyebrow, and I glare at him. "No? Interesting... Well, I guess that means I know you in ways they don't."

What does this have to do with anything? And why is he being such an ass? This isn't the Tyler I remember. He used to be sweet, gentle. Now, he's hard edges and hot flames, anger radiating off him in waves.

Tyler narrows his gaze and glances down my body in a way that's meant to analyze, but instead it sends a shiver through me.

I hate that he has this effect on me.

"You look out of the corner of your eye instead of directly when you're telling a lie." He scans my face and his eyes stay fixed on my mouth. "And the centers of your cheeks blush when you're agitated—or excited."

I'm on fire with fury, ignoring the flutter in my belly his words elicit. How dare he pay attention to my bodily signals?

"I do not blush when I'm excited."

He leans in farther, his strong fingertips bracing the counter across from me. "You do. Would you like me to demonstrate?"

His words are a threat and a temptation.

This conversation is going in the wrong direction. I've got to get the upper hand. At the very least, a grip on the way he makes me feel. What is it my therapist always says? No one can *make* me feel anything. I'm in control of my emotions.

Tyler watches, listens in a way no one ever has. I used to love that about him, but now I see the downside to it. I don't want him butting around in my thoughts and emotions. Damn him for trying to get into my head.

"Leave me alone, Tyler." I turn and reach for the bag of bread.

"No." It's not the volume of his voice, but the tone that has me turning back. "We can't live together, which means you need to tell me the truth if we're getting you safely out of here."

I cross my arms. No way am I telling him anything.

He glances away and sighs. "I'll keep it to myself, if that's what you want. But you need to be honest with me. It's the only way. Like it or not, we're in this together until you move out."

* * *

Tyler

My words suggest I only care about getting Mira out of Cali's place, but it's more than that. Mira was my first—first crush, the first girl I had sex with—and for some reason, she means more. I need to know she's going to be okay.

I see Mira's rough side like everyone else, but I'll always wonder about the softer part of her she doesn't show anyone. The playful, sweet girl I once saw lurking beneath the surface.

So yes, I want her out, but I also want to help her. I'd swear she's not telling the truth, and if I can get her to trust me, even a little, maybe I can get us out of this fucked-up situation.

She rubs her arms. Her shoulders hunch forward slightly, an atypical response from the girl who holds her head high, no matter the situation. It's as though the weight of the world has fractured her resolve.

Mira walks past me into the living room. For a moment, I think she's going to keep walking and shut me out. But she doesn't. She stops in front of the couch and sits in the center.

I walk over and take the recliner across from her,

waiting for what's to come, because with the way she's holding herself tight, her arms tucked close to her sides, I sense her vulnerability. I have a knack for pissing Mira off. If I want the truth, I had better keep my mouth shut.

She doesn't speak for a long moment. She turns to the side and stares out the window, the saddest look I've ever seen pulling down her pretty features. That look hits me square in the chest, knocking the air from my lungs. I want to protect her, destroy whatever has given her this look of utter defeat.

I figured she was lying about something. I believed she'd gotten herself into trouble, but what is this really about? Mira doesn't cower or back down easily. Whatever's got her worried is big time.

She raises her eyes and singes me with a glare, which takes me aback for a second. It's the kind of look I'm used to from her, but she just did a one-eighty on me. I'm all ready to protect and maim for her, and she's looking at me like she wishes *I* were dead.

Is there any wonder she twists me in knots?

"What I'm about to tell you does not leave this room, Tyler. Ever. This is a secret between the two of us. No one can know."

"Been there, done that." Kind of rude, but true. No one knows we slept together. Well, except for the high-school kids who must have seen Mira leave the bedroom with bedhead.

The centers of her cheeks turn pink, and my heart stirs to life.

Still works. Still awesome. I love that I can draw a blush from her. There are some perks to living with Mira after all.

"Don't be an ass."

"Too late."

She rolls her eyes. "Do you agree, or not?"

"I won't tell anyone. Now spill it."

She sits forward and tucks a leg under her, her breasts bouncing with the motion. That one movement tosses my brains to the wind.

Focus, man. I reluctantly drag my gaze to her face.

"You know how close Lewis and I are?" I nod, and she glances away, biting the inside of her cheek. "He doesn't know what I'm about to tell you. When I say no one can know—I mean *no one.*"

That gets my attention. Lewis and Mira are tight—*were* tight. I'm not sure what they are anymore. I thought I knew what they were in high school, but that seems all wrong, since she indicated she never slept with any of her friends. Which was a surprise. I could have sworn Mira and Lewis were a couple at one time. But then, I didn't actually believe that rumor until Holly suggested Mira was sleeping with both of us. I wish I had known there was nothing going on between them. If I'd known the truth, Mira and I might have parted as friends.

She focuses intently on me. "I don't owe money for gambling."

This is the most information I've gotten out of her. "But you do owe money?"

She nods. "Lewis has been telling me to stay away from my mom for years. If he knew, he'd freak out."

"You've been giving your mom money?" Her jaw drops, and I shrug. "She wanted whatever you had pretty badly. Money's a big motivator."

"I helped her pay off some bad people. She told me they'd kill her if she didn't give them the money within a week. I believed her. The dregs she hangs out with are scary, and she seemed desperate." Her gaze wanders nervously.

"What else?"

"Then she asked for more." Mira shakes her head. "Honestly, I don't know how my mom pays her bills. She never works. I kept giving her money, but I started coming up short each month. One month I couldn't pay my rent. I borrowed from a place in town. I paid the money back with my next paycheck."

She glances down and tucks a loose strand of hair that escaped her ponytail behind her ear. "I told my mom I couldn't help her anymore after that."

I hold my breath, waiting for what's to come, because my gut tells me this gets worse.

Mira looks straight at me, her expression unguarded, despite the steel she tries to exude. "I didn't hear from her for two months. After a few weeks I started to worry. I searched for her and when I found her...She had a broken arm, a black eye...She wouldn't talk to me. She blamed me for what had happened."

Mira plays with the frayed edge of her jean shorts, her next breath shaky. "I didn't know whether or not she got hurt over the money, but I couldn't risk it again. I told her that if she needed cash, I had some saved, which I didn't." She looks up as if to convince me. "I had a job and no one depending on me. I thought I could handle it, but I got more behind. Eventually, I asked my mom to seek help. She's had a cocaine problem on and off. I figured that's where the money was going. I gave her pamphlets for places that provide support, but she wouldn't take them. She refused to get help. I didn't know what else to do."

"A cocaine problem *on and off*," I say, disbelieving.

Mira's mother—the drug addict—uses Mira, and Mira is

desperate for her mother's love. Of course Mira feels she can't say no.

I shift my jaw, attempt to tamp down my anger. I pull at the collar of my shirt and sit back, staring at the wall. I want to rail on her mom's ass for using her daughter. Instead, I say, "Lewis told me you're seeing a shrink."

Her eyes grow dark. "I'm not crazy, Tyler."

"I didn't say you're crazy." And she isn't. Mira just has too much on her shoulders. Addicts are heavy burdens. My mom worked in the casinos for decades. I've seen her lose friends to drug and alcohol addictions. She put the fear of God into me and Cali, warning us to never get mixed up in that.

"You can't help your mom if she's still using, Mira. You need someone to talk some sense into you."

Her eyes widen, her face turning red.

Okay, that might not have come out right.

"Screw you, Tyler."

Fuck, why do I bother trying to help her? "You already did."

She turns away. "Will you never forget that night?"

I don't know why I brought it up. It's a jerk move. A part of me must still be pissed, which I don't like to admit. "Can you?"

"No," she says, surprising me.

Her arms loosen and she looks at me. "I know my mom is a problem. Lewis has told me for years to sever the tie. I couldn't do it then. I still can't imagine it. She's the only family I have."

"You have Lewis and his parents."

"But they're not *real* family. They don't have to love me."

"No. They love you because they want to."

Mira stares at me for a long moment, as if she actually heard me. Shocking.

"I'm trying, Tyler," she says. "I'm not giving her money anymore, no matter what happens, okay? Even if she won't talk to me. Or if..." Her chest rises shakily on an inhale. "When those men found me in the woods, it was supposed to be my last drop-off. I was going to tell her I couldn't do it anymore, but then..."

"Those assholes kicked the hell out of you over the money you owe for *your mother*."

Her mouth twists in a frown. "I'm clear on the details. You don't need to remind me. I know how bad things are. I'm finished with it all. In fact"—she sits forward, hesitancy in her eyes—"I'm getting a new job. Two if I can swing it. I'll work day and night to pay off my debt. I already sent out job applications, and I have a good lead at Blue."

My shoulders tense. The fuck?

"*Blue Casino?* The place that fired my sister? The place where Gen was nearly raped? Are you fucking crazy, Mira?"

Annoyance fires behind her gaze. "I can't be picky, can I? It's a position as an assistant to a director. Kind of a long shot, but it pays well. If I work nights as a dealer and days as an assistant at Blue, I'll be able to save a ton of money over the next couple of months."

I hate the idea that she applied for a job at Blue. That's like jumping out of the frying pan and into the fire. "You can't work at Blue. That place is bad news."

"This is an executive position. It's not on the floor. Nothing will happen up there. Besides, I doubt I'll even get the job."

I shake my head, not paying attention to her logic or *illogic*. "No. Not there."

"You can't tell me what to do, Tyler!" She leaps to her feet, one hand supporting her ribcage for a second before planting on her hip, as if her ire won't be deterred by the beating she's still recovering from. "I told you because you were being a pain in the ass about everything and snooping around. Now I wish I hadn't. I should have known I couldn't trust you."

She can't trust *me*? I stand and march across the room to the counter, grabbing my wallet and keys. I climb a couple of rungs of the loft staircase, jerk a short-sleeved button-down off the floor, and slip it on over my T-shirt.

"You wanna be on your own? Fine. I'm outta here."

Chapter Eleven

I order another beer from the waitress at Avalanche, while my buddy Phil curls a slice of pizza in half and shoves a good majority of it in his mouth.

"You're living with a chick?" he mumbles over the food.

I glance around the crowded pizza joint, hopping with locals getting their drink on, and search out our waitress. It's only been thirty seconds since I ordered, but I need that second beer.

Mira has to leave. That, or we're going to kill each other. Which means I need to find her another living situation. All my local buddies have suddenly shacked up with their girlfriends. My options are limited, but Mira's aren't. She could live with Lewis's parents, where she grew up. She's just choosing to be stubborn.

Because she is a pain in my ass.

"I gotta get her out, man. Can't live with that girl. You don't know what she's like."

"Didn't you say she was beautiful?"

Did I mention that? Dammit.

Phil raises his eyebrows, and I pluck at the front of my T-shirt. *Is it hot in here?* "That's not the point."

Phil takes a gulp of beer and wipes his hands on the thin napkins. "Best way to get rid of a woman is to find another."

"I don't need another woman," I grumble. "I need the one who's contaminating my hideaway to get out."

"No, I know, man. That's what I'm saying. Bring another chick around. This girl, Mira, she'll get pissed and take off."

Oh, fucking hell. Why did I bother telling my old high-school buddy the situation? Phil's an amazing mountain biker, but he isn't the sharpest tool in the shed.

"It's not like that. She won't get jealous. She's not into me," I say, biting off my words. There was a time when Mira *was* into me and I didn't realize it, until I was practically inside her.

I shake my head. This isn't the same.

Phil swigs his pint, studying me. "Doesn't matter, man. We're all animals when it comes down to it. She'll get territorial. Men duke it out until they land on top." He snickers at his joke. "Women, though—dude, they're manipulative and vocal. They yell and stomp until you cower. Don't cower. Whatever you do, remain on top. Bring other women around. Mira will get the picture. She'll realize she's lost her territory and either take off, or stay away from the house as much as she can."

Jesus, I'm being lectured about biology by my local buddy, who never left Lake Tahoe. The worst part is, some of this crap makes sense.

"You're missing the point, Phil. I don't want to live with Mira. If she gets pissed and stays away from the house, she's still under the same roof. And how is replacing Mira with some other nameless girl a solution? I'm not like you and the rest of our friends. I don't want to live with a woman—well, my sister is different. You know what I mean."

Phil holds up his hands. "Hey, I'm the idea man. You got a problem with performance, that's your problem."

The attractive blond waitress takes that moment to set my pint on the table, her mouth twitching as she clears a glass. I shake my head her way, as if to say, *Don't listen to this jackass.*

The waitress leaves, and I lean toward Phil. "You want to keep your voice down. I don't have a problem getting it up. Where the hell did you get that idea?"

Phil shrugs. "You said this girl, Mira, cut off your balls."

Does he remember everything I say? Clearly I've been talking out of my ass. "I meant figuratively. Believe me, getting it up isn't the issue. Everything's on high alert. That's part of the problem," I mumble.

"Oh, hoo." Phil slaps his hand on the table and leans back in his chair. "So we get to the bottom of it. You want her and she doesn't want you, so you don't want to live with her."

"What? No. That's not it at all." *Dammit, is that it?* "The point is we are completely incompatible—"

"Seems one of you is compatible." He glances at my lap.

I stop in mid-speech, staring incredulously at my jackass friend.

First of all—dude, why is my buddy checking out my balls? Second, he may be right. It causes me no small amount of agitation that I still have a physical attraction to Mira. Puts me in a downright fucked-up mood.

This conversation is giving me a headache. Somehow Phil's suggestion is sounding more and more tempting.

I scan the surroundings. Avalanche Pizza is a major hangout. Girls come here in their short shorts and flip-flops, wearing skintight tanks and full makeup. It's a casual pickup joint is what it is. Why not scope someone out and bring her home tonight—test Phil's theory? It couldn't hurt. His idea is dodgy at best, but under the circumstances I can make an exception.

I swig the last of my second pint. I haven't had a hookup in a while, but it might be just what I need.

* * *

LACY TRIPS OVER THE THRESHOLD. "OOPS," she whispers loudly in my ear.

"Easy, girl. Why don't we sit you on the couch?"

When I picked up my and Phil's waitress at Avalanche Pizza, I thought she'd be fun. Hot body, pretty face, sweet demeanor—an all-around ringer for a good time.

The only problem? Lacy is a lush.

As soon as her shift ended at eleven, she started pounding pints. *Phil* had a tough time keeping up. I gave up entirely. Someone had to drive us home.

Lacy was so smashed by the time we left, I decided to take her to my place and get her sober. Hooking up wasn't on my mind. Trashed girls don't do it for me, but that doesn't mean I leave them to their own devices. Not when I covered the bill for her drinks. I'm partly responsible.

I guide her to the couch and she sinks like a rag doll.

This is a disaster. I should never have listened to Phil. "I'll get you a glass of water."

"Beer?" she slurs.

I have it in the fridge, not that Lacy will see any. "Sorry, I'm all out."

I bring her the water and sit next to her. She rolls into

me, and for a moment, I don't mind. It's been a while since I held a girl. I'd forgotten how nice it is.

I wrap my arm around her shoulders and she slips her hand up my shirt, caressing my stomach and chest. I'm okay with the easy touching—still not into the drunk hookup, though.

"Lacy, we should think about getting you home once you've had a couple of glasses of water. Is there anyone there? A roommate, maybe?"

I don't feel comfortable dropping her off by herself in this condition.

"Nope. Want to come over? I bought a new mattress. It's massive." She nips my chin with her teeth. "We can do all sorts of fun things on it."

"Ah, no. I was thinking of crashing. I'm pretty tired."

The corners of her mouth turn down. "Oh."

The next thing I know, Lacy's lips are on mine, and she's reaching for the snap of my jeans. The kiss isn't bad, considering how trashed she is, but it also makes me feel...nothing.

Not one spark. But even if my mind doesn't do drunk girls, my body has never had a problem reacting to them.

Until tonight.

I've got a hot chick reaching for my junk, and there's no response from my better half. I actually wish this girl would pass out so I don't have to deal with the situation. Which is insane. What is happening to me?

The sound of the doorknob jiggling grabs my attention, but Lacy's still got an arm lock around my neck, her tongue down my throat. The door opens before I can untangle us.

Mira walks in and freezes, her keys dangling from her hand. Her gaze goes straight to where Lacy is palming me.

Close quarters inside my sister's place. The couch is only a few feet from the front door.

Lacy finally notices someone has entered, and comes up for air, giving me back my mouth.

"Hey," I say to Mira. Might as well milk the situation. This was my plan, after all.

Lacy shows some modesty and pulls her hand from my pants, sitting upright, or as upright as she can while weaving from a heavy buzz.

Mira's mouth tenses. She strides past us into the kitchen, flipping on the lights. She slams cabinet doors as though she's looking for something, or wants to make a lot of noise.

"Is that your girlfriend?" Lacy whispers loudly.

"Roommate."

"Oh." She smiles. "Good." She glances around as if only now taking in how small the place is. "Is there anywhere we can go?"

I consider the loft, just to get out of the line of fire, but I don't think Drunk Lacy will make it up the ladder. And I'm not sure I want to find out what Lacy has in mind. I don't like turning girls down. They tend to get more aggressive, as Lacy exhibited before Mira's entrance.

At the same time, a part of me wants to continue testing this theory of Phil's. For a moment there, I got the sense Mira wasn't simply pissed to see me, but pissed to see me with another woman. And that shows promise. If she thinks running into this sort of thing is what she has in store living with me, maybe she'll suck it up and move home to Lewis's parents' place.

"It's pretty tight in here," I tell Lacy. "We're stuck on the couch. My roommate will probably go in her room soon anyway."

Her face twists in a flirty pout.

I play with Lacy's hair as Mira stomps into the bathroom. A few minutes later, she sweeps past us, slamming the bedroom door behind her.

"Damn," Lacy says. "You sure she's not your girlfriend?"

"Completely." I lean in for another kiss.

I'm suddenly optimistic about having Lacy stay the night. Still not going to sleep with her, but I wouldn't mind holding her and kissing her. I miss that. And because there's no spark, I have zero need to worry about the repercussions of *this* relationship.

Chapter Twelve

Mira

I rub the sleep from my eyes, squinting at the sun glowing through the cheap curtains of Cali's bedroom window. I can't believe Tyler. *Asshole.* That girl was unfastening his pants. Pretty obvious what I walked in on last night.

I flip over and punch my pillow to fluff it up.

Okay, I just want to hit something.

He couldn't find someplace else to take his hookup? I could have come home at any point during their little interlude. You don't do that with a roommate around. It's an issue of respect.

I swear he brought that girl back just to piss me off. I never should have told Tyler what was up with my mom. Had I left him guessing, he probably wouldn't have bugged me about the job stuff. We might not have fought.

He looked like he expected me to walk in on them—like he planned it. I might be reading into things, but he could have at least stayed at her place instead of bringing her here.

But even that thought bothers me. *Arghh.*

I tilt my ear toward the door. No noise filters in from the living room. It's early—seven, maybe. Tyler is probably still asleep. I rest my chin on top of my pillow above my folded hands and stare at the clock.

One, two, three minutes tick by.

If Tyler is going to be an inconsiderate jerk, why should I be a courteous roommate? I'll go mad if I stay in here all morning, waiting for his date to leave.

I grin. I'm willing to bet that I've had more experience at being a bitch than he has at being a jerk.

I leap out of bed and throw on slipper socks, jerking my hair into a ponytail. Tyler wants to bring a girl home and make out on our couch? Fine. But he'll have to deal with his early-rising roommate.

I open the bedroom door and saunter into the living room. And my stomach sinks, all thoughts of retribution fleeing.

Tyler is on the couch, the girl he was with last night half lying on top of him. He has his arms wrapped around her waist, her head tucked beneath his chin. They're sleeping, his handsome face tipped back onto the armrest, looking boyish and sweet.

Fortunately, they're dressed; otherwise I would have to kill him. The thought of Tyler naked with another girl—I won't even go there. Seeing him like this leaves me in enough pain. He left town. I wasn't supposed to be subjected to this sort of thing.

Damn him. I glance away and swallow the knot in my throat. Tyler with another girl stabs me in a place I never feel pain. It's deep, shadowed, and protected so well that not even the stuff my mom pulls penetrates. But Tyler manages to spear the spot in one shot with his insensitivity. Because I want to be the girl wrapped in his arms.

I walk past them into the kitchen and pull out a bowl and cereal. I'm not quiet as I set milk on the counter and fill the teakettle with water. After a minute or two, I hear light rustling and the sound of hushed conversation. The girl walks into the bathroom, closing the door behind her.

I sit at the dining table, ignoring Tyler a few feet away in the living room. His date exits the bathroom and waits by the front door as he puts on his shoes and grabs his keys. After a moment, the sound of the front door closing reverberates throughout the house.

I set my spoon down, my hands balling into fists.

Tyler has been gone a long time. Of course he's moved on. Logically I know this, but seeing it is so much worse.

I take a deep breath and try to clear my head. My heart doesn't recognize Tyler coming home for what it is. Temporary. He'll be gone soon. This being forced together is a blip, one small scene in his brilliant life. It means nothing to him.

I munch woodenly, chewing the cereal that feels coarse and rough against my tongue, attempting to harden my heart against the pain that living with Tyler causes.

I don't know how long I stare out the backyard window before the front door opens and Tyler walks in. For a moment, I glimpse uncertainty in his eyes.

"Morning." He plasters on a cheery smile.

I stand and walk into the kitchen, dumping the rest of my cereal in the sink. "You can't bring girls home while we're living together," I tell him, my back turned.

The sound of his keys clanking on the counter comes from behind. I look over to find them in the exact spot he pulled them from earlier. He returns his shoes to the resting place they were in when I walked out this morning.

He has a routine. That I notice pisses me off.

"Excuse me?" he says. "Pretty sure I can. Last time I checked, I'm not tied down."

I twist on the faucet and run water over my cereal bowl, washing it vigorously. "That's not the point. This place isn't big enough for sleepovers."

I sense him walking up behind me, the way he did yesterday morning. Too close, his body grazing my back. "You got a problem seeing me with other women?" he says above my ear, his voice low and sultry.

I set the dish down and step around him to the other side of the kitchen, careful not to touch him. "Of course not."

He leans against the cabinets, his handsome face set in a determined expression, arms crossed over his broad chest.

"As soon as I get another job, I'll be working a ton. I'll hardly be around. Can't you put it off until then?"

A beat passes as he continues to study me. I hate it that I don't know what he's thinking right now. I'm pretty sure I won't like it.

"Nope, don't think I can. Besides, my sister and Gen accommodated their boyfriends. You can deal. *Or*—here's a thought—you could move in with the Sallees."

No way. If those men are dangerous to me, they'll be dangerous to the people I care about. Tyler's a young guy. He could take care of himself in a fight. "Gen and Cali are best friends. Of course it worked for them. You and I—"

He crosses the couple of feet that separate us, making the pulse at the base of my throat hammer. I grab the edge of the counter. "You and I what, Mira?"

My mind goes blank. I don't know what we are to each other. We are so much more than we should be, and so much less than what he shared with that random girl who just left.

"Nothing, we're nothing. Just—don't bring girls around while I'm here. Or be prepared for me to return the favor. You'll see how crowded things can get."

Chapter Thirteen

I pull up to the Sallees' house, still annoyed at Tyler. He's
goading me, and it's working. But I don't wilt. He won't
win this.

I throw the car in park and peer at John tinkering in the
four-car garage he uses for small wood projects. The rest of
the house is a two-story, peaked Tahoe-style home with
views of the forest. Located a block or so from the lake, their
house is nice sized for Lake Tahoe, but not ostentatious.

John and Becky are wealthy, but you would never
know it. They live and act like your average middle-class
family. They have what they need and no more. The
single-bedroom home Lewis recently built for himself is
also modest. The Sallees are not about money—they're
about family and taking care of the people you care about.
Which accentuates the problems I have and the family I
come from, who've historically been selfish sons-of-
bitches.

I step out of the car and breathe in the scent of Tahoe,
and another essence unique to the Sallees' property—a mix
of pine needles, hot cement, and the oleander Becky

planted on the side of the house. A wash of summer images fills my mind. Happier times and so darn simple.

Water-gun wars with Lewis and his friends were serious business when we were kids. They knew instinctively how to nail me right in the face, so I used sneak attacks and Becky as my safe zone. The guys wouldn't get Becky wet, and if they did, she'd laugh and order them to knock it off. If I think back hard enough, I can smell Becky's cocoa butter sunscreen, remember the worn tank top and shorts she used to wear while gardening or lounging on a chair watching us play. My best memories come from this house and family, not from the reservation where I was born.

Not that the reservation is a bad place. Some of John's closest friends and coworkers live there. But like any place, there's always a small subset that doesn't conform, doesn't try. That's the group my mom hung out with, in addition to the crappy people she spent her time around when she was off the reservation. They were worse.

John's back is to me, but I can tell he knows I'm here. For one, my truck is as loud as a lawnmower. Also, he stilled when I pulled up. He's been waiting for me.

He turns and smiles as I approach. "Hi, darlin'. Was beginning to worry about you."

I wrap my arms around his waist, and he plants a kiss on the top of my head. John is tall, though not as tall as Lewis. His eyes have deep grooves from the easy smile he throws around, but with high cheekbones and a strong jawline, he's a handsome bugger.

As a younger man, John Sallee carved a swath through the ladies of Lake Tahoe and the reservation with his jet-black hair and killer smile, until Becky knocked him on his ass. John didn't stand a chance with Becky. Almost thirty years later, she's still stunning, and no pushover. Becky is the best of both worlds. She is beauty and grace, and strength. She would never let a man walk all over her. She would lay down her life for her family. She's affectionate, confident, and smart. Everything I wish I was.

"I took a short drive before I came," I tell him.

The full story is that I wanted to make certain no one followed me, so I took a detour to get here. A man dressed all in black was walking down the street away from Cali's cabin when I left. I didn't catch sight of his face, but his height and build looked familiar. Scarily familiar. He could have been anyone, but the chill I got at seeing him made me paranoid.

My injuries are healing well, but I haven't forgotten what those men did to me. I'm sure the people I owe money to already know where my loved ones live, but I'm not going to point an arrow at them.

John's face grows taut. "I'd like you to give me a call if you're going to be late."

I'm twenty-two, but he still worries. Like a dad. And because I've gone missing before with disastrous results.

When I was sixteen, I didn't return from a visit with my mom when I said I would. Lewis found me at my mom's place being beaten by one of her boyfriends. Since then, John and Becky assume the worst if I don't show up somewhere on time.

They love me. Sometimes I don't see it, because I'm afraid to look. Afraid it will disappear before my eyes.

I press my face to the collar of John's shirt, as if to give him another squeeze, when really I'm pushing back that darn burning behind my eyes that seems to come and go often lately.

What's gotten into me? I'm all sappy. It's ridiculous. Of course John cares. He's always cared. I'm off-kilter, my emotions close to the skin because Tyler's back in town and pissing me off at every turn.

This reunion with Tyler isn't what I thought would happen when I dreamt of us together in my high-school fantasies. He is not madly in love with me. He might actually be in *hate* with me. The chemistry I felt back then is still there, and super befuddling. But then, nothing was ever simple when it came to Tyler. He wasn't what I expected the night I seduced him. He isn't what I expect now.

I breathe in John's calming scent. A mix of the laundry detergent Becky uses and the spiced aftershave he's worn for as long as I can remember. Completely comforting, completely home.

I look up and smile. "Sorry. I wasn't thinking. I'll call next time."

His face brightens. "Come on." He tosses the yellow work rag in his hand on a stool, and we walk to the door that leads from the garage into the kitchen. "Lewis and Gen are already here. They'll be happy to see you."

My shoulders don't tense the way they used to when Gen first started coming around. She is beautiful—like serious model material—tall and gorgeous, and something about her classic looks reminded me of the girls I went to high school with. I assumed she'd act like them too. Catty, bitchy. But she isn't like that at all. And the more I'm around her, the more I realize it.

Despite my initial reaction, I like Gen. It scared me, the intensity Lewis showed toward her at first. He homed in on her like a laser. I thought I'd lose him to this girl. But I should have trusted my reserved, almost-brother's instincts. Gen is great. To my surprise, I actually enjoy having her around.

Inside the house, Becky pulls something from the

oven as John closes the door behind us. She baked, but not the good stuff. This looks like sliced goop with spices on top.

"Sweet, girl, there you are." Becky smiles over at me. "Just in time for eggplant appetizers. Lots of vitamin B in these babies to keep us healthy and happy."

I give her a kiss, eyeing the eggplant warily. "Really? What happened to those little quiche things you make?"

"Oh, those are frozen food. This is homemade, and it's good for you."

I shoot her a look.

"Stop. Give it a try."

"Okay, but we need to regulate the healthy food around here. Sometimes a little fat does a body good."

"Mira," she scolds in a not-at-all-serious tone.

"I have a sweet tooth, and you're throwing eggplant at me. My body is going into shock without the preservatives and processed sugar that have sustained me for the past twenty-two years."

Becky laughs and sets the pan on the counter. "Lewis," she calls. "Get over here and eat the food I've slaved over. Mira isn't giving it the love it deserves."

Lewis walks into the room and catches the look I level at him. His face calm, he surveys the purple globs. "Something new, Mom?"

Becky scoops one onto a napkin and hands it to him. He takes a bite, chewing, his gaze thoughtful. "Good." He looks up. "You should try it, Mira."

Huh. Lewis is a bit of a human garbage disposal, but he'd probably say something if it were truly bad. And I don't want to hurt Becky's feelings.

I take the napkin Becky hands me. I'm hungry, so I dig in...to salt, mash, and some flavor that's...not right.

I force back a gag and look over at Lewis. He's hiding a grin behind his fist, his face turning red.

Bastard.

I swallow the goop that feels like it's congealing in my throat. "Becky, I love you, but don't ever make me eat that again."

She punches her fists to her waist. "Mira, it can't be that bad."

"Have you tried it?"

Her expression turns to chagrin. "Well—no."

I raise my eyebrow.

"Fine," she says, scooping one up and taking a bite. Becky's mouth twists to the side, then she casually walks to the sink, leans over, and spits out every last bite of food in her mouth in a very unladylike manner that has Lewis and me laughing.

I smack Lewis on the arm. "Jerk. You totally set me up."

Still laughing, he hugs me.

Becky gracefully dabs her mouth with a napkin. "That's disgusting. It's going in the trash."

John, who's been watching us while pretending to rummage through the junk drawer, walks over and gives his wife a hug. No one but Becky is a fan of her healthy phase, but we love her anyway.

Becky glares at John. He raises his hands in surrender and walks away, grinning.

Smart man.

Normally I love eating at the Sallees' and getting my grub on. Given Becky's latest invention, maybe she'll dump this health-food kick.

"One bad recipe doesn't mean anything," she says to no one in particular. "I'll find a delicious eggplant you guys will love."

Or maybe this phase *won't* be over so soon. Guess I'll be starving for a while.

Lewis and his parents head out back to look at some plants Becky wants the guys to relocate, and Gen saunters in from the living room. She's holding her cell phone, her pretty dark hair swept back in a ponytail, highlighting her hazel eyes.

"You're lucky you were on the phone," I tell her. "My gut might never recover after that supposed food product Becky tried to foist on us." I point at the tray of food that has yet to be disposed of. If Becky thinks the dog will eat it, her ego is about to get burned. Buckles, who loves Gen and follows her around everywhere when she's at the house— traitorous dog—is too smart to fall for that crap.

"I didn't have a good feeling about that appetizer," Gen says. "I may have strategized my phone call with my dad around the kitchen timer."

I stare agape. "Wow, Gen. I wouldn't have thought you so devious."

She grins broadly. "Impressed?"

"Yeah. I underestimated you. Remind me never to make you my nemesis again."

Gen chuckles and starts searching the kitchen cabinets.

I scratch Buckles, named after the patch of white fur that halos his waist. He finally deigns to grace me with a nose rub. I lift his chin until we're staring human eye to dog eye. "Would it hurt you to greet me at the door every now and then?"

He puffs out a doggy breath and walks over to stand beside Gen.

So not cool. And if Gen wasn't so sweet, I'd be offended that even the dog prefers her company over mine. Not that Lewis prefers Gen over me, exactly. She's his girlfriend. Of course he wants to spend time with her. If I had someone in my life, I'd want to be with him too. Not that I'd know what that's like. Tyler certainly isn't it.

"So, Gen," I begin hesitantly, deciding now's a good time to bring up Blue. Because we're alone, and because I'm a giant wuss, hoping Lewis's girlfriend will tell him I applied so that I don't have to. Lewis is far too comfortable yelling at me. Meanwhile, Gen is safe from his wrath, because he worships the ground she walks on. "I applied for an admin position at Blue Casino."

"Really?" she says, looking over her shoulder, the pantry door wide open. She twists around, her expression a mask of concern. "You know I had a bad experience there, right? Like, *really* bad."

I glance away and wipe crumbs off the counter. "I do. Sorry about that. I never said anything, but I felt really horrible when I heard."

A manager attempted to sexually assault Gen when she worked at Blue as a cocktail waitress. It was a near miss, and it rattled everyone. It rattled *me*.

But what happened to Gen won't happen to me. I'm not sweet like her. Not vulnerable—except when ganged up on by a handful of junior-high-school bullies, or oversized men in the middle of the woods...or when my crush shows up in Lake Tahoe, out of nowhere.

Okay, I'm as susceptible as the next person, but I'm a little more street-savvy than Gen. The point is, there's no chance of anything happening in the middle of the day inside a populated office.

I meet her concerned eyes. "I'm sorry you went through that. But what happened to you was on the casino floor. This position is upstairs among corporate Blue."

"Yes. And that's where Drake worked. I don't think—"

"I need this job, Gen."

A weighty silence fills the room. Gen studies me. I'm tense. Stressed and worried about how I'll dig myself out of the things I've gotten myself into.

She sighs, possibly reading the look on my face. "Drake is on a forced leave of absence from the casino until his trial. You should be safe, but there could be others at Blue. He got away with so much. I just—I don't know—I always thought there was something funny going on there."

"The casino's got to be on the lookout. They can't afford more bad publicity."

"Maybe." She doesn't look convinced.

"It's a long shot that I'll get the job, but I have to do something. I'm not making enough money dealing to pay off my debts."

"Lewis or his parents would—"

"No." I shake my head.

It may not make sense to Gen, but there are things I've been working on with my therapist. I've been stuck, clinging to Lewis and his family. They rescued me; that doesn't mean they have to bail me out for the rest of my life. I'm trying to take responsibility for my actions. Borrowing money from shady moneylenders to get my mom out of a scrape that's probably linked to something illegal? Not smart. I did this, and I need to get myself out of it.

Gen looks around, seemingly grappling with something. "You've got to do what you think is right. I'm worried, is all. The Sallees love you and want to help."

"It will be okay, Gen."

She closes her eyes and sighs. After a moment, her finger taps the counter. "If it turns out you get the job at Blue," she says slowly, "let me know. I've got a friend on the inside. Maryanne. She's a supervising cocktail waitress on the floor, and she's a good friend to have there."

"Nessa and Zach still work there too. I wouldn't be alone," I say.

Zach met Nessa when she first started working at Blue, and she's slowly become a part of the gang. She's even a regular at Zach's taco dinner nights. Nessa and I aren't close, but we've hung out a few times.

Gen props her head on her hand, her elbow on the kitchen island. "You know, there might be other jobs. Have you looked everywhere?"

"I've looked, but this is Lake Tahoe. Other than the casinos, there's not much that pays well for someone with only a high-school diploma."

She gives me a sympathetic nod. "I'll give Maryanne a heads-up. See if she can do anything to get you in." She blinks, forehead furrowing as if she's having second thoughts.

"That'd be great," I say before she can change her mind.

I grab a sliced apple from the appetizer dish and shove it in my mouth, frowning as I chew. I rely on a heavy dose of junk food from the Sallee pantry. Becky's health kick is like a forced diet.

Gen shakes her head at the appetizer plate and returns to hunting the cupboards. She pulls down a bag of rice crackers. Not the most promising processed food, but better than fruits and vegetables.

I grab a cracker from the bag. "So you don't think it will be weird if Maryanne puts in a good reference for me? Upstairs suits and floor employees work in parallel at my casino, not so much together."

And that's another thing. I put feelers out with a few people at work. They said it wasn't likely the casino would allow me to keep my job if I decide to work at another casino. Some kind of conflict of interest. I'm going to try to pull strings, but it doesn't look good.

"Nah," Gen says, opening the fridge and rummaging around in one of the bins. "Maryanne's badass. She manages the floor waitresses, but she's also influential upstairs. I think management is afraid of her." Gen pauses. "She's kind of scary. Totally hazed me when I first got there." Returning her attention to the bin, she says, "I'm not sure what changed. Could have been the Drake thing, but she's shown a different side and now we're friends." Gen reaches deep into the fridge, her face brightening as she pulls out something wrapped in plastic. She slaps it on the island.

My eyes light up at the half-eaten block of cheese. I've scoured this kitchen high and low for days with nary a sign of trans fats. Gen's putting in serious time at the Sallees' if she knows where to find fatty stashes I'm not even aware of.

"I like Maryanne," Gen continues. "She reminds me of Cali and Tyler's mom. No-nonsense and down-to-earth. Just don't get on her bad side."

I've always wondered what Tyler's mom was like. That Gen knows and I don't is another reminder of the distance between me and Tyler. We may live together, but that doesn't mean we are close.

And I don't know why that makes me sad, but it does.

Gen hands me the slice of cheese I'm ogling. "If anyone can get balls rolling, it's Maryanne."

Chapter Fourteen

A week later, I realize Maryanne doesn't just have pull at Blue, she's a rock star. She put in a good word for me about the assistant position, and I received a call back, which is a miracle when I think about it. The job description for the assistant to the human resources director doesn't state it, but candidates typically have college degrees, or at least prior experience in the field, and I have neither.

I pretended I didn't want to go to college when the Sallees offered to pay, because I wasn't sure I could do it. The only time I felt book smart was when Tyler helped me with math in school, and I chalked that up to his tutelage.

Using a lint roller Cali left behind, I swipe the black pencil skirt and white blouse Gen lent me for the interview this morning. I own black heels, so I didn't need to borrow those, not that I'd fit in Gen's shoes. She's slender, but tall. The skirt is a little big in the waist and hips, and I had to roll the sleeves of the blouse, but the outfit works. My size-six feet in Gen's size-eight heels would not.

I arrange my hair three different ways this morning: a ponytail, a bun, a French twist, each one so not me and worse than the last. I'm trying too hard, and I worry that the minute I walk into Blue, people will recognize me for the fraud I am. Somehow, I have to get through this interview and prove against all the odds that I belong.

I pull out the pins from my latest hair disaster and settle for it parted to the side and hanging down my back in waves. Same way I always wear it. If you can't be true to yourself, who can you be true to? Might as well begin with your hair.

I walk out of the bedroom and Tyler is at the kitchen table typing on his computer. He's shirtless, his hair sticking up on one side—basically, early-morning hot.

I groan internally. It's the worst torture to have the one thing I ever sought for myself dangled in front of my face. Close, yet infinitely out of reach.

Even if I could have Tyler physically, as he seems to have turned into this manwhore, I've always wanted more with him. That was the problem.

Despite my threat, Tyler brought a different girl home every night this week, the asshole. I don't know how long the girls stayed or what he did with them. I didn't want to know. I closed myself off in my room, earbuds in my ears, blocking it out of self-preservation. I'm trying to numb myself to Tyler. I could keep to my threat and bring home dates. I've not ruled it out. I'm just busy, that's all.

Tyler looks up and does a doubletake. His gaze takes in my outfit appreciatively, until his eyebrows pull together in suspicion. "Where're you headed?"

"You really think that's your business?" I grab my black purse that has a little too much wear for the outfit, but whatever.

"Yes. I'm keeping your secrets, aren't I?"

I stare incredulously. Was he always this manipulative? He used to be so sweet and accommodating.

What could it hurt? He can't tell me what to do, no matter how much he seems to think he can. "I have an interview."

Tyler slowly lifts his hands from the keyboard of his laptop and turns to me, revealing a full-frontal of his muscled chest. He's lighter than I am, the dusting of hair on his arms a golden brown above a faint tan. His shoulders are wider than they were in high school, his chest chiseled and defined. Tyler was a beautiful boy back then. I try not to focus on how devastatingly handsome he's become, but sometimes I can't help it.

I swallow, forcing my gaze to his eyes. He seems too focused on interrogating me to notice my distraction.

"Where's your interview?"

He'll find out eventually, whether Gen mentions it, or he figures it out because he reads me. Never thought I'd think it a pain in the ass to have a guy be so observant.

"Blue," I tell him, and check my phone for the time. The last thing I want is to be late for my interview.

Because I can't resist another glimpse of his chest—or his reaction, which I anticipate to be colorful—I glance up. He's frowning, his shoulders and the muscles in The Chest taut and lightly bulging.

Can't he wear a T-shirt? How am I supposed to concentrate with him dressed like that?

"Mira, we talked about this. You can't work at Blue," he says calmly, though his posture and the tension radiating off him tell another story.

"Sure I can." I apply lip gloss and press my lips together. His eyes focus on my mouth, his attention momentarily distracted.

Good. I'm glad I'm not the only one. I was beginning to think I was the only female Tyler Morgan didn't want to take home.

Tyler turns back to his computer and begins typing rapidly.

That's it? No argument?

Well, that was no fun. Thought I'd get a bigger rise out of him than that.

I roll my eyes. He's hot, he's cold, he's pissed, he's distracted. This new Tyler is all over the place and I can't keep up. So I won't even try. I grab my things and slip out the door.

* * *

I'M NOT sure what I thought an interview at Blue Casino would be like, but I didn't think it would resemble a television casting call. The sheer number of people in the waiting area is making my head hurt. I don't like to be alone. But crowds make me woozy. I think it has something to do with people getting too close. Freaks me out.

I smooth a lock of hair away from my face, as though I'm not bothered by it all. The guy next to me smiles. One of *those* smiles. The kind that says, *I'd like to know what color your panties are.*

He's in a tailored suit, a shoulder briefcase resting beside his fancy leather-clad feet. He pulls out his phone and scrolls the screen, glancing every few minutes to see if I'm watching. I'm not, but I sense his gaze landing on me every time he does it, and it's not helping my paranoia about fitting in.

The woman next to me, about my age, but way classier in a flared skirt with a matching cropped jacket, is modern and sophisticated. I'm self-conscious in my too-large pencil skirt and nicked-up purse.

I tuck my bag under my seat with my heel and fold my hands in my lap. What the hell was I thinking, applying for this job? Everyone waiting for an interview is out of my league. *Stupid, stupid*...I shouldn't be here.

The hiring manager scheduled appointments close together to screen for candidates in rapid-fire ten-minute interviews. I arrived early, and I'm seriously tempted to leave. No way will the director call me back after he meets me and sees the way I'm dressed. And once he goes over my background experience? It's all over. I had no business applying for this job. This was a waste of time.

"Mira Frasier?"

My shoulders jerk at the sound of my name. Like most Washoe, my last name is as European as the people who stole our land. It's all I've known, familiar, yet never fitting. Like me, here, now.

For a moment, I sit, considering my options. Flee? Which isn't really my style. I'm more a face-it-down-no-matter-the-consequences type of person. But at the moment, fleeing seems like a good alternative to the humili-ate-self-in-extreme-fashion-and-lose-what-little-pride-you-have-left option.

But then I remember the money I owe...and why I'm living with Tyler. Yeah, I will grovel to get this job.

I take a deep breath and stand, smoothing out the ripples in my skirt. Flirty guy rakes his gaze over my body, staring at my ass as I bend to grab my purse off the floor. I ignore him and every other polished yuppie in the waiting area. I hold my head high as I follow the receptionist down a wide corridor.

The receptionist is wearing a tailored navy suit that

hardly sways when she walks, but her hair is this crazy, deep red—almost violet—color. She fits the environment. Professional business thinly veiled by casino smut. We round a corner and a woman stands at the entrance of a large office, greeting me with a kind smile. I'm surprised. In my experience, most managers are men who sit behind over-large desks, expecting to be waited on.

The manager is about my height, so average, with a slightly fuller figure, but curvy in all the ways guys appreciate. Her hair is a shiny, dirty blonde, her eyes a golden brown. She has great coloring. I always thought blond with brown eyes was pretty.

"Hi, Mira. I'm Hayden Tate, the new human resources director." She holds out her hand, and I shake it. I follow her into the office and sit across from her moderate-sized and unpretentious desk.

Large shelves on either side of the room line the walls, filled with books, with more books stacked on the floor. There's a colorful abstract on the wall that doesn't fit the rest of the Blue décor, and I wonder if it's something Hayden Tate brought in from home. The painting is a red, shadowed abstract of a woman's torso as she holds herself, her shoulders curled in. None of the Blue paintings contain figures. They're all squiggles or blotches, or whatever paint spread on canvas passes for abstract art. This painting is raw somehow. I can't decide if the woman is holding herself together, or falling apart.

"I apologize for the crowd out there," Hayden says, and takes a seat, as my nerves return. "This department has experienced major losses of late." Her eyes flicker away and she straightens a stack of papers, her movements strained. "We're speeding up the hiring process for the assistant position, which will require possible evening and weekend work, depending on what the casino has going on. Would that be a problem for you?"

"No." I shake my head. "I'm used to working long hours. Weekends are fine."

I have too much time on my hands, now that Lewis is busy with Gen. I appreciate Cali letting me stay at her place, and I've even gotten used to the idea of living with Tyler temporarily. But with him on a manwhoring mission, I'd love any excuse to stay away.

Hayden studies my face, and it takes all my willpower not to fidget.

She glances at a sheet of paper on the desk in front of her. "It says here you've worked at a local casino for the last four years. You advanced from a hostess position to a dealer." She looks up. "I see two other positions in between the dealer and hostess jobs, each with increasing levels of responsibility."

To keep from getting bored, I looked for new jobs that challenged me. And I needed more and more money over the years to support my mom.

"This is a desk position," Hayden continues. "Not that there isn't room for growth, but I want you to understand the parameters of what I'm offering." She lists the job duties, which, I must admit, sound foreign.

"I understand," I tell her, nodding as if these are all tasks I can handle.

"We're short-staffed in human resources, as well as in our hospitality department. The assistant I hire will provide support to both departments until a replacement can be found for hospitality."

I'll be filling two jobs I have no background in? Whatever; it's not like I'm actually going to get the position. My résumé clearly shows that I don't have the skill set she requires. She must give every applicant the same spiel.

"Now that you know what I'm searching for, why don't you tell me about yourself, Mira. Why are you looking to move from gaming to management?"

I give her a story about how I'd like something with a higher ceiling for growth, when I really just need more money.

"That all sounds good," she says. "I'll keep your application in mind as I wrap up the first round of interviews."

Hayden has been nice, but this whole interview felt scripted, as if she's going through the motions. A part of me hoped I'd get lucky with this job, but I never really believed I had a chance. Not after I saw my competition in the lobby.

Time for a new plan, because this lead is a bust.

The sound of knuckles rapping on the door comes from behind. Hayden looks up. "Drake," she says in greeting, a rigid smile on her face.

I don't know Hayden, but she isn't hiding her unease at seeing the man standing in the doorway.

She called him Drake. He can't be the same Drake that Gen told me about—he's supposed to be on leave.

"Good morning." Drake gives Hayden a cursory glance, his gaze settling on me.

He's a fairly handsome man, wearing a dark suit with a blue checked tie that turns his amber eyes more demonic than I'd like. The look he gives me is assessing, a full-on check-out. Worse than the looks from the guy in the waiting room, because there's a sense of possession behind this man's gaze. As if he believes he could have me anytime he wants.

These thoughts run through my mind, but they aren't what has my stomach lurching, my hands sweating. It's the man who approaches Drake in front of Hayden's door who has my full, terrified attention.

I'm ready to leap over the desk and put any large object between me and this other guy.

Because I know him.

Denim jacket guy.

The man who hunted me in the woods, pinned me to the ground with his rough body, then proceeded to beat the crap out of me. *That* denim jacket guy.

Denim Jacket mumbles something into Drake's ear while peering at me, and Drake's gaze turns even more assessing, if that's possible. He smiles, but it's more smirky than kind, as if he, like Tyler, knows all my secrets. Only I trust Tyler a hell of a lot more than I do this Drake guy, which speaks volumes, because Tyler's on my shit list.

"Here for an interview, *Mira*?" Drake says.

He used my name, though we haven't been introduced. Because he knows of me, or because Denim Jacket said something?

I need to get out. Like *now*. I glance around, but it's either cower in the corner behind Hayden, or make a run for it past the two large men blocking the doorway. So, basically, suicide. No way am I escaping the situation without a confrontation of some sort.

Hayden glances between me and Drake. "You two know each other?"

"In a manner of speaking," Drake says.

I sense Hayden's gaze on me. My face is flushed, and I won't look at Drake or Denim Jacket. She walks around her desk and stands beside me in an almost protective manner.

How is this Drake guy connected to the evil piece of crap next to him? None of this makes sense.

Both Gen and Tyler warned me not to come here.

Applying for this job may be the worst decision I've made yet. Because now that I've run into Denim Jacket, I'm certain I should have stayed home. Or moved out of the country.

But I have nowhere to go. No one to go to...

Stay calm. There's no point in running. I'll never get this job. I just need to wait out the interview until it's over. Denim Jacket won't do anything to me in a public place, right? *Right?*

"Mira is applying for the assistant position," Hayden says.

Don't tell him that. These men don't need to know any more about me than they already do.

Her chin rises a notch. "She's a strong candidate and I'm happy to have her come in today."

No, no, no! I'm not a strong candidate. What's she saying? She's making the situation worse.

"But my interview is over," I butt in, and grab my bag as I stand. "I was just leaving." I attempt to scoot around Hayden.

Hayden narrows her eyes on Drake. "You know, Mira" —she drags her focus to me—"I'm beginning to believe you're the perfect candidate for the position." My jaw drops. Hayden stares at Drake and says, "You're as qualified for this position as I was for mine."

I glance between Drake and Hayden. Something is going on. And I'm sure I want no part of it.

"Planning to hire someone unqualified as your assistant, Hayden?" Drake taunts.

Normally I'd take offense at that statement, true or not. But no way am I stepping in the middle of their conversation.

Hayden crosses her arms. "It's been done before. And

you never can tell a candidate's merit based on a piece of paper. Some have hidden strengths that can't be predicted by a degree. Wouldn't you agree, Drake?"

He doesn't smile. He glares at her, and I feel the urge to protect *her* this time.

I've never been the protector. Have always looked out for number one, and to hell with everyone else. Well, except for Lewis. Okay, and Zach too...and the Sallees. All right, there are a few people I care about.

"Anyone can obtain a college degree, but people with ethics and a moral code are more important," Hayden continues.

Drake smirks and brushes invisible lint from the sleeve of his coat. "As you say, Hayden. Come see me when you're finished." He walks away.

Denim Jacket doesn't immediately follow. He smiles, staring at me. "I'll see you around, Mira."

Maybe I should reassess the idea of leaving town. It's sounding better and better.

Hayden walks across the room and shuts the door behind the men, pressing her back to the wood. "Can I be frank with you?"

Frank? What have I gotten myself into? I don't want her to be frank, I want to get the hell out of here. I'm in some warped world. Everything is turned upside down. This place is supposed to be professional, not a hitman hangout.

Hayden continues before I determine how best to let her down. "I'm new here. Very new," she says as she makes her way to her desk. "As in, they just hired me to fill in for the last human resources director they fired." Her words are coming fast, in a rush. "I thought it was strange that I was hired fresh out of business school. This position would normally be filled by a candidate with the degree, plus years of practical experience, but that's not what they did. They needed someone immediately. And they hired *me*." She sits and motions for me to do the same. I reluctantly do as she bids, resuming my seat across from her. "After I took the job, thinking I was the luckiest girl alive, I discovered why the position had opened and why they needed it filled so quickly."

She leans forward and lowers her voice. "The casino is under investigation for sexual harassment. The last HR director failed to respond to multiple complaints about one of the employees." Hayden's gaze moves toward the door, silently saying what she's apparently not willing to admit out loud but that I already gathered. That Drake was the employee.

"Honestly, I'm like you," she says conspiratorially. "I have the right attitude and drive. I'm scrappy, but I don't possess the qualifications for the position. Management didn't care. They hired me because I'm a woman and they needed to quickly clean up their image. And because they thought I'd be malleable." She smiles humorlessly. "I represent Blue Casino's PR effort to save the company."

"You're a woman, so they can't be misogynists if they hire you as one of their directors," I say, returning her sarcasm.

She sits back. "Exactly."

All this—it's not what I bargained for when I came in today. I knew things would be awkward due to my lack of qualifications. I did not predict this outcome. Running into Drake—*the* Drake. Running into my tormentor from the woods. It's all too much.

"I'm sorry for you, Hayden, I really am." I'm about to tell her I can't work here, even if she truly wanted me to and wasn't simply taunting Drake, but I can't help adding,

"Maybe you should consider resigning. Seems to me like you work with a bunch of assholes."

Hayden laughs. "Mira, you're perfect."

"Excuse me?" I cussed and insulted her employer. Is she nuts?

"I'm looking for more than an assistant. I'm looking for someone with a good head on her shoulders. Someone who can assume a leadership position when needed, who possesses good judgment under stress. These recommendations"—she taps the paper in front of her—"point to the type of person I'm looking for. Maryanne Boeman is well respected at this casino, and she gave you a strong character reference."

How did Gen manage that?

"Your work experience at a top casino is also helpful."

She can't be going where I think she's going...

Hayden folds her hands on her desk. "Mira, I'd like to hire you as my assistant."

Chapter Fifteen

At Hayden's declaration, I say the first thing that comes to mind.

"Why would you want to hire me?" I wave behind me. "You heard what Drake said. He called me *unqualified*."

I don't know Drake, but I got the sense he knows me, or knows of me.

Why did Denim Jacket have to be here today of all days? He was casually dressed. I don't think he works here. Or maybe he does, but not upstairs.

This isn't good.

"Which is why I want you," Hayden says.

This is the most bizarre interview I've ever had.

"Look," she continues, "I'm not sure what Drake is up to, but I suspect things. He's onsite for a couple of days to hand over the finer tasks of his management position in person. He shouldn't be here at all, but the CEO has a soft spot for the guy. The CEO feels the charges against Drake will be dropped. But even he can't allow Drake to work while he's being investigated."

She looks at me as if she's pleading a case. What she

doesn't know is that there's no way I can take her up on her offer. This is a waste of both our time.

"You have a healthy dose of leeriness toward Drake. Right away, that makes you a strong candidate for the job. If Drake gets off in the courts, you won't be swayed by him, unlike so many of the women in this casino."

Whoa, that gets my attention. "Women actually *like* that guy? After what he did?"

"As far as I can tell, yes. Quite a few."

What is wrong with people?

I shake my head and focus on the more important issue. I can't take this job. I can't be anywhere near these men. But I stick with the practical argument. "You've seen my résumé. I don't have a college degree, and I've never worked in an office."

"You're qualified in all the ways I need you to be." Hayden sits back in her chair with a scarily determined look on her face. "I trust anyone who doesn't trust Drake. You're clever and hardworking, or you wouldn't have risen at the casino where you've worked. I can train you, and I'd rather train someone who has my confidence."

Oh my God, she's serious.

But no. No way. I can't agree to what she's proposing.

"Plus"—she smiles devilishly—"you're a woman, which should make management happy. Better for the image. And you're a smart enough woman to remain apprehensive of that man." She pokes her finger toward the door. "Not to mention the others like him in the company."

"There are *others*?" Gen mentioned something about the possibility. It seemed hard to believe, but now...

"Oh, many." Hayden pauses. "Maybe I shouldn't tell you that."

"No, don't worry. It doesn't matter. I can't take this job."

Hayden blinks, her expression revealing the first sign of uncertainty before it's quickly wiped from her face. "Whatever your reservations, I'll eliminate them."

Hayden is pretty and feminine, with a delicate voice, but the girl plays hardball.

I wish I could work for her. She'd be a cool boss. I respect the fact she's not willing to back down to these jerks, but—I shake my head. "I really can't. Even if I could..."

I glance toward the door. Even if Drake is on leave, there's no way I can work in a place with Denim Jacket around.

"As a director, I have influence, no matter what Drake led you to believe through his intimidation tactics. I'm sorry about that interruption. He likes to make people feel small. But I don't frighten easily, and the casino has to support my decisions. I'm holding their image together. You and I working as a team would form relationships with other trustworthy coworkers to get the job done."

This doesn't seem professional, it seems crazy. There's something spectacularly wrong with this place, considering the assault allegations—which I know to be fact—and running into the hitman who attacked me in the woods. But that statement alone—the part about *other trustworthy coworkers?*—it's like there's a war being waged at Blue. Good versus evil. What the hell?

Hayden's not backing down, so I'm going to be blunt. "Really, Hayden. I appreciate you offering me the job. I know it would be a huge step up for me, but it doesn't matter. The reason I can't work here isn't only because of Drake. That man he was with...I shouldn't be near him. Matter of fact, I need to stay as far away from him as possible."

"I see," Hayden says, though her expression says otherwise.

Of course she doesn't get it. I'm not making sense. I haven't given her any of the pertinent information. And I'm not going to.

A gleam takes over Hayden's eyes. I don't like that look. "Scrappy" is right. "Mira, Drake will be out of the picture for a while. What if I made sure that other man didn't return either?"

I shouldn't encourage her, but I'm curious. "You can do that?"

"Yes."

I can't really be considering this job. With Drake potentially stopping in from time to time, a man with a connection to Denim Jacket?

I shake my head. It's no good.

"And I'll offer you a signing bonus," she adds. "How does five thousand dollars sound?"

Ahhh, crap. Just—*crap.*

Of all the things she could have said to convince me to take the job—things I could easily shoot down—she has to say the one thing that makes a difference.

* * *

I RETURN to the cabin to find Tyler pacing the small living room the way Lewis was the night Tyler brought me here. Worse, Tyler is dressed and his hair is combed.

All is not right with the world.

Tyler's hair is perpetually disheveled and he rarely wears a shirt around the house—or maybe that's just since I arrived. It wouldn't surprise me if he walked around half dressed to antagonize me. But today he's professional-looking? Something's up.

"Where've you been?" he asks, as if he doesn't already know the answer to that question.

I set down my ratty purse. "You suffer a brain injury while I was away? You know where I was. I had an interview."

"At Blue. You were there the entire time?" he asks disbelievingly.

What is this, the Inquisition? I'm still coming to terms with what went down at the casino. I don't need Tyler pestering me.

"Yes," I say, and shake off my heels, padding barefoot into the kitchen for a glass of water. When I turn around, Tyler is directly in front of me, crowding me at the sink.

I draw in a breath, which has me inhaling his scent—Tyler and soap mixed together. The scent I love.

For once, Tyler steps back, as if realizing he's standing too close, or maybe he detects the sparks my body is shooting off. "You were there a long time. Did something happen?"

I shrug. If I say no, that would be a flat-out lie, and for some reason I don't want to lie to Tyler. He's good at sniffing them out. Funny, no one else is.

"You're shrugging. What does that mean?"

"Nothing." I brush past him and head toward my bedroom. "Just, yes, stuff happened, but it's no big deal."

Tyler follows me and braces a shoulder against the doorframe after I enter the room, his expression severe. "Let me decide if something's a big deal or not."

My fingers pause on the top button of my blouse. Part of me is turned on by his words, the manly protector bit. There's no hesitation. He actually thinks he knows what's best for me. But I miss gentle Tyler, especially when this alpha side is in my way.

"You mind? I'm trying to change here."

Tyler's stare drops to my hands on my shirt and he blinks. He turns around, crossing his arms stiffly. "Don't try and spin the conversation in a circle, Mira. I don't have time for it. Interviewing at Blue was a stupid idea. Then you go and stay there for two hours? I want to know why."

I finish pulling on jeans and a T-shirt, and glare at his back. "What do you mean, you don't have time for this? You're jobless. I think you have the time. And why do you want to know? Were you worried about me, Tyler?"

I'm being sarcastic. Obviously. Tyler would never worry about me.

He turns slowly, his face twisted in a grumpy, sardonic smile that is somehow extremely sexy. My mind flashes to memories of that mouth on mine, and I shake my head, rattling it out of my brain.

"Of course I wasn't worried," he says. But there's something faltering in the way he says it. "But I won't be held accountable if something happens to you. So you need to stop making stupid decisions."

I hold up my finger. "Did you just call me stupid?"

He taps his thumb on the doorjamb, but offers no apology.

"I don't need you to look out for me." I move to walk past him, but he doesn't budge, and his body takes up the entire doorway.

"You mind?" I say to the smooth biceps peeking from beneath his short-sleeved button-up, blocking my path.

If I wasn't so pissed, I might be able to admire his muscled arm. But the offending appendage belongs to Tyler, which means I'd like to bite it.

God, he's frustrating. "Move it," I screech.

Strong hands grab my shoulders and push me back until the backs of my knees collide with the bed, my butt landing on the mattress. "Not until we have a little talk, Mira."

A shiver runs down my spine, settling in my lower belly. Tyler sits beside me and I suck in a breath. He's too close. It's been a bitch of a day, and I'm weakened.

"What happened at Blue?" His voice is low, gentle.

That voice, the way his presence softens me—they were what made me allow him inside years ago. And it's dangerous. Look how well that turned out for us.

"Nothing," I say stubbornly.

A finger settles beneath my chin, turning my face toward a masculine jawline that no longer hints at the boy I once knew. "Tell me."

Up my gaze goes, drawn to eyes I could never resist, the strength and sincerity behind them as mesmerizing now as they were six years ago.

"I took the job."

Chapter Sixteen

Tyler

The fuck? She cannot be serious. "What do you mean you took the job? You went in for an interview, Mira. Places like Blue don't hire on the spot. What the hell did you do?"

"God, Tyler! What are you insinuating?" She squirms away from me and stands, brushing past me into the living room.

Haven't lost my touch. Except normally when women make celestial exclamations I'm doing something that gets them going, and they use words like *God,* and *Jesus, Tyler,* mixed in with a few cries of *more*. But that hasn't happened in a long time, because in spite of appearances lately, I haven't actually hooked up with a woman in forever.

I follow Mira into the other room, where she spins to face me. "Is it so hard to believe someone would want me?" Her voice comes out strong, but her eyes are all vulnerability.

She thinks no one wants her? Is she crazy? Everyone wants Mira.

I attempt to calm my anger—with her, with myself. "You can't take that job, Mira."

She glares at me, the fire in her eyes lighting up the room. She's fucking beautiful. "I can. I did."

Not what I want to hear. And I don't need the stubborn attitude either.

I pinch the bridge of my nose. I've got to get a grip. There's a solution here if I cool my head, think this through.

Mira needs a better-paying job than the one she has. I get that. I'm trying to not consider the possibility that she took the job at Blue to piss me off. Both Gen and Cali were sexually harassed at Blue, yet Mira takes a job there? She knows it's the most dangerous place for her to work. But telling Mira what to do isn't effective either. She'll do the exact opposite.

I've got to fight Mira on her own playing field. She expects me to boss her around and act like an ass, because that's what I've done so far, which, admittedly, is pretty messed up.

So I'll do the opposite.

Which means I can't tell her to quit her job. Goddammit, *think.*

I need to protect her—I mean—*fuck,* where did that come from? I need to make sure she's not doing anything dangerous. The only way to get her out of Cali's place is to make sure she's safe.

I pop my neck and scrub a hand down my face. Fine. I'll keep my mouth shut about her new job. But I've got my own plans. Good thing I didn't waste time after she left this morning. I made a few phone calls, put some things into motion that will ensure Mira doesn't get into trouble.

I grab my keys from the counter and slip on my Vans, tying them.

Mira's gaze tracks me. "Where are you going?"

Hah, wouldn't she like to know? Fine. I'll tell her. Let her mull this one over. "Blue Casino."

"What? Don't you dare, Tyler. I need this job." She scurries after me as I head to my car.

I jerk open the rusted door and turn to her, taking in the flush of her cheeks, the beautiful intensity of her eyes, which typically melt my resolve, but not today. "Don't worry, Mira. Your job is safe. I have something else I need to do at Blue."

* * *

Mira

I NEVER DISCOVERED what business Tyler had at Blue, but it didn't matter because I received an official offer letter for the assistant position. Whatever Tyler did, he didn't ruin my career prospects.

I've spent the last few days preparing for my new job. I went into work and told them the situation and they let me go, just as my coworkers said they would. My boss was pretty bummed, but she understood the pay-raise aspects. Lewis wasn't happy either, at first, but once I assured him Drake was on forced leave until the sexual harassment charges were investigated, he mellowed out. Lewis is confident that Drake will get his ass nailed to the wall. He's not worried the guy will get off.

The only thing that has me worried now is Tyler's behavior. He's been dodgy, disappearing for long periods of time. It's better if we stay away from each other, but there has to be a hitch. Tyler went from being all up in my business to letting things go. I don't trust it. I can't tell if he's mad, or if he has something up his sleeve.

Tyler doesn't get it. I couldn't turn down the money Hayden offered. The five-grand signing bonus is almost half the amount I still owe. What sealed my fate was the salary she quoted. It's almost double what I was making as a dealer. I couldn't afford *not* to take the job.

Tyler may be worried I'm getting myself into trouble, but this will work out. I'll have my debt paid off in no time. Then I can move out and he will be rid of me. Crap, he'll be thanking me.

I arrive at the casino more nervous than I can remember ever being, though the interview for this job came in a close second. I don't want to screw up, and as much as Hayden pumped up my ego with why she wanted to hire me, I can't help worrying I'll let her down.

I enter the elevator, and am pondering how to keep it together and not look like an idiot newbie when an arm shoots between the closing doors and a security guard steps inside.

Not just any security guard.

Tyler.

"What are you doing here?" I whisper harshly. "And why are you dressed like *that*?"

I've never had a thing for security guards—men in firefighter uniforms, why, yes, yes indeed—but security guards? No, they are not what I consider sexy among the uniformed hotties. They're like the bottom-dwellers of the uniform hierarchy.

But Tyler's uniform clings to his muscled shoulders and chest, his fitted shirt tucked into a narrow waist with—I peek behind him—his amazing uniformed ass on display, dammit.

He's a hot security guard. And he works here. Obviously.

Son of a bitch, he tricked me.

"I could ask you the same thing. Wait," he says, cocking his head to the side as the elevator doors close. "I already have."

I bite my lip, holding back the urge to stomp my heel. "Tyler, this is not a joke. I'm in trouble, and this is my way out."

He casually shoves his hand in the pocket of his hot security guard pants. "I told you, Mira, it's to my advantage to keep you safe, so you can move out. Which means I'm not letting anything happen to you while we're living together."

All the anger melts from my body. "Why? We both know how you feel about me. Why are you doing this?"

He takes in the red wrap dress I borrowed from Cali, his gaze moving on down to my legs—where it lingers. He shrugs. "Do you know how I feel about you?"

I thought I knew, but the way he's looking at me and the way my chest is rising and falling at the expression in his eyes... I'm confused.

Tyler may recognize the attraction I have for him, may even feel some of it in return, but he'd never act on it. He doesn't trust me, and he's made it clear that he's moved on.

The floor numbers spring up the digital display before settling. The elevator doors open. "You used me, which I didn't mind, by the way." He winks. "But I really don't want to live with you. No offense."

"I didn't use you," I tell him, and walk into the reception area.

I wanted to have sex with Tyler, because I was young

and thought I loved him. Of course, he doesn't know that. He thinks I slept around.

Tyler was going to leave. He was being an ass to me, accusing me of sleeping with other guys—I used it as the excuse I needed to run and protect my heart. To leave him before he left me.

"Doesn't matter if you used me or not. I was willing," he says.

We stop in front of the reception desk, sizing each other up.

"Can I help you?" the receptionist asks. It takes me a second to register that she's talking to us.

"I'm Mira Frasier, the new assistant to Hayden Tate."

"And I'm Tyler Morgan. New floor guard."

The receptionist looks from me to Tyler, her gaze skipping down Tyler's uniformed chest in a stealthy glance. "We've never had guards up here, but you've come at the right time. They're letting someone go this morning, and he needs an escort. You think you can handle it?"

"I'm here to serve," Tyler says, and whips out a charming smile.

The receptionist grins, barely cracking the plaster of makeup she's wearing.

I might hurl.

"Right this way, Mr. Morgan." Her mouth turns down. "Ms. Frasier, please have a seat. I'll let Ms. Tate know you're here."

I want to tell her there's no need, because I remember the way to Hayden's office, but I sit and wait. Violet—that's not really her name, but it's what I'm calling her in my mind from now on—is too distracted by the handsome new guard to pay me any attention.

Tyler said he's doing this to make sure I'm safe so I can

move out as soon as possible, but this is extreme. Especially when he seemed content to wile away his days on his computer and his nights drinking beer and hooking up.

I don't care what Tyler thinks—I don't need his protection. And forget Violet, who's decided to go MIA so she can drool over Tyler. I don't need her escort to Hayden's office. Hayden's expecting me. She can't be offended if I show up at her door.

I stand and walk down the corridor. Rounding the corner to Hayden's hallway, I catch sight of Tyler. Escorting Denim Jacket.

I go stock-still, frozen in the middle of the hallway.

Denim Jacket leers at me as they approach. I scoot to the side of the hall, my shoulder pressing the cold, white surface. "Back so soon?" he says as he and Tyler near.

I swallow the dry ball in the back of my throat and try to hold his gaze. He walks past me, a smirk on his face.

Tyler stops. "Hey, you okay?"

I nod, though my heart is racing. I don't know why this bully affected me above all the others I've encountered in my life—kids in school, my mother's ex-boyfriends—but he did. He does.

"You don't look okay." Tyler glances after his charge, who's making steady progress toward the exit. "Is it that guy? You know him?"

It's the look on my face, or I don't know, Tyler is psychic, because his expression hardens. "Is that *him*? One of the guys who attacked you?"

"Don't do anything," I say in a panic, which sounds utterly weird. I never show alarm. "I mean it, Tyler. You're escorting him out. He's leaving. It's a nonissue. Don't make things worse."

I'm so close to paying off the money. I just want this

over with, and they've left me alone as long as I make my payments. If I turn this man in to the police, would it make things worse? Would he or his partner come after me again? Or my family?

It's not worth it.

Tyler leans forward, his hand finding my waist. The pressure of his touch is possessive and warm. "He made it an issue when he put his hands on you."

Chapter Seventeen

Tyler

That piece of shit Blue axed is one of the assholes who hurt Mira?

Motherfucker.

They issued me a wand and I have a permit to use Mace while in uniform, but I'd like to take this guy with my bare hands and fuck him up. The only thing holding me back is that if I lose my job, I can't look out for Mira in this cesspit.

"Jesus Christ," I mutter to the ceiling. *Deep breath.*

Mira peels her shoulder off the wall. She holds her head high, but her eyes are glossy and frightened. "It's fine. He's gone."

Fuck, it's not fine. She's not fine. I've never seen Mira so scared. The only time I've seen her this way was in the woods and right now. Goddammit.

I go to reach for her, but she steps away, walking shakily down the hall. She glances back in the direction of the asshole who frightened her, before steeling her features and knocking on a door. A woman greets her and she enters the office, the door closing behind them.

I turn toward my charge, anger burning inside. I'd like to rage all over this guy, but I need to keep a cool head.

I jog to catch up to him and slap a hand on his shoulder. "Easy, buddy. Not going anywhere without your armed escort." I'm not really armed, but I wouldn't mind using my wand on his kneecaps.

He glares at me, then stares ahead.

"What'd you say your name was again?" This fucker needs to be put behind bars for what he did to Mira.

"Didn't."

Easy enough to get the information from Blue. "That girl back there?" I say. "Stay away from her."

Asshole gives me a crooked grin. "She's not your type. Too much spunk. Girls like that enjoy a strong hand."

I squeeze my fists together until my knuckles crack. I thought this position would be the perfect way to make sure Mira was safe, and I was right. Look who popped up on her first day—the very guy who made it necessary for us to live together.

Even if this guy hadn't hurt Mira, I could use an excuse to bash something in. The guilt I carry over Colorado, living with Mira—they have me wound up tight. Add in this fuck, and taking out pent-up aggression while performing my "job duties" doesn't sound like a bad idea. Maybe this is the perfect job for me after all.

I assess the dude. He's not as tall as I am, but he's bigger in the shoulders. "Your hands go anywhere *near* her and I'll remove them. From your body."

Asshole chuckles. "Big threat." He glances at me out of the corner of his eye. "That little girl you're protecting got herself into some serious trouble. If you know what's good for you, you'll stay away from her. Nothing good comes from hanging with girls like that. But don't worry. I'll take good care of Mira when the time comes."

I pull out my rubber wand and crack the back of his knees.

Asshole crumples to the ground, laughing. "Good one, buddy. You forget where you're working? That stunt will have you walking the plank too."

Fuck, I forgot about the security cameras. I don't bother to look around. Doesn't matter. Worth it. "Get up and keep walking."

He chuckles again as he ambles to his feet. My detainee doesn't make any more inciting remarks as I escort him to the exit, but he looks over his shoulder as he walks out the glass doors. "I'll be sure and tell Mira you said hello the next time I see her."

Keep it together. I let out a slow breath.

He's taunting me. I'm more intelligent than that, not some Neanderthal. I need to plan how I'm going to deal with the threats to Mira's safety. Getting fired from the job that allows me to keep an eye on her will not help.

* * *

PRETTY SURE MY mom would have a conniption if she knew I was working at Blue. She spent most of her adult life slaving away at the casinos to keep me and Cali in clothes. This is not where she expected us to land when she put us through college. Fortunately, I doubt Mira will keep working at this place after her run-in with Asshole this morning. The girl has a death wish, but she's no dummy. Though I'd feel a hell of a lot better if I could see her and confirm it. I haven't seen Mira all day while they've put me through the rest of my training for the position.

So far, my boss is steadily introducing me to just about everyone. For some reason, people find it fascinating that a biologist with a master's degree would choose to work as a crap-dollar-an-hour security guard. Personally, I don't see what the big deal is.

"This here's the security depot, also known as security central."

My boss, a fit, middle-aged guy with one of those handlebar mustaches, takes me inside a double door off the corporate offices. These are the only two doors in the entire corridor, with the exception of an emergency exit at the end of the hall.

I check out the cavernous space. Security central is right. It looks like the central brain of the CIA. Hundreds of television screens large and small show every inch of the casino, but not the executive floor. Apparently, few cameras reside up here, the majority being reserved for gaming, which is why I didn't get fired for whaling on Asshole in the hallway this morning.

A dozen people man the security stations, communicating through microphones attached to headsets. The air in here is charged, as if the extra electrical equipment has thickened it with current. I was prescreened for everything under the sun when they hired me. They also gave me a long talk about the rules for the casino staff, but I'm given another lecture by my boss about confidentiality and gaming policies.

"So this is where we'll work?" I ask.

My boss erupts in a loud hoot. "Oh, man. You're a funny one. No, man, no. This place is for techies. You and I are strictly ground crew. Digging through the trenches."

He jabs me in the rib. "Come on. I'll show you your territory."

When they gave me the position of floor guard, I'd hoped they meant upstairs on one of the actual floors, but apparently the title stands for "casino floor." We walk out of security central and my boss takes me on a circuitous route through stairwells and private doorways; I might actually need a map to find my way back.

The more I consider Mira, the more I worry this day won't be her last at Blue. It would be just like her to keep the job despite the danger it poses. And if that's the case, I need a backup plan.

"What did you think about what I said earlier?" I ask my boss. "Think they'd give me detail in the corporate offices?"

"Nah, man. Why would you want to be there? Gaming is where the action is. Or the suites." He waggles his eyebrows. "A good prostitution bust is what you need to break you in."

What the...? "Yeah, man, that sounds cool"—*not*—"but I heard there's action among the execs."

My boss glances over. For all the easygoing demeanor he projects, I get the feeling he's pretty damn astute. "Be careful there, buddy. The corporates pay us. No good comes of talking smack."

He opens the door to the casino floor. The sound of slot machines drowns out our footfalls on the carpet with buzzers, bells, and sirens.

"No, man—" Great, I'm here a few hours and I'm already starting to sound like this guy. I'm trying to blend, though. "That's not what I mean. I heard there was a bit of a crackdown on people messing with the waitresses."

My boss winks at one of the cocktail waitresses. His

face hardens as he looks over knowingly. "Drake Peterson. Always hated that guy. Fucked with my girl, Kendra."

"Ah, man, that's low. So you know why I'm thinking there might be a need. I got my own girl at Blue. She works in corporate." Total lie, but I'm willing to use any angle, and the girlfriend story looks like it could be a winner. "That's where I heard the guy worked. It would be great to be around and know she's okay."

"I hear ya, I hear ya. But see here, they haven't requested extra heat on the exec floor."

Extra heat? What are we, special ops?

"I gotcha, but maybe we can be proactive. Ask if they could use the extra muscle." Yup, I said *extra muscle*. I'm a *security guard* now.

My boss slaps me on the back. "Good one, Morgan. I'll ring up the powers that be, and check it out. The more armed mass they request, the more my rank increases—you know, with all the subordinates working for me."

I nod, attempting a meek expression. My boss likes his control, but he's a good guy. "You know, I escorted a dude out this morning for Ms. Tate, the human resources director —you wouldn't happen to know that guy's name, would you?"

"Ronald something. Short-termer." My boss nods to a group of bellboys a few feet away, who I'm assuming I'm about to be introduced to.

"Well anyway, Ms. Tate might be a good person to contact. She seems to appreciate what we do."

"True that, man. True that. She's new here, but she's a good egg. I'll check it out. In the meantime, let me introduce you to more people."

With any luck, my boss will be successful and I'll work closer to Mira. For protection, nothing else.

Chapter Eighteen

I arrive home expecting to see Mira, but even though her truck is in the driveway, the house appears dark and lifeless.

Why wouldn't she be here if her truck is here? Did she go somewhere with Lewis?

I kick off my shoes by the front door, and that's when I sense it. Her presence.

I turn and push on the bedroom door that's partway open. Mira is sitting on her bed, in her work clothes, staring out the window, her back straight, hands folded in her lap. She doesn't seem to realize I'm there, though I've made enough noise to alert her. She's completely zoning, which shouldn't be a big deal. I'd probably walk away and let her be, if it weren't for that incident in the hallway at Blue this morning. Or the expression on her face. Sadness, despair.

Fuck, she's killing me. I tug at my T-shirt and look away. Am I really doing this?

Yeah, I guess I am.

I push the door open the rest of the way to give Mira another opportunity to notice me and kick me out, but she

147

doesn't even blink. I walk over and sit beside her on the bed. Right up next to her so that our thighs touch, because she's starting to worry me and I'd rather piss her off by crowding her than see that look on her face any longer.

"Mira."

Her delicate throat rolls in a swallow, her eyes barely flickering my way.

"You okay?"

Her chest deflates and she nods, but I don't believe her.

I rack my brain for some way to reassure her, because she looks like she could use it. "It's probably a good thing we saw that guy this morning. Now I know what he looks like in case he ever comes loitering. You could go to the police. It will be easy to get his name and address since he worked at Blue."

My words don't seem to help. She pinches her lips like she's about to cry. Jesus Christ.

I'm no pussy when it comes to women's tears. I grew up the only male in a two-woman household. I've seen PMS tears, angry tears, and manipulative tears (Cali in all her glory). That shit does not faze me. And I've accumulated smooth words over the years to deal with the female water-works. But right now, the despair Mira's throwing off is enough to break me.

I do the only thing I can think of to make both of us feel better. I reach around her shoulders and draw her to my chest. Her face rests against my T-shirt, and that's when the dam breaks.

Mira is a quiet crier. Little squeaks here and there, her back rising in delicate hiccups. The way she's crying—as if she's used to hiding it—has me doing something I never could have envisioned a few weeks ago.

I wrap my arms around her and press my lips to the top

of her head. I lift her face and wipe tears from the smooth curves of her cheekbones. "Shhh, it's okay. Everything will be okay," I say in a low, calm voice that is the opposite of the storm inside me.

My mind is in turmoil. I don't know that things will be fine, but I will say anything, *anything* to make her feel better. To bring back the feisty Mira I know and love—*hate*. The scrappy Mira I love to *hate*.

Only this doesn't feel like hate.

It feels good to hold Mira in my arms. As if that's where she's supposed to be.

Mira pulls away and wipes her face with the back of her sleeve, leaving a smudge of mascara on the fabric. She stares at that smudge, and I swear she starts crying harder.

"Mira, tell me what's wrong."

"Seriously, Tyler? You really want to know all the fucked-up things in my life?"

I nod. I actually want to know. I've always wanted to know what goes on in Mira's head.

Her hand balls into a fist in her lap. "Where do I begin?" She laughs without humor. "How about running into the guy I thought would either rape or beat me to death in the woods. That was a good way to kick off the day. Then there were the snickers from my female coworkers at various points throughout the afternoon...When I couldn't work the fax machine, or the phone transfer system—oh, yeah, and when I broke the automatic pencil sharpener." I lift a brow. "Don't start with me, Tyler. I *visited* John and Lewis at Sallee Construction. I never sat behind a desk. I don't know anything about collated versus stacked. And what the hell is a dictation machine? Then there were the men giving me creepy looks, which were the opposite of the glares I received from the women."

She looks at me plaintively, her chest rising and falling. "I overheard them, Tyler. The women whispered that I dressed like a homeless person." She hiccups on the last word, and a new round of tears erupts.

Shit, shit, as my new boss would say. I dug myself into this one. I look around desperately. The walls aren't offering any advice, the bastards.

I brush my knee closer to her leg and lean my forearms on my thighs. "First, a dictation machine allows someone to record a message, like a letter or whatever, so that it can be typed. Software programs can do that for you now, along with the typing."

She looks at me in question.

"I was a teacher. We didn't have a regular secretary. I did my own paperwork," I say. "As for clothes, if you've never worked in an office setting, it's understandable you don't have the right clothes. We'll go shopping this evening. Some of the stores stay open late. We should be able to find you something. And the women stare because they're jealous. Take it as a compliment. The guys, though...Names. I need names."

"Really?"

She's okay with me fucking up the guys in her office who leer at her? 'Cause I will.

"You'll go shopping with me?"

Oh. "Yeah, I'll go. I can't promise I'll be much help. Don't expect me to pick out colors or anything, but I'm pretty good at holding up walls."

Her eyes study me, an almost shy expression lifting her pretty face.

If it's this easy to make Mira happy, and this easy for her to wrap a little piece of herself around my heart, I'm a dead man.

* * *

Mira bends over in a slim off-white skirt. "Can you see my underwear through this?"

She has the perfect ass. Like, literally, the most well-formed ass I've ever seen. Round but firm, curvy but proportional. I'd like to grab that backside she's pointed in my face and nip it with my teeth.

Killing me softly, that's what she's doing. "Christ, Mira," I growl.

She looks over her shoulder and straightens. "Oh, sorry." Her blush seems totally genuine.

For a pretty girl, she doesn't know her effect on men. Or maybe she just doesn't realize her effect on *me*.

Mira doesn't ask for any more advice about how the clothes look, because, yeah, all I do is check out her body. I try to pay attention, but the stuff underneath is extremely distracting.

She buys a few clothes and a new pair of shoes, checking all the tags multiple times and buying only sale items. I want to rip the tags off the merchandise so she can't look and stuff a wad of bills in her hand. I hate that she's worried about money. And I can't do anything about it, because that would be weird, me buying her clothes.

"Let me buy you ice cream. I owe you after you hung out with me while I shopped. Lewis would never do that. He hates shopping."

So do I, but I don't mention it. Makes me look like a giant softy who will do whatever it takes to make this girl happy. And that's not me. Not anymore. Mira just looked so sad earlier. There's no doubt she's going through a rough time right now. Any decent person would have offered to help.

"I never turn down ice cream."

Mira shoves her shopping bags on the floorboard of my Land Cruiser, and my eyes skim over her as she scoots into the passenger side. I cringe as the torn upholstery snags the fabric of her top. She's not injured tonight, so I don't know why this bothers me, but it does.

"Can I ask you something?"

"Sure," I say absently, paying attention to the road instead of the girl who makes me feel things I've never felt for anyone else. Protectiveness. And such longing that my chest aches.

"Whatever happened to your dad?"

I shrug. "He bailed on my mom."

"Do you still talk to him?"

"He calls now and then. We have a relationship, but we're not close."

It's odd thinking of my dad. He's more a stranger than a parent. I'm pretty sure he can't help the way he is. He never provided for us. Couldn't seem to keep a job that paid enough. My mom worked hard when he was around, trying to take care of all of us. Things were easier once he left.

"We're more like casual friends," I add. "He calls to see what I'm working on. That's about the extent of our conversations. And he doesn't get Cali at all. She's too emotional for him. My dad is ridiculously intelligent, to the point of being oblivious."

My dad never knew how to show affection, especially with my mom. I worried when I was younger that I might end up like him. But I'm not like him. I have no end of feelings around Mira. There are *too* many when it comes to her.

I chuckle. "I don't know. Maybe my dad has a touch of Asperger's or something. It wouldn't shock me. Cali's crazy book smart too, but not so much common-sense smart.

Correction, make that book smart as long as we're not talking math. In that case, she's remedial at best."

"I'm the opposite. I'm street smart, but not book smart." Mira says this so matter-of-factly that I can't help but look over, my brow furrowing.

"I disagree. You were good at algebra in high school once I pointed out a few things. You're a quick learner."

She tucks a lock of hair behind her ear, a shy smile pulling the corners of her mouth as she points out an empty parking space in front of the ice cream parlor.

I pull up and we get out of the car. I follow Mira to the glass door of the shop, holding it open for her, wondering what exactly I'm doing. This feels like a date, but that's not what this is. I felt bad for Mira. She had a bad day. She's not getting under my skin.

We select our ice cream cones—hers pralines and cream, which somehow fits. It requires a sophisticated palate. Totally contrary to what I'd expect of Mira, so of course that's the one she selects just to fuck with my head.

I ask for a strawberry/cookies 'n' cream double-decker, and I hand the server a twenty. My own flavor combo is an acquired taste.

"Hey, I wanted to pay for that." Mira stares at the twenty-dollar bill as it disappears into the cash register and the attendant hands me the change.

"You can get me next time," I tell her.

She tucks her cash back in the small turquoise wallet I notice is missing the zipper tab. Why these little things—the broken suitcase, buying only sale items, a beat-up wallet—bother me, I don't know. But they do. They really fucking do. She lived with a wealthy family most of her life, but that doesn't seem to have changed the way she lives or her mindset about what she has.

This girl shouldn't have the responsibility of caring for a druggie mother. She shouldn't be in debt because of said mother, and forced to fend off people like Asshole.

We take a booth, and I study her face. "Why won't you tell Lewis the truth?"

She pauses before licking her cone. "He doesn't understand why I help my mom. And it's not his fault I owe the money. It's my responsibility to pay it back."

"It's not your fault you owe the money, either."

Her eyes flicker to me. "Of course it is. I borrowed it."

"Everyone needs help sometimes."

She doesn't say anything at first. She shifts in her seat. "Lewis already gave me money for the loan. I asked him for half. I'll pay off the rest."

"Only half? For your nonexistent gambling problem. That's a good one, Mira, considering you have issues around spending money on yourself."

The side of her mouth notches back in annoyance. "Do you know how awful it felt to ask him for money that indirectly pays for my mother's cocaine problem? It was wrong of me to do it. I shouldn't have gone to him. If he knew the truth, he'd be so angry. He's been telling me to stay away from her for years. To cut the tie. One of these days he's going to cut the tie with me instead."

"He wouldn't do that," I say automatically.

She stares at her ice cream without saying anything.

This conversation has gotten entirely too serious. I never meant to tell Mira about my dad, whom I never talk about. And I didn't mean to bring up anything painful for Mira and make her feel worse about the situation she's in.

"You should give Lewis more credit. He's a good guy. He wouldn't ditch you because he was mad. You don't get rid of family, and that guy thinks of you as his sister."

"Exactly."

Huh? She's agreeing with me?

"You don't give up on family," she says lightly. "What kind of person would I be if I gave up on my mom?"

I just fucked myself there. "A smart one? Look, of course you don't want to hurt your mom, but you can't let people use you. And that woman uses you."

"I know. I'm working on it. I'm making changes." She gives me a weary smile. "Let's not talk about this anymore, okay? Let's just enjoy our ice creams."

I nod. I don't want to make Mira feel worse, so I drop it.

But my efforts to spare Mira from thinking about her mom are for nothing. When we return to the house, as if her ears pricked at our conversation at the ice cream parlor, Mira's mother is sitting on our porch patio, smoking a cigarette. There's no car in the driveway, but the jalopy she pulled up in the other day is parked down the street.

I glance at Mira, who's collecting her bags from my car and watching her mom nervously out of the corner of her eye. "Want me to ask her to leave?"

Mira peers up in surprise. Because I would ask her mom to leave? Hell yes, I would. That woman doesn't deserve Mira.

She shakes her head. "No. I'll talk to her."

Chapter Nineteen

Mira

My mother looks furious, and haggard. "Where've you been, girl?"

I glance at the front window of the cabin, my shopping bags in hand. Tyler walked inside so I could talk to my mom. I don't see him, but I take her through the side gate to the back of the house anyway.

My mother's eyes narrow on the bags in my hands as she shuffles along the dirt and pine needles, her gait slower than I remember. "Shopping? Is that how you been spending your time while I been lookin' everywhere for you?"

She turns abruptly and knocks one of the plastic bags from my hand. "Your mother got people after her, and you're out shopping?"

For a moment, I am filled with guilt and shame; then reality sets in. I have nothing to be ashamed of. I paid off the debt that had my mother's life in danger, according to her. "I have a new job and I needed clothes."

"A new job, eh?" Her gaze is calculating. "The pay any better?"

"Yeah." I pick up the shopping bag she knocked to the ground, and clench it in my hand.

"That's good. You've been saying you want to earn more."

I wouldn't need to if it weren't for her, but I keep that to myself.

"I could use money myself right now. Been hard up since you didn't show the other day. That boy"—she frowns toward the front of the house—"he said you got in a scrape." She scans my body. "You seem okay."

"I'm okay," I agree.

"Good. How much you got on you? You went shopping, so you must have a lot."

I swallow. This is the moment I've been dreading.

"Mom..."

"What is it? Spit it out, girl. I don't have all day."

"I—I can't give you any more money." I'm rattled, my voice not at all smooth.

"Why not?" she snaps.

"Because I don't have it to give." It's the plain truth, but the meaning is double. I don't have extra cash. It's all going to paying off my debt. And I can't keep helping her at the expense of my life.

She nods, her mouth twisting. "I see how it is, Mira. You got enough for yourself, but nothing for your mom."

"That's not how it is. I'm cash-strapped too, but I also don't want our relationship to be all about money. I'd like to spend time—"

"*Relationship?* What relationship? You're a selfish little bitch is what you are."

I can't breathe. Heat and pressure build behind my

eyes. "Please don't say that." My voice comes out on a whisper.

"Oh, I got more to say, but I won't. Won't waste my breath." She knocks into my shoulder on her way past me.

I stare after her. "Mom, please don't leave."

I am pitiful, even to myself.

My mother ignores my words and slams the gate closed behind her.

I turn and face the tall pines in the backyard, trying to regain my composure. I knew this was coming. Knew she'd react this way when I told her, but it doesn't make it hurt any less.

I wipe a tear from my eye and straighten my shoulders.

At least Tyler didn't witness the humiliation of my mother leaving me. Again.

Chapter Twenty

Tyler doesn't ask questions about my mom's visit, and I'm grateful. I go to work the next day less self-conscious in my new clothes, though still hurt about my mom. I did the right thing for both of us, and that's what's important. My hope is that someday we can build a relationship based on a genuine foundation, and not me giving her money all the time.

I train with Hayden all day and don't see Tyler until evening. He's at the dining table, booting up his computer, when I walk in.

"How was your day?" he asks.

"Better." I set my purse on the couch.

Tyler stares at me, then at his laptop. He shuts it abruptly. "What do you think about going for a bike ride?"

I don't say anything at first. Tyler and I have never done anything fun together. The shopping expedition was more a forced situation. "Um, I don't own a bike."

"You don't need one. Just change and meet me out front. If we hurry, we can catch the sunset."

I stand there, just staring.

He glances up from putting away his computer. "Hurry up, Mira. The sun doesn't wait for anyone."

Without another word, I do as he says. When I meet Tyler out front, he's on his bike, a sweatshirt over his long-sleeved T.

I zip up my fleece jacket and pull a knit cap over my head, the waves of my hair tickling my cheeks. "I still don't own a bike, Tyler."

"Not a problem. We'll do this like we did the last time. It's only a few blocks to the beach."

Like the last time. In the woods? When I rode on his lap? "I'm not sure this is such a good idea."

He studies my face. "Chicken?"

I roll my eyes. "Yeah, right." But I totally am. Doesn't stop me from walking over.

He opens his arm. "Sit sideways so your legs stick out the side. I'll take care of the rest."

I do as he says and slide across the top of his thighs. There's no way for us to make this work without me wrapping my arm over his broad shoulders and sitting high up, right above his crotch.

He lifts me and makes some kind of adjustment. I focus my gaze anywhere but on his face, inches away.

"Don't be afraid to hold on tight," he says with a naughty wink.

He's flirting with me? Right as the thought crosses my mind, Tyler takes off with a jerk and I yelp, wrapping my arms around his neck and pressing my chest to his.

"Good hold, but I need to breathe." He chuckles.

"Okay, speed demon, then slow down. You're going to kill us." I close my eyes as we pass our neighbors' houses in a whirl and turn down a side road to the main strip.

"Have a little faith. I won't let anything happen to you, Mira." There's a serious undertone to his words.

I glance up to see him staring at me. My stomach tightens, my heart speeding up. It would be so easy to fall back in love with Tyler—assuming I ever fell out of love with him.

* * *

Tyler

THIS BIKE RIDE is a wee bit different from our last one together. For one thing, I'm infinitely aware of every curve of Mira's body pressing down on places that don't need more encouragement to make their presence known. And her vanilla scent is driving me nuts.

I don't know why I asked her to come with me. I hadn't planned on going for a ride, but when she walked in the door my chest did a little lurch and my blood started rushing through my veins. I couldn't stand the thought of another evening spent avoiding each other. I said the first thing that came to mind. Considering I have her in my lap, it turned out to be a genius idea.

I ride to the stairs to the lake that are located closest to our cabin.

Our cabin? Since when did Cali's house become my and Mira's place?

Mira slides off and stands beside me. "We're not too late," she says, staring at the sun as it sets behind the mountain range.

I hike my bike on my shoulder and jog down the steps to the sand, resting it up against a cement block that was once a part of a pier. Mira's still at the top of the stairs, staring out.

"You coming?"

She climbs down and approaches my side, gaze flickering back to the sunset. "It's pretty."

I brush her long, dark hair over her shoulder. Her hat hugs the top of her head, leaving her hair to frame her face. She is so beautiful. "Come on." I grab her hand and pull her up the beach.

Mira doesn't recoil from my touch or try to ease away, and for some reason that makes me happy. We arrive at the large rock where I like to stare out at the lake, and I let go of her hand. We are not a couple. This is not a date. But it's nice.

Mira and I sit there long after the sun has set, until it's so dark, I realize we had better get back. The road is well lit, but I don't want to take a chance riding with Mira on my lap in the dark and competing for road space with cars.

I stand, and without a word, Mira does too. We make it all the way back to the cabin in total silence. It should be awkward, but it isn't. I lock my bike in the backyard, and meet her inside.

She looks up shyly. "Thanks. That was nice."

"You're welcome. Any time you want to ride my lap, just let me know."

She shakes her head. "You had to go there," she says, but she's smiling.

My lips twitch. "You know who you're dealing with."

Her smile fades. "Do I?"

I swallow. "Better get back to work." I head for the dining table.

"Work?" she says. "Is that what you've been doing over there?"

I scan the textbooks and journal articles I've been researching. I needed something to keep me busy once I arrived in Lake Tahoe, but the small project I started has taken on a life of its own. "Yeah, I guess I have. It's something I've been thinking about since I began teaching. Never had the time before, but now..."

"Now you do, except you're working at Blue and that must take time away from it."

It's true. I haven't been able to put as many hours into my project since I started working at Blue, but my job as a security guard is temporary. Soon Mira will move out and it won't matter if I spend a few hours less on my project. It will still be there waiting for me when she's gone.

"Eh, I needed a break from it. This way, I come home and I'm excited to dig in. No big deal."

There's a pause, then, "Thank you, Tyler. For getting the job at Blue." She walks into her room and closes the door.

I stare off for several minutes, wondering what the fuck I'm really doing with her, with my life.

Chapter Twenty-One

Mira

"Jaeger, will you blend more Bullfrogs? The girls and I are almost out, and yours taste so much better than mine," Cali says to her boyfriend.

We're at Jaeger's place, hanging out on his dock in the afternoon sun. The weather is uncharacteristically warm for this time of year, and we're taking advantage of it in our bathing suits, drinks in hand. Jaeger recently built the dock, and it's pretty awesome, with custom benches and cushioned lounge chairs. Oh, and it's huge. There are eight of us now that Nessa has arrived, and we're sprawled out everywhere.

I worried when Gen invited me. Zach and Lewis are like brothers, but I hardly know Cali and Jaeger, even though I'm staying at Cali's place. The last time I saw them all, I'd just had the crap beaten out of me. Not my shining moment. And then there's Tyler. Strangely, I feel more comfortable around Tyler. The only way I can credit it is our forced living arrangement, and the truce we seem to have formed. We must be getting used to each other...but that's not right either, because I definitely don't feel relaxed around him. I'm hyperaware of him.

"Sure, babe," Jaeger tells Cali. He sets down his beer and stands, stretching his arms above his head.

"Wait for it...Wait for it," Cali whispers to me and Gen as she studies her boyfriend.

Gen rolls her eyes and shakes her head at me, as if Cali has lost her mind.

No idea what's going on. My Bullfrog is full, and so is Cali's as far as I can tell.

Cali stares as her boyfriend walks to the stones leading up the shore. His place overlooks the lake, but it's a hike to get there. Jaeger begins climbing the couple hundred feet to his house.

"Ahhh," Cali says, admiring her boyfriend's ass as he lunges up the rocks. "So, so hot. You think he'll do it again in a half hour?" she whispers to Gen.

"Cali," Gen says, admonishing, humor in her voice.

Jaeger is tall and muscular. After being around another tall, athletic guy, I see the appeal.

I steal a glance at Tyler, his light golden chest and smooth skin catching my eye immediately. He's confounding me lately with his supportive side. I can't figure out why he's been so nice ever since I imploded on him after my first day of work. He's reminding me of the Tyler I used to know.

Tyler is sitting next to Lewis, cringing at his sister's blatant ass-ogling. Jaeger and Tyler are good friends. So yeah, it must be awkward.

"What?" Cali says to Gen. "His ass is the most perfect thing in creation. God put his stamp on that backside. We're *supposed* to admire it."

"Anyway." Gen rolls her eyes again and looks at me. "How are things going at the casino?"

Cali continues watching her boyfriend until he disappears from sight.

"Things are okay," I say hesitantly.

I am grateful for my job at Blue. I'm making more money than I thought possible when I decided to find a better-paying job. Drake is basically gone while he awaits trial, so I don't worry about him. But something doesn't feel right at the casino, and I can't put my finger on it.

Gen leans forward. "No one's been mean, have they? I forgot you'd be on a different schedule than Nessa and Zach."

I glance at Nessa. She arrived a minute or two ago, but she's still holding her beach bag, and Zach has her in a bear hug, her feet dangling above the ground. She's laughing hysterically as he rattles her up and down like a salt shaker.

"No, it's fine." Which is the truth. Guys ogling me while women talk crap is pretty much what I'm used to. Different setting, same situation.

I've given up trying to figure out why I cause that reaction in people. I've talked to my therapist about it, and she thinks I'm somehow allowing my deepest fears to shine through. It's that circular thing. I'm worried about being abandoned, so I push people away. Sometimes consciously, sometimes subconsciously. It's not the case with everyone, but I get this reaction often enough that I'm convinced my therapist is on to something.

Jaeger returns to the dock and Cali smiles brightly. He walks over with a pitcher of Bullfrog, a lime and vodka drink they all seem to love, and tops off our plastic tumblers. I have to agree—the Bullfrog is pretty fantastic on an Indian summer day. We get a few of these in the fall, but pretty soon it will be too cold for shorts, let alone bathing suits.

Jaeger leans down and kisses the top of Cali's head. "I know what you're up to, and I like it." He nuzzles her neck, and she squeals. "I'll be your errand boy all day long if you give me looks like that."

I thought I wanted to gag at the loving looks Gen and Lewis shoot each other, but these two are way worse.

And I am so jealous.

* * *

Tyler

I'm TRYING to not stare at Mira's body in a bikini, but it isn't easy. I'm trying even harder not to listen in while she talks to Gen and Cali about work. I'm not going to lie. I worry about her. Which is probably obvious after I dropped everything to get a job at Blue Casino so I could keep an eye on her.

I'm telling myself this is all to keep her safe so she can move out, but I can't help thinking I have another interest in this. *I* don't want to see her get hurt.

When Mira's mom staked out our place the other day, waiting for her until we returned from shopping, I went inside to give them space. There's a chance I might have overheard their conversation through a window I cracked open while they spoke in the backyard. I'm not happy about what I heard. When her mother called her names and accused her of being selfish, I about flipped my lid. I wanted to rail on that woman, but I kept it together. I have to draw a line at how far I'm willing to go to protect Mira. But it was hard to stand by and not say anything.

It's a pretty fucked-up situation. From Mira's viewpoint, that woman is her mother. I mean, talk about getting screwed in the mom lottery. I'm lucky. I have an awesome mom. And then there's Mira. Her mom shouldn't have had children. But if she hadn't, Mira wouldn't be here...

I've completely lost the thread of the conversation between Lewis and Jaeg. I'm nodding, chiming in with an "mm-hmm" now and then, but not paying attention. Mira walked over to the edge of the dock a minute ago, her feet dangling in the water—and that's my entire focus. Her shoulders are slumped slightly and she has a wistful look on her face. All I can think about is how she might be doing—and our sunset bike ride together last night. Something changed between us yesterday evening and I don't know what.

Mira is probably the most intense girl I've ever met. I thought I knew her, but now I'm not sure about anything—my feelings most especially.

I saunter to where she sits, because it's not something I can control. She's alone, beautiful, complicated, and—shit, I don't know why I'm so drawn to her. I just am. It's like those forces of nature that can't help their attraction. They glom on to each other whether they like it or not, positive and negative charge, bubbles on surface water, and that's how it is when Mira is near. She's the force I can't resist.

Lately, I haven't wanted to resist, which is seriously fucking scary. I don't *want* to want her. I know her better now, and I think I was wrong and a jerk for accusing her of sleeping with multiple guys when we were in school together, but that doesn't mean I trust her.

Despite this, I go to her, because she is a bubble on the surface, and my bubble wants to rub up and get cozy.

"Hey," I say as I sit beside her, knees spread wide over

the edge of the dock, lightly touching her leg. A guy needs space. But yeah, I just want to touch her. "Lewis have you convinced about the lake monster?"

She grins with her mouth, but the power of that smile is in her beautiful eyes, the corners crinkling as she looks out at the lake. "He tell you that story?"

"No. I overheard Gen tell Cali about it. Sounds like a bunch of crap to get her so scared he could..." She looks over at my pause. "You know."

She smiles saucily, and my heart races. She used to grin at me like that when we studied together—the smile I thought was only for me. "I don't know. Why would a guy try to scare a girl, Tyler?"

It's cool. I'm not affected by that sexy look anymore. Okay, that's a total lie. But at least I can hold it together and not go crazy over her the way I did when I was younger.

She knows what I meant. She's taunting me.

I lean down until my lips are close to her ear, the scent of her hair branding my senses and stunning my brain for a moment—*fucking pheromones*. "So that he can touch her... you know, for comfort."

Her breath hitches and she swallows, running a hand nervously down her bare leg. My gaze follows, because she's in a bikini and her body takes my breath away. I've tried to avoid looking, with her sitting across the dock, but this close, there's no chance I won't stare.

I realize, after I've spoken, that I've just defined what happened between us the other day, when she came home from work upset. I had wanted to comfort her. I could have stuck with words, but I didn't. I touched her, held her. Because that's the way I want to soothe Mira when she's distressed. Words aren't enough.

"Lewis is full of crap," she says. "He loves that Ong lake

169

monster story, but he twists it depending on who his audience is."

"Are you saying he had ulterior motives?" I can't hold back the twitch at my lips as I watch her reaction.

"I don't know, Tyler. What do you think?" she says sarcastically.

Hmm, I'm wondering if she thinks I had ulterior motives when I comforted her the other day. And when I asked her to go on the bike ride with me. I didn't. I truly wanted to make sure she was okay. And spend time with her. I did enjoy touching her, though. "I think I'd rather not talk about my sister's best friend—who's like a little sister to me—and her boyfriend hooking up."

"I think I'd rather not talk about my brother figure and his girlfriend hooking up."

"Now that that's settled"—I bump her shoulder and she rolls with it, her body straightening and coming to rest just shy of my own—"why are you so pensive over here?"

Mira sips her girly drink without looking at me. "You don't want to know."

Now I *have* to know. "Try me anyway."

She looks up, her eyes penetrating, and suddenly I'm wondering if she's right. I don't want to know. The look on her face is a bit sharklike. "Why'd you return to town?" she asks.

Definitely should have kept my mouth shut.

I let out a deep sigh. I've not even told Cali what happened in Colorado. Am I seriously going to share this with Mira?

"Some things went down that I needed to get away from. Clear my head."

"Can you be more vague?"

I frown. Saucy as usual. "I was in a relationship." My

heart constricts just from thinking about Anna and what happened. I can't believe I'm telling Mira this. Deep down I secretly think Mira is a part of why things were never quite right between me and Anna. Mira stole my ability to love a girl.

"We were...engaged," I say.

Mira's body tenses beside me. She looks over her shoulder, but the others are engrossed in conversation. "Does Cali—"

"Cali doesn't know. No one does. My engagement was a new development. We'd only just decided...Well, anyway. I hadn't gotten around to telling anyone. Doesn't matter. It ended soon after."

Mira stares at her cup. "Sorry."

Am *I* sorry? I am so fucking sorry for what happened to Anna, but not that our engagement ended, and that's why I'm a dick. If I'd cared more, loved Anna the way I should have, would things have ended up the way they did?

"Me too," I say.

She studies me, and this time she seems depleted, as if my confession has sucked the life from her.

I'm feeling hollow myself.

I want to tell her it's okay, that I'm okay. But I'm not.

Chapter Twenty-Two

Mira

Tyler's confession a week ago that he'd been engaged hit me hard. It's what I expected when he left our hometown, but again, I wasn't prepared to hear firsthand about him falling in love with someone else. Realistic or not, I dreamt it would be me he'd declare his undying love to one day. The knowledge that he was prepared to marry another cuts deep, and I've been covering the wound through long hours at work and avoiding him at home. Only my long hours at work haven't been as good for my spirits as I thought they would be.

This past week at Blue has been a combination of jack-assery (on my part) and stress. Hayden said I'd be her assistant in human resources as well as the assistant to the hospitality manager until they found a replacement. Well, Hayden and I have been so busy putting out human resources fires—as we're both new and learning the ropes—that Hayden only recently sent out an advertisement for the hospitality position. To add to the pressure, Blue is preparing for a large music festival, which has resulted in a boatload of extra work for both of us. In short, I'm a one-woman band, performing two jobs when I don't know how to do either properly.

After I graduated, I went straight from the Sallees' home to living on my own and working hostess and floor jobs at a casino, no office work required. Among the Blue executives, I'm a beginner at everything. I've made so many mistakes that even my male coworkers have stopped leering and look at me with pity.

It's a sad state of affairs when men stop ogling me like I'm a piece of meat. I mean, I never liked it, but damn.

I stare at the laminated instructions attached to the printer. I'm just changing out a black ink cartridge. Easy, right? I can totally do this.

Awesome. Now I'm giving myself positive affirmations over office equipment.

My therapist has me saying positive affirmations. Stuff like *I am lovable, I am special, I am worthy of loyalty*. Supposedly, if I say it enough, it sinks in, and this halo of doom I walk around with—that everyone and anyone will leave me—will dissipate and I won't push people away with my negative vibe. My therapist is quick to state it's not my fault that these things happen. I had bad luck in the parental department, with the exception of the Sallees, who've done their best to make up for what my biological parents lacked. But she says it can't hurt to build a positive internal dialogue.

My therapist has some crazy theories, but I like her.

You know what? Positive affirmation or not, this office stuff is intimidating. Like this, for instance. *Do not throw used toner cartridge into open flame, as this may cause the remaining toner to ignite.* I mean, seriously, what is this —gunpowder?

Whatever. I can do this. I am capable. I am smart.

"Open toner replacement cover. Pull toner cartridge out of supply port," I read aloud.

Done and done.

I walk to the supply cabinet and grab the box with the new black toner.

"Hey."

My body jerks and I slap a hand to my chest, glaring at the handsome figure in the doorway. "Tyler! Don't walk up on a girl like that."

He steps into the room. "Why so tense? I've been standing here for the last minute watching you talk to yourself."

Okay, embarrassing. "Don't you have anything better to do?"

His lips purse in thought. "Maybe, but this is more entertaining."

"Changing printer cartridges is entertaining?"

"Watching you do it is."

I glare at him. "You can leave now."

"Nah, I think I'll stay." He crosses his arms, his mouth turned up in a grin.

Awesome. An audience. And Tyler of all people.

Whatever. It's just a printer. So what if said printer comes up to my chest and resembles R2-D2? I've got this. I read the instructions.

I open the cartridge box and ignore Tyler in his hot security guard uniform, which has less to do with the uniform and more to do with Tyler's amazing body filling out the tailored fabric.

Damn it. Now I'm thinking about how good he looked in his swim trunks.

I take a deep breath. No way am I going back to the instructions with Tyler staring over my shoulder. That would give him more ammunition to make fun of me. I remember what the instructions said. Mostly. How hard can it be? Something about removing the seal and shaking the cartridge while holding both ends, probably to get the toner to loosen up.

See? Common sense. I can do common sense.

I remove the seal as instructed, which comes off easily, and toss it in the trash can. Holding both ends of the toner all casual-like, as if I'm a pro—

"Wait—"

I give it a good shake.

And splatter black powder all over my shirt, the floor... the wall?

Fuckballs.

I hear soft snickering, and turn to see Tyler pinching the bridge of his nose, seemingly holding back tears. Dammit.

"You might want to wait to remove the seal until *after* you've shaken it," he says.

I pat at the black powder on my blouse. "And you're just now informing me of this?"

"I tried to stop you. You acted like you knew what you were doing. Or were you pretending?" His eyes say he knows the answer to that question.

"Jerk."

"Hey," he chuckles, closing the door as another worker tries to peek inside, "don't get mad at me." He steps closer and surveys the debris. "It's not so bad. Keep your voice down and we can get it cleaned up without anyone knowing."

Tyler removes the toner cartridge from my hands and inserts it into the machine, expertly closing the cover and resetting a couple of buttons.

He looks at my white blouse covered in inky soot. "That's a goner."

"You think?" I say, pure sarcasm.

I hastily grab paper towels from inside the storage cabinet and wipe the soot from my hands. Tyler tears off a paper towel as well and starts dabbing at my sleeve, my chest, which I realize is also splattered with toner. Excellent.

He reaches for a spot near my collarbone, and his knuckle grazes my nipple. It's cold in here, and I'm agitated, and well, I'm a bit nippy.

I must gasp—I sure as hell stand stock-still—because Tyler stops what he's doing. He stares at his hand an inch from my breast now, frozen in mid-wipe. He doesn't say anything. The awkward tension is so thick you could cut it with a knife. Then his gaze lifts to my eyes, his chest rising and falling heavily.

His empty hand moves up and I watch it warily. Suddenly, the tension doesn't feel so much like awkward, more like another type of tension I'm not used to, but sense on a regular basis around Tyler. He cups my jaw, the tips of his long, warm fingers grazing the nape of my neck.

I close my eyes. I know where this is going. I feel it. The irresistible pull. I can't look. I'm on a rollercoaster about to drop off the highest hill, and I won't look to see if he follows through with the promise in his eyes.

Warm lips meet mine and the faintest moan escapes my throat.

Oh God. I've waited so long. I didn't know I was waiting, but I have been. Waiting for Tyler.

His fingers slide into my hair, his hand angling my head while his mouth delves deeper, the touch of his tongue hitting me in places far more south. I'm dizzy, my heart pounding in my chest as our mouths collide, retract for soft kisses, then melt together again. I don't dare lift my hands and touch him, afraid I'll break the spell.

The sound of a throat clearing has Tyler breaking away. He stares at me with heat in his eyes before glancing over his shoulder.

"Hello, Ms. Tate. I was just leaving," he says hurriedly, his voice gruff. He glances at me with an enigmatic look, then steps out the door, while Hayden passes into the room.

I don't remember the door opening. I didn't hear anything except the pounding of my heart as Tyler kissed me—in front of my boss.

This is a classy place, and I'm making out in the copy room. Great, just great.

"Hayden," I say. "I'm so sorry. I don't know what happened."

She shuts the door, and turns to me. "He's cute," she whispers, though it's only us in here.

"I—what?"

"I mean, you guys shouldn't—you know—at work, but you definitely should. I almost walked out. I felt like I was intruding." She fans her face. "I need to get out more, because that was"—she nods as if agreeing with herself—"hot."

Who is this teenybopper? Hayden is my young, but formal, MBA boss, not this slightly flushed girl gossiping about a boy.

"I spilled toner. He was, uh, helping me?" It comes out as a question, because I'm not sure how we went from cleaning up to our mouths inhaling each other. Hayden grins suggestively, then glances at the arm I raise as proof.

She winces. "I've got a cardigan you can borrow."

"Thank you." I wipe the last of the toner off the wall and move to the door, my body gliding, half-dazed. What just happened with Tyler? And does Hayden really not care?

"Mira—" Hayden touches my arm, startling me. "I'm all for romance, but you can't do that here."

"I'm sorry. It won't happen again."

She nods decisively. "We can't give them any reason to doubt us." She doesn't say whom. "I have some clout, because I'm helping the casino's image, but I don't want to give Blue a reason to fire me. And you shouldn't either."

"I promise, Hayden. What you saw was..." I can't finish my sentence. I don't know what just happened. Something I never thought would.

Tyler kissed me. And I felt it everywhere.

We live together, but he's never initiated anything like that. I don't know why he did it here, now, but I'm not complaining. Except—I can't lose my job, or endanger Hayden's. She's right. We can't step out of line at Blue. But man, I hope...

I won't finish that thought, because whenever I hope for something, my wishes never come true. Only I've been dreaming of kissing Tyler ever since he returned, and that dream came true.

* * *

"Nessa," I say as I dip a chicken tender in barbecue sauce. I just got off work and we're in the Blue cafeteria, in the basement, eating dinner before she begins her shift. "Do you think dreams come true? Like farfetched ones?"

Nessa sprinkles salt on her french fries. "Sure. But I guess it depends on the dream. If you're planning on flying to the moon...?"

"No, of course not. It just seems like, well, wanting something ensures it'll never happen."

Nessa studies me for a moment. She's in her Blue cocktail uniform, the bustier of her sequined top pushing up her small breasts into half-moons. She has the tiniest waist and beautiful, straight black hair. I have to pull my wavy mass into a ponytail first thing in the morning, otherwise it's a nest. "I guess sometimes that's true, but I think it has more to do with the thing you want not being right for you. Like, even though you want it, you're not meant to take that path, you know?"

Her words are honest, and they really suck.

My heart has always told me Tyler is right for me. But whether I'm pushing him away, or he's pushing me away, it's never worked out.

Then today happened.

Something changed, or maybe we've been moving in this direction from the very beginning. Tyler kissed me. It was new and familiar at the same time, and so honest it spoke more than any words we could have shared.

No wonder Hayden walked in on us without me noticing. The fire alarm could have gone off and it would have taken me a minute to figure out where I was. Tyler's kiss was heat and emotion, and it drained the brain cells from my head.

"What if there was a chance to have what you thought you couldn't? A person you always wanted to be with."

"Um—go for it?" she says as if it's a no-brainer. "If I

could...Well, let's just say, if I liked a guy, which I'm not saying I do, but if I did, I would jump at the opportunity to seal the deal."

I swirl my chicken in the barbecue sauce, my cheeks growing warm at the idea of going down that path again with Tyler. "Really? What if that's all there was?"

I've been there before, and it hurt so badly to watch Tyler leave town. Can I go through it again?

"Better to have loved and lost, you know? I'm pretty sure someone really smart said that." She grins, proud of herself.

She's right, though. I've dreamt of being with Tyler for what feels like my entire life, and now there may be an opening. A small one, because he seemed as surprised by the kiss as I was. But if he's having second thoughts about me, about us trying again...I'd like to give it a chance.

Who am I kidding? I totally want him. There's no question.

"You've changed," Nessa says, her expression serious.

"What do you mean?" Are my emotions showing on my face? Or worse, has the kiss gotten around? I haven't noticed a grapevine, but I'm new. People talk.

She tilts her head. "You seem happier."

I smile shyly. "Thanks."

My therapist has helped me deal with my mom issues. And this new job—despite my office bloopers—has challenged me and gotten me excited about work. There are still things going on, but I feel happier.

"Your mom has put you through the wringer, Mira. No one could go through what you've had to and not be affected by it. But I'm really proud of you for getting help. You've been cool about Lewis spending time with Gen."

I'm not proud of how I behaved when Lewis first started

dating Gen, and it sucks to have the reminders. "I never thought I'd say this, but I'm glad he's with her. At least he picked a good one."

"True. You never know with those guys." Nessa's mouth firms and she grabs her soda, taking a sip.

The only guy left in our crew is Zach. Is she saying she doubts Zach's ability to pick a nice girl?

I can't argue with her there. Zach is a flighty one. At first I thought he might have a thing for Nessa, but it never went anywhere. In fact, they seem more buddy-buddy than ever.

"I don't think you should give up on a happy ending," she says. "Focus on good things, and good things will happen." She giggles. "Deep, huh?"

"Maybe not, but I think you're on to something."

Chapter Twenty-Three

I arrive home from work after dinner with Nessa, and a black sedan with tinted windows pulls away from the front of our house. It's out of place in our neighborhood, and it reminds me of another time when something was out of place. Deep in the woods, when the men popped up out of nowhere.

I wrap my arms around my chest and walk quickly up the driveway. Once inside, I lock the front door, unsettled. I've grown used to having Tyler around. There's a sense of security to it. I can't help but feel disappointed he's not here, especially after what happened in the copy room. I'm not sure what the kiss meant today, or if his absence now says anything, but I'd like to know.

I take a shower and shave my legs. I'm totally not preparing for anything. It's just that my legs are a forest. Basic girl hygiene is all this is. I smooth on vanilla-scented lotion and grab a pair of low-slung sleep shorts from the bedroom dresser, along with a sleep cami.

Towel-drying my hair, I leave it down. I could blow-dry it, but what if Tyler walks in and thinks I'm primping? The last thing I want is for him to think I've cleaned myself up for his benefit. His ego is inflated as it is. I don't want him to think I'm waiting for him.

When he walks in, I'll act as if he didn't kiss the sense out of my head. That way, if he's changed his mind about this kissing business, there's no discomfort. On the outside I will be totally cool.

Inside, not so much.

I pull on ugly, fluffy sleep socks and kick my legs up on the couch, phone in hand. I could watch TV, but I need something to take my mind off Tyler. I open my poker app and check to see if SuperMom is connected. She's an Oklahoma stay-at-home mom who kicks my ass weekly.

SuperMom is online, which is no surprise. I think she plays poker with whoever will participate while she takes care of the kids. I don't let the "mom" in SuperMom fool me anymore. She's sweet, but she's a shark, so I'll have to concentrate. Which is what I need. A good mind-number.

Six or seven hands in, I recognize the sound of Tyler's Land Cruiser pulling into the drive. There goes my concentration.

Me: *Gotta go, SuperMom.*
SuperMom: *Okay. Kids finally down. Stop by later if you have time for another ass-whooping.*

She's so modest. I needed another ass-kicking like I need more reasons to make an idiot of myself at work, but at least SuperMom is nice. I bet she's a really cool mom. Mine hasn't gotten in touch with me, and it's what I expected. I was prepared for her silence, but it still hurts. This time, though, I'm not letting my pain take me down the wrong road. If my mother wants a relationship, she needs to meet me on fair terms.

I don't move from my spot sprawled lengthwise on the couch, my legs crossed and resting above the armrest on the opposite end. I check my email, some Yahoo! sensational news posts, which I'm too distracted to focus on. Finally, the sound of the front door cracking open has my shoulders tensing. I immediately loosen them and click through another news article. I almost dropped my monthly data plan, but it's the only extravagance I allow myself. My only connection to the outside world. I couldn't let that go.

I hear Tyler close the door and sense him approaching the couch.

Finally, when I can't take it anymore, I glance up—and can't look away.

Tyler is standing above me in jeans and a T-shirt, staring at my bare legs. His gaze skims to my eyes.

Mayday, mayday—It's on.

Tyler tosses his keys on the counter—same spot he always leaves them—without removing his gaze from my face.

He leans down and grips my ankle above my fluffy socks. I stare at his large, hot, electrifying hand as it slowly slides up my leg. My heart is racing, about to catapult from my chest, which is seesawing up and down because I can't control my breathing. With his other hand, he reaches for my phone, which I realize I'm clutching like a knife, and gently pulls it away from me and sets it on the floor.

The hand on my leg makes its way to my hip, and a puff of air escapes my mouth. The urge to reach for him is excruciating, but if he wants this, he needs to make it happen. I won't be the one to seduce him this time.

I stare into those pale blue eyes that are suddenly a lot

darker, with the pupils covering most of the irises. Both of his hands are on my hips now, and he's watching them as they glide up the sides of my waist, his thumbs slipping over my breasts, until his palms cover my chest above my raging heart, up to my neck, and finally to my jaw, which he cradles, staring at my lips.

I'm going out of my mind, crawling out of my skin. If he doesn't kiss me soon, I don't know how much longer I can keep from grabbing him.

Tyler leans down and his lips touch mine, so sweet, so tender, my entire body shakes. This kiss is different from the one in the copy room, which was hot and desperate, like water filling the cracks of a desert floor. This kiss is poignant, with so much longing behind each gentle brush.

I wrap my arm around his neck and pull him close, because I got the message. He wants this, and so do I.

Tyler braces a hand on the back of the couch and covers me with his body. My leg slips to the floor and his hips seat between my thighs. I can feel him hard and big against a very tender place that happens to be pulsing at the moment, but he doesn't move or grind. He runs his fingers through my hair, thumbs rubbing my temples. "Mira..." He lets out a sigh, as if no more words need saying.

I feel cherished, and it's nearly killing me. I want him so much, and I'm terrified of him at the same time. But I won't allow fears I've harbored to control this moment.

I won't hide how I feel this time.

His mouth seeks mine, but his lips are soft, his tongue twining and teasing. I run my hands down his sides to his thighs, where I grip him with the passion that's been burning for so long.

Tyler groans in my mouth and slides his hand down my chest, over my breast, where he pauses to cup and run his thumb over my nipple. I wiggle, because it's impossible to stay still when he does that. His hand moves down my waist to the hem of my top, and he pulls it up and over my head without hesitation.

That was my sleep cami, and I'm not wearing a bra.

It's been a long time since I've done this, and I'm nervous. If I'm half naked, he needs to be too. "Take off your shirt," I say.

Tyler braces his leg on the floor and reaches between his shoulder blades to pull his shirt over his head, immediately returning his mouth to mine. Only now we're chest to chest, and I don't think there's anything in the world that feels better than Tyler's warm skin against mine.

His fingers run over my shoulder, down my arm, to my hand, where he squeezes, warming that place in my heart I've protected. I kiss the slight indentation on his chin, the scruff that prickles my lips at the top of his throat, back to his mouth that's soft and demanding. He kisses me like he's worshipping my lips, the emotion pouring off him so intense, I nearly break away to catch my breath.

I don't. I kiss him back with everything I've ever felt for him.

Tyler's chest rises on a deep inhalation and he pulls away, shifting his weight, which makes us both wobble on the couch. His gaze is heated as he stares at me for long seconds, his eyes dark and intense—and if I'm reading it right—concerned. After a moment, he breaks eye contact to look around. "Where do you want to do this?"

This is really happening. He doesn't ask if I'm sure, just to name the place. And oh, God, why is that so hot?

Then I remember Tyler hooking up with the last woman on this couch, which I attempt to flush from my mind, but now that it's there..."Not here."

"Your room."

"No. Yours." I want all of Tyler, his body, his heart...his bed. I don't care that he's in the loft. Better because it's his space. All him.

He stands quickly and pulls me up. My chest is completely bare, and even though Tyler has seen it before, instinct has me covering myself.

He doesn't say anything. He watches me slip off my socks and walk barefoot to the ladder. He quickly does the same with his shoes and socks, and follows me.

I feel him behind me as I climb, the heat of his body so close, his hand on the small of my bare back, protectively holding me in place. I scale the rest of the way and crawl across his bed, which takes up most of the loft floor.

Tyler slides to my side and tucks me up against him. His mouth is immediately on my lips, his hands tugging down my sleep shorts. I have one instant of hesitation. A spark of worry that this is all we'll ever be to each other, the same concern I mentioned to Nessa earlier.

"Wait." I push his chest with my hand, and he pulls back.

Tyler and I have only ever been lovers, never more. I want more. I stare at his handsome face, taking in the lines of his cheekbones, the strong chin, the beautiful eyes that are all emotion.

He kisses my cheek tenderly, studying my gaze. "Okay?"

His expression is so gentle, and if I'm reading it right, loving. He's asking if I'm all right.

Nessa's advice was to seize the moment. I haven't been living, I've been surviving. This, right now, is living.

I wrap my arm around his back, press my lips to his, and pull him close.

Tyler's hands return to my shorts, and he slips them off my body, the article disappearing off the side of the bed. The only barriers between us are my lacy boy shorts and his jeans.

I run my hands down the ripples and contoured muscles of his chest and arms. He's not overly bulky, but his shape is so perfectly masculine, I can't stop tracing my hands up and over his smooth skin—and down. I want to go down.

My fingers tug on the band of his jeans, to the snap at the front. Tyler rolls on his back, and I unfasten his pants. He pushes and kicks his jeans off and over the side, before his mouth returns to my body. This time on my chest, where he marks a path with his lips around my breast and nipple. He remains just shy of that sensitive peak and it's killing me.

I arch and pull him closer. Tyler palms my ass and tucks me up against him, right where he's hard and long, then wraps his mouth around my nipple, sucking and rolling the tip with his tongue.

Oh. My. God. He's gained skills.

I should be upset about this, because it reminds me he's been practicing on other women, but you know what? I can't muster the energy to care. He feels amazing.

Tyler gives my other breast the same insane attention, his body rocking between my legs, making me crazy. "Tyler, I..." *Want more. Now.*

His response to the words I can't voice is to run his mouth down the center of my stomach, over my panties, where he kisses me *there,* the naughty boy.

Some strangled, inarticulate sound escapes my mouth as he moves between my thighs. He spreads my legs and nuzzles the inside of my thigh, pressing soft kisses to extremely sensitive skin.

"Tyler," I say, this time more insistent.

I feel him smile against my leg, and then my panties are sliding off my body. He shucks his boxer briefs, along with my undies, and plants kisses up my leg. I don't know where he's going with this, but he better get on with it because all that "expert" attention he's giving me has me wanting things. Certain things. Inside me. *Now.*

Before I know what's going on, a warm, wet tongue licks up the center of where my mind is expecting other parts of him to be. I gasp.

He looks up, his eyebrow quirked. "More?"

I stare at him because, oh my God, what is he doing to me? I'm going to melt into the mattress if he keeps this up. I actually have to wrench my brain back to the question.

Do I want him licking me there?

Considering how amazing that felt, um, yes. Please. Do I want him, after all the time we've been apart—emotionally, physically—to be inside me, connecting in the most intense way I can imagine? Yes. More so.

And then back to this other business I've heard so much about but have never personally experienced.

Because the only sex I've ever had was that one time with Tyler.

"I want you...inside me," I say hesitantly.

His expression turns serious, as if my words bother him.

I gulp, panic rising in my chest. He can go back to what he was doing. I just want to feel connected to him.

Before I can ask what's wrong, he's climbing up my body, pressing me into the bed as he reaches for the bookshelf and opens a box. He fumbles around, then tears open a condom and slips it on.

Tyler settles between my legs and I can feel him *there,* right where I want him. Only, my body is shaking, and this time it's from nerves. The last time Tyler and I did this, it didn't end well. I mean, it felt good. But I wasn't prepared for the emotions it brought.

His hands rest on either side of my head, his thumbs lightly brushing the arches of my cheekbones. He stares into my eyes and my worries drain away, because the look on his face is pure tenderness, maybe more. I don't glance away. I want him to see how much he means to me. That this was never just sex.

Tyler rocks forward, moving inside me, and I'm all sensation, my head tilting back, arms gripping his shoulders. He feels large, the connection tight, but so good.

He dips to my neck and kisses a trail to my mouth, his lips moving urgently, the opposite of his body, which is slow and sensual.

I'm tingling everywhere, an urgency building where we're connected. Tyler slips his hand between us, and rubs me in a spot that has me seeing stars.

I break off our kiss right as something rips through me, tearing me into a million pieces. My head rocks from side to side and I'm moaning. It's too much, but I don't want it to end, because I've never felt anything like it before.

Tyler's pace picks up, and all I can do is hold on, my limbs still tingling from the wave that rocked me off my axis. Orgasms are my new favorite thing, right after Tyler. Well, he's always been my favorite, but now I want him *and* orgasms. Because oh my God.

He's peppering sweet kisses over my face, down my neck, until his eyes shut tightly and his body tenses, a deep moan escaping his lips.

I kiss his jaw, his mouth, until he collapses on top of me,

his arms holding his body high enough so he doesn't crush me. He's heavy, but I love it. I love the feel of him above me, inside me. Close.

A wide grin spreads across my face as I snuggle into his neck and chest. I missed out on so much the last time we were together, too scared and worried about the feelings he'd evoked that night. But not this time. This time, I want to bask in what we just shared.

And I can't wait to do this again. With an orgasm, because that was awesome. I didn't know what I was missing.

I'm in a lulled state of happiness when I sense a shift. Tyler's body hasn't moved, but something has changed. And then he does move.

He sits up, his eyes flickering to me, without holding. "You okay?"

He said those same words after we had sex in high school, except this time, I really am okay.

"Yeah. You?" I smile, but Tyler's expression is blank.

"I'm good, just hungry. Can I get you anything?"

I sit up, because he rolled off me and I really don't want him to leave. I pull a sheet to my chest, not hiding the confusion on my face. "Um, okay."

"Cool. Peanut butter and jelly sandwich?"

I nod, but something isn't right.

Tyler ties off the condom and puts on his clothes. *All* his clothes. As if he's not returning to bed. A fist clenches my chest, but I don't say anything. I am frozen in fear.

Please don't leave.

He climbs down the loft ladder and I hear him rustling around in the kitchen, opening the fridge, the cupboards. I chew nervously on my thumbnail, listening. After a couple of minutes, he climbs back up and sets a plate with a sandwich and a glass of milk by the bed. He remains on the ladder, running a hand through his thick, dark hair.

"Mira, I've gotta go. I made plans. I wasn't expecting... Anyway, my friend is waiting for me."

I look away, sucking in a breath to hold back the well of tears behind my eyes. Why is he doing this? *Why?*

"Sorry, I know it's bad timing. I'll see you later, though, okay?"

I don't answer. I don't look at him. I won't tell him it's okay, when it's not. And he damn well knows it. I can hear it in his voice.

I listen to the sound of him climbing down the ladder. The closing of the front door is what sends the choking in my chest to the surface.

The largest tears I've ever shed drop to my cheeks. I curl into a ball on the bed, hiding my face in Tyler's pillow, smelling him, loving him, and hating him at the same time.

After all we've been through, why would he do this?

Chapter Twenty-Four

Tyler

As soon as Mira and I had sex, the cloud muddling my head these last few months whooshed through my body and out my pores, forcing every emotion I've stifled to the forefront, along with my reasons for suppressing them. Why I'm here in Lake Tahoe. Why I quit my community college teaching position and hightailed it out of Colorado.

Because I'm a fucked-up mess.

I couldn't love Anna. I haven't been able to love anyone.

Anna deserved more. She was sweet and gentle. I cared about her more than any girl I'd been with these last few years. I thought I'd never love any woman again. That I was incapable. Anna was good for me, and I told myself I could make her happy. It was ludicrous to get engaged, but I needed to move on, even if I hadn't realized at the time what I was moving on from.

All those emotions I thought myself incapable of came pouring out this evening with Mira. Love, anger, lust.

Why did I return to Lake Tahoe? I can't even remember my reasoning. I have buddies all over the country from my years at university. I could have stayed with any one of them, but I came home. To a place that isn't even my home, now that my mom has moved to Carson City.

It's frightening to imagine I subconsciously returned for Mira. And yet, when we made love—'cause there's no other way to describe what happened—and these last few weeks... the tension between us...*fuck.*

I came for her.

I didn't want to think about the reasons we shouldn't get involved. I convinced myself we could have sex and it wouldn't matter, but that was a lie. My feelings for Mira are wholly different from anything I've had with anyone else. The pain and wrongness of leaving her is killing me. I want to crawl back and beg her to forgive me for being such a dick, but there's a reason I freaked out and ran.

After Anna, I'm not worthy of any woman.

I came to Tahoe thinking Mira was the one who needed to change. But Mira is trying to save her mom, she's giving her best friend space to be with the girl he loves, though it kills her, and she's staying away from the Sallees to protect them from the trouble she's in. Mira is the altruist. She is everything I thought she was when I first got to know her, and nothing I believed of her when I ran from this town six years ago.

I blink at the house in front of me. I've managed to drive to Phil's on autopilot. I shot him a text as soon as I left Mira, but I haven't checked to see if he received it. I considered going to Jaeg's, but Cali is there. She'll skewer my ass for walking out on Mira; Cali's very protective of her fellow women. At the moment, I don't blame her.

I step out of the car and knock on Phil's front door, scrubbing a hand down my face.

Phil answers, takes one look at me, and opens the door wide, letting me in. "That bad, huh?"

Phil's live-in girlfriend, I discover, is out on a girls' night. It's just us, and instead of our usual beers, he tries to give me a shot of tequila.

I shake my head. "No, man."

"Dude, what's gotten into you? I've never seen you like this."

I clasp my hands between my knees, legs spread wide on the couch across from him. "You remember that girl I told you about before I left town?"

Phil takes his shot and sits on the small couch next to me. "Yeah, you said she dumped you, but you didn't have a girlfriend in high school, so that made no sense. And you wouldn't tell me who she was."

"I'm living with her." I stare at Phil, waiting for recognition.

He sits forward. "This Mira chick is the one who fucked you up?"

I nod, framing my forehead with the tips of my fingers.

"I thought you decided to get her out of your place?"

"It's not my place, but yeah, I tried. It didn't work. I —we..."

After a long pause, Phil says, "You screwed her?"

I raise my head. "Dude, that's my girlfriend you're talking about."

Phil holds up his hands. "Whoa, she's your girlfriend now? What are you doing, man?"

My head falls back into my hands. "I don't know, but I think I just ruined everything."

Phil proceeds to tell me to forget about Mira. To get her out of my system. Hook up with someone else. I tried all that after I left Tahoe the first time. It didn't work. And honestly, I don't have the energy to fight this anymore. I'm not sure I deserve Mira, but I'm tired of walking away from her.

I stand abruptly. "I gotta go."

Phil stands too. "What? You can't go back. She'll ruin you. Look at what she's already done." I glare at him, and his face eases. "She means that much?"

I sigh as the heavy pressure in my chest escapes. "Yeah."

We argue, she's feisty, but Mira and I are connected in a way I've never been with anyone else. I *see* her, and I'm amazed by the person she is.

She means everything. I don't know how I could have been such a blind ass that I didn't realize it.

* * *

Mira

I LIVE with the fear of people leaving me. My mom's abandonment when I was three had that effect. Yet when Tyler left me naked—emotionally, physically—there is no description for the hollow pain in my chest, or for how utterly pissed I am.

After I uncurled from the fetal position on his bed and gathered my clothes, I hobbled my way down the ladder to my bedroom, where I dressed and packed an overnight bag. I can't live with Tyler. We just end up hurting each other.

I pull up to Lewis's place a half hour later, and Gen's car is in the driveway beside Lewis's truck. The lights are on inside the house. I hate the idea of intruding on them, but I need a place to crash. And I'd actually like to talk to Gen. It's why I came here instead of Zach's.

Lewis and Zach would totally freak out and try to crack skulls if they knew some guy hurt me. I'm angry at Tyler, but I'm pretty partial to his brain remaining intact.

I need Gen's help. She may be pretty, but she is tough. She once told Lewis, who's never had to work at holding on to a girl, to shape up or she wouldn't be with him. She'll know what to do about Tyler. Because walking away from him goes against every fiber of my being clamoring to remain close.

But I can't. Not after what he just did.

I walk up the steps to Lewis's small A-frame house, and peer into the broad front windows. He and Gen are sitting on the couch watching television, his arm wrapped around her shoulders. He leans over and whispers something that puts a smile on her face.

Maybe I should stay with Zach. Or maybe I can talk to Gen, then crash at Zach's? Or drop by Nessa's? She has a roommate, but she probably wouldn't mind me sleeping on the couch.

Gen's head pops up. "Mira?" she says through the open window. She springs to her feet and Lewis does too, a worried look crossing his face.

"Hey," I say as I let myself in, attempting to look upbeat. "Sorry to interrupt, I..." I what? Needed a friend? Needed to get away?

All of the above.

"Come in," Gen says before I can finish. She grabs my arm and leads me into the kitchen, where she pushes me onto a stool at the counter. She rustles around in the cabinets and pulls out mint Oreo cookies and a tub of Red Vines.

"What can I get you to drink? We have Jägermeister"—she makes a gagging face—"or rum. I haven't had a chance to stock the place with good alcohol yet, only the sugar products. We're left with what Lewis has around."

"Um, I'm not sure I need anything." I don't drink much, especially not when I'm sad. Reminds me too much of how my mom copes.

"Mira." Gen lowers her voice. "You look really upset. Are you okay?" She glances over my head. "I'm only asking because Lewis is about to come over and interrogate, so unless you want him involved, we should pretend like we're having girl time." She holds up her hands. "That is, unless you need to talk to him? It just seemed like—well, I've seen that look before. Crap, I've worn it. You look heartbroken."

I let out a sigh. She's right. I came here to talk to her. "Rum and Coke. And pass the cookies."

Gen's mouth compresses and she nods as if I've confirmed her instincts. She quickly mixes two rum and Cokes, pouring them into wineglasses. "We'll pretend it's fine wine," she says, and hands me mine. "Give me a sec and I'll get us some alone time."

"You don't have to—"

She shakes her head. "No, it's fine."

Gen walks over to Lewis and talks in a low voice. He raises his head and glances over. I take a sip of my drink.

"Mira," he says as he walks toward the stairs. "Gen says you want to talk about girl stuff." He cringes, though I don't think he realizes he's doing it. "I'll be upstairs if you need anything."

I don't even want to know what she told him. He probably thinks I have PMS or something. But he glances back a couple of times, so maybe he suspects more.

Gen returns and grabs her wineglass.

"I don't want to lie to Lewis," I say.

I'm already uncomfortable with the one piece of information I'm keeping from him. I don't want to add to the list.

"This isn't lying. This is girl time. I told him you have personal girl issues to discuss with me. No lie there. You can tell him what's up later, if you want. Once I've helped you figure out what you should do. You know, the right way. Not the guy way."

I smile, despite my sadness. This is why I came. "Yeah, Zach and Lewis aren't good for chatting about this kind of thing."

"Boys."

"Right."

She sips her drink and leans forward conspiratorially. "So, which boy are we referring to? Have I met him?"

I slide my finger over the rim of my glass. There's no way to say it, except to say it. It's not going to sound good no matter how I put it.

"Tyler."

Gen chokes on the gulp she just took, holding up her hand while she hacks and grabs a towel from the oven door. *"Tyler?"* she gasps.

"It's not like that, or maybe it is." I feel my brows furrow. "We have history."

"He was strange around you," she says, her eyes unfocused as if she's thinking back. "I asked him about it once and he said he didn't want to talk about it, which I of course translated to mean there was a lot to talk about. But I never would have thought it was..."

I'm tired of hiding the way I feel about Tyler, and I

need Gen's advice. For so long I had ironclad walls around my emotions. I finally let Tyler in, and he hurts me. Nothing good comes of a relationship where two people hurt each other. But how do I build up the walls once I've taken them down? Every feeling I've ever had for Tyler is exposed.

I grab a Red Vine and twist it in my fingers. "Tyler was my first."

Gen sets her glass on the granite counter on a loud ping. "He was *your first?*"

"It's been awkward living together."

"Um, *yeah.* Why didn't you say anything? We could have come up with a different living arrangement."

"What could I say? 'Sorry, Cali, I don't want to live with your brother because I lost my virginity to him'?" I shake my head. "How do you tell that to someone's sister?"

"I see your point." She pushes my drink toward me, and I take a sip. "Obviously something happened. More than you guys being forced to live together. You've managed it so far these last couple of weeks without looking like someone ripped your heart out."

I mentally flinch. I used to be so good at hiding my emotions. All that changed once Tyler returned to town.

"Living together, we've, uh, rekindled some things."

I explain what it's been like, the attraction between me and Tyler, him taking a job at Blue, the kiss in the copy room. And tonight. I give her the CliffsNotes rendition of the way Tyler left me after we had sex.

"Damn. I'm sorry, Mira."

"What do I do, Gen? I care about him. I finally open up to the guy, and he does this. I'm not perfect, but I don't deserve what he did."

"No, you don't. Never put up with someone treating

you poorly. No matter who it is, or how much you care about him."

Gen put the smackdown on Lewis when my relationship with him came between them. I *might* have been a tad needy of his time. And I *might* have pressured him to put me first. It sounds terrible when I admit it to myself now, but I was so scared I'd lose him. I still am, though giving Lewis space has proved that people stick around because they want to, not because they're forced. You know, free will and all that. I've given Lewis space and he hasn't gone anywhere. He's still there for me.

I look up and sigh. "I'm trying to set boundaries when it comes to how people treat me, specifically my mom. She's the only person I've allowed to hurt me, but now with Tyler...leaving me like that—it's harsh."

And plays on all my fears.

"What's this about Tyler?" Lewis asks, surprising us from behind. We were huddled so close, I didn't notice him walk up. He has an empty glass in his hand and he's walking toward the sink. "Did he do something, Mira?" There's an edge to Lewis's tone.

I look at Gen, and she shrugs.

"Trust me, Lewis, you don't want to know what's going on with me and Tyler."

"Yeah, well, I'm sensing something bad. If you don't tell me, I'll have to go over and pull it out of Tyler. Physically."

"Ya see? This is why I didn't say anything." I pull my hair into a knot at the nape of my neck and slump my shoulders. "Tyler and I—we...Crap, Lewis. It's such a long story. Tyler was my first. Back in high school." Lewis's eyes go wide, and there's a tic at the side of his jaw. I'm talking fast, scrambling my words in an effort to peel off the Band-Aid. "It's been, ehh, difficult living with him. We, ah, we—"

Lewis holds up his hand and closes his eyes. "Stop. I don't want to hear it. Just tell me one thing. Did he hurt you?"

"No. Not physically. It's fine, Lewis. I just needed girl-friend advice."

Lewis grabs the edge of the counter, the tips of his fingers going white. "Because if he's not behaving himself, you need to *tell me*."

Lewis is pretty mild-mannered, but when there's a threat, he can be scary.

"It's not like that," I say. "We have a bit of a tumultuous past. I thought we'd overcome it, but obviously I was wrong."

Only that doesn't seem right, either. Tyler has looked out for me—he's grumbled about it, of course—but he's been there. I don't understand why he left tonight, but I'm not going to try and figure it out. He did, and it was cruel.

"Well, he needs to behave. I don't care what you did, if he hurts you—"

"Lewis—" Gen presses a hand to his chest, and his gaze drops to her as if he's momentarily startled. She pulls him aside and they talk amongst themselves for a minute.

This isn't why I came here. I don't want Lewis to be angry with Tyler. I'm not happy with him, but this is between us.

"Mira." Lewis is staring at me, and I realize they're both waiting for me to say something. "Do you need me to do anything?"

"No. Thank you. Actually, Lewis, there is one more thing."

Lewis has been supportive, and we're still close, despite his new relationship. I should have confessed sooner, but I wasn't ready. I'm not sure I'm ready now, but holding on to fears has gotten me nowhere. "Please don't be angry, okay?"

Lewis sits on the stool beside me. "Go ahead," he says gently.

"I lied about why I owe the money," I blurt. Lewis's face is immobile, but a shadow crosses his eyes, as if he suspects what I'm about to say. "I've been supporting my mom financially since I graduated."

Lewis lets out a loud breath and looks away.

"The payments have gotten worse these last couple of years. She told me her life was in danger, and I borrowed a large amount. I couldn't pay it back fast enough...You know the rest of the story."

Lewis doesn't look at me.

Desperation bubbles up my chest. I wanted to finally be open with him about my mom, but now I'm not sure I should have told him.

"You've been so adamant about me staying away from her." My voice falters and I take a deep breath. "And then I went and did this. It didn't seem a stretch that you'd get fed up. I worried that you'd cut me out of your life the way you've asked me to cut her out of mine. I know it's not rational, but..."

Lewis stares at his still-empty glass. I'm rambling, trying to explain, to make him understand.

"Lewis? Please say something."

He sets the glass on the counter, spins on the stool, and walks to the front door. The screen slams into the frame at his exit.

I ordinarily bottle up tears, but these days, they spring from my eyes like it's their business, slipping down my cheeks. I lower my head to the counter and feel Gen's hand on my shoulder.

"It's okay, Mira. It's going to be okay. Give him time. He's not happy, but he knows how difficult the situation is with your mom."

I hear her words, but the only thing that penetrates is that the two people I want in my life the most have walked out on me.

Chapter Twenty-Five

I go to Zach's house and tell him everything about my mom and the money, because there is no reason to keep it a secret any longer. He is totally pissed that I lied, but then he cooks us popcorn and we watch back-to-back episodes of *Game of Thrones*.

That's what I like about Zach; he gets things off his chest and forgives. It's a good quality. But while we are watching *GoT*, my chest is scoured and sore, and I'm having difficulty swallowing.

Tyler freaking left me. Right after we...And now Lewis is so angry. Will he ever talk to me again?

A piece of popcorn bounces dead center off my forehead.

"Snap out of it," Zach says.

I smile halfheartedly. No way am I getting into the dirty details about Tyler with Zach. Explaining it to Lewis was bad enough. But this is nice. As terrible as things are, I still have friends, and that's something. Some of my worst fears have been realized tonight with Lewis walking out once he

205

heard the truth, and Tyler...what he did, so wrong. But I'm still standing. And I'm not entirely alone.

I stay with Zach over the next few days, going in to work and doing my best to act like the guy I've always cared about didn't tear my heart from my chest, and that my best friend isn't so mad he won't speak to me. I've also visited John and Becky and explained to them the situation with my mom. They weren't happy that I lied, or that my mom has been using me as her personal bank account. I *did not* mention that I think the guys who beat me up were hitmen for the dude I owe. There's only so much parental units can take without wigging out, no matter how far into adulthood you get.

"No going out alone until you get the money paid off," John said. So obviously, he was concerned about that very issue without me having to confirm it.

I could literally see the pain on his face when I told him I wanted to pay off the debt by myself. He argued with me, rubbing a red mark into his forehead. It was killing him not to be able to take care of this, but somehow I feel that if I'm forced to get out of the rest of this situation myself, I won't allow it to happen again. That I'll no longer be susceptible to my mom's manipulation.

I'm not stupid—if I think my life or anyone else's is in danger, I'll ask John and Becky for the money. But for now, the guy I owe was happy with the after-tax money I received from my signing bonus. He's allowing me to pay the rest in installments over the next few weeks. I guess he figures if I'm dead, he gets nothing.

It's another long afternoon in the office as I work overtime to prepare for the festival. Despite the mountain of work Hayden and I have, we've managed to remain afloat.

It's amazing how productive I can be when trying to keep my mind off things.

I take a deep breath and press the buttons on the copy machine to print the last fifty copies of music festival fliers. One way or another, I'll get through this—my debt, building a different relationship with my mom, fixing things with Lewis, and even letting go of Tyler, if that's what it comes down to. I don't like it—I might cry myself to sleep every night for the next year—but I'll get through it.

I don't need someone who doesn't want to be in my life.

"Frasier, you going to the mixer tonight?"

William, a finance guy a few years older than me, stands in the doorway, tapping the doorframe with his sapphire Blue Casino signet ring of accomplishment.

Blue throws management mixers in the Mont Belle Lounge a couple of times a month. They claim it's a chance for management staff to loosen their ties and form good working relationships. I think it's in poor taste, given how crazy everything is right now. If people have time on their hands, they should help me and Hayden out with our crap ton of work. Just sayin'.

"I'm working late." I read the error message that pops up on the copier and refill the bin with bright yellow paper.

We're understaffed and unprepared for this music festival, but Blue has thrown it every year for the past fifteen years, so sexual harassment investigation and staffing issues or not, the show will go on.

"Get off early," William says. "Your work can wait. That's the reason they have these things..." He steps into the room, crowding me, though he's a safe six feet away. "So we can mix."

Ew. Obvious innuendo.

Over the last week or two, people have stopped snickering at me and started, dare I say it, respecting the work I'm doing for Hayden and the hospitality department.

I guess the leers from men are back as well.

"Can't. Too busy. Enjoy, though." I grab my stack of fliers, give him a short, tight smile, and move to walk past him.

William grabs my arm. Not hard, but his fingers are wrapped all the way around and graze my breast. I flinch and take a step back. He lets me go, but says, "You can always change your mind. There are a few of us who wouldn't mind spending time with you. Give us guys a chance." He plasters on a charming smile that makes me shiver in revulsion.

I have no words. Except *no*. Not ever. Putting aside the fact that I still have all these feelings for Tyler, William and his ilk are creepy. He's good-looking, but there's something about him and the group he works with. They remind me of a pack of rats, scurrying around the casino, their oily confidence sliming the place up.

"Thanks, but I'm swamped." I send him my best not-interested bitchy smile, because his presence is setting off all kinds of alarms in my head, and walk around him and out the door before he can deliver another cheesy line.

When I turn down the hallway, Tyler is walking toward me, a determined set to his features.

Staying at Zach's, it's been easy to avoid Tyler's calls for the last few days; not so easy to avoid him at work. I don't know what he wants, but the only way I can resist Tyler in my weakened state is to stay away from him. I'll have to face him at some point, just not right now.

I spin in the opposite direction and steer myself into Hayden's office, which is closer to the copy room than my small space.

Hayden looks up from her computer as I shut her door and listen for footsteps to pass. "Mira? You okay?"

I juggle the fliers in my arms. We've blasted the festival all over social media and posted it on the Blue Casino marquee, but good old-fashioned fliers are still a mainstay for local businesses.

"I'm fine. Sorry for interrupting. I wanted to make sure these are what you had in mind?" She's already approved them, or I wouldn't have printed a gabillion, but I need an excuse for barging in.

Hayden's brow furrows. "You don't look fine. Is someone giving you a hard time? That security guard I saw you with? I thought you were interested in him, but if he's bothering you, tell me."

"No, he's fine. He's a good guy." And I realize the truth of my words. Tyler has always been a good guy. Even when he's an ass. For God's sake, he couldn't even bail on me properly after sex. He had to make sure I was fed and hydrated.

"You'd let me know if there was anything wrong, right?"

"Of course."

I work late, looking over vendor lists and making sure I've emailed everyone the information they need for their contribution to the festival. By the time I wrap up, our office is a graveyard, with the exception of Hayden, who is also working late. Everyone else has gone to the mixer.

I rap lightly on Hayden's open door. "I'm taking off." She sits back, her shoulders sagging. Hayden has been burning the candle at both ends and she looks exhausted. "Not going to the mixer?"

She spreads her hands in front of her computer. "Too much work. You?"

Sometimes I wonder if Hayden avoids our colleagues as much as I do. "I'm beat."

"Have a great weekend." She returns to her computer and starts clicking away with her mouse.

Crap, the weekend. I can't sleep on Zach's couch forever. On the other hand, the men who attacked me in the woods haven't bothered me since that run-in with Denim Jacket my first day at Blue. Lewis wanted me at Cali's because Tyler was around, whereas Zach works nights. But with the tension so thick around Tyler and the threat of those men reduced, I'm wondering if I should move in with Zach. I wouldn't be opposed to the idea, but I think Zach might be. He enjoys his lady callers, and he's been keeping a low profile with me in the house.

I need fresh clothes from the cabin. I'm not looking forward to an encounter with Tyler, but it's probably time I get it over with. I'd rather it occur at home than at work.

When I unlock the door to Cali's cabin, it's pitch-dark inside. I flip on the lights, and Tyler is sitting on the couch, his head tilted back against the cushion, staring at me as I enter.

"Fuckballs." I slam a hand to my chest. "Tyler, that is so creepy. Why are you in the dark?"

He glances around as if just realizing the sun has gone down. "Sorry. I was thinking. It got dark and I didn't feel like getting up to turn on the lights."

I set my ratty purse on the counter and slip off my shoes, carrying them into the bedroom, my hands shaking. I'm terrified of the warmth of emotions I feel around him, even after what he did. I change into jeans and a light-weight sweater. When I return to the living room, Tyler is still on the couch, facing me.

"Mira, we need to talk."

Chapter Twenty-Six

Tyler

Mira crosses into the kitchen and grabs a soda. She pops the top and sits at the table, opposite my laptop and stacks of books. I really should clean up that crap.

I shove my computer to the side and push papers out of the way, taking a seat across from her. She's wiping condensation from the side of her soda can, avoiding me. I can't say I blame her.

"Mira, I'm sorry."

Her chest rises and falls, but she won't look up.

I shift closer, annoyed at the table separating us. "I fucked up. I shouldn't have left the way I did. Can you forgive me?"

"It's fine, Tyler. No big deal."

The fuck?

I stand, walk around the table, and squat in front of her, placing my hand on her knee. I sense her flinch, but she doesn't push me away. "No. It's not fine. *We* are a big deal to me."

Her gaze darts to my face. She stares into my eyes as if to gauge my earnestness, then focuses on the table, tuning me out.

I sigh and knuckle my forehead. "Look, can we sit on the couch? I need to tell you something important. It'd be easier if we weren't so far away."

"Tyler, there is no way we are—"

Memories of making love to her swarm my head. *God,* I want that, but I'm not trying to go there. "That's not what this is about. You need to know what happened in Colorado. It's why I freaked out and left the other day, which I'm so fucking sorry for."

She studies my eyes again, almost as though they're her sole read on my sincerity. Instead of looking away this time, she nods and rises. I follow her to the couch and we sit at opposite ends, but it's better than the land block of the kitchen table.

I lean my elbows on my thighs, my hands overlapped in a fist between my legs. How do I tell her? I've never talked to anyone about what happened, or my responsibility in it.

I swallow back the rock in my throat. "I mentioned I had a fiancée." Mira nods. "She was a good person. Someone I probably didn't deserve."

Mira squirms beside me, and moves as if to get up. "I don't want to hear about how you lost some great love. *God,* Tyler—"

"No." My voice is firm. "That's not it. I didn't love her. That was the problem. She deserved more, and I didn't love her. But she wanted me to."

She looks at my face and slowly settles back into the cushion.

"I thought—I thought I couldn't love anyone except my family. I hadn't felt that way for a girl in a long time. I thought I never would again."

I turn to her and look her in the eye. "I haven't loved anyone since high school."

Mira shakes her head, almost imperceptibly, but that's not going to stop me from telling her the rest. She needs to understand. This needs to be said.

"I loved *you*. I've never been able to feel that way for anyone else. Not even Anna. She was everything I thought I wanted. We both tried. She tried harder. I wanted to give her what she needed. I thought we could make it work, so I asked her to marry me. It was a desperate attempt to fix things. If I couldn't love this girl, who should be perfect for me, I didn't think I'd be able to love anyone."

My gaze never leaves Mira. "I regretted asking Anna to marry me the moment the words were out of my mouth, but I didn't take them back. I let it drag out for a week, convincing myself it was the right thing to do."

I lean my head against the back of the couch and close my eyes briefly. "I think she knew how I really felt. She didn't say it, but..."

For a moment, I'm lost in the past, the burning I haven't been able to shake these past several months flaming in my chest.

"What do you think?" Anna asked, the last Saturday I saw her. "My friends are organizing it. I'm game if you are."

Her friends had invited us to river-kayak. Anna wasn't sporty, but she tried. We'd gone on a few hikes together. She would slip and stumble, and I couldn't hide my frustration. It wasn't because she didn't do well in the outdoors. It was because deep down I wasn't into us, and my lack of emotion came out in other ways.

"I've got papers to grade, but go ahead," I told her. I'd already begun to pull away. Had been considering how to talk to her about our new engagement and explain I'd made a mistake.

Anna didn't normally get involved in outdoor trips like this, especially not without me. I'll never know if she was trying to prove something.

"I think I will," she said with a mischievous smile.

I smiled back, because she was so gentle and sweet, and I got the sense she wanted to impress me. I didn't care one way or the other if she went river-kayaking, but I thought it funny she'd do something so out of character.

"Tyler," Mira says, snapping me out of the horror of that day. "Are you okay?" She scoots closer without touching me.

"No."

I rub my forehead. I've not admitted that to anyone since I returned to Lake Tahoe. I didn't have to admit it to my friends in Colorado. They already knew I was a mess.

"She did something, this girl I didn't love but had asked to marry me. I think she thought if she did certain things, I'd grow to love her the way I should."

I look at Mira, pleading with my eyes, willing her of all people to understand. I don't blame Mira for what went down in Colorado. But maybe, just maybe, if Mira felt a small fraction of what I did for her—what I still feel for her —she'll understand why I couldn't love Anna.

"What happened, Tyler?" Mira's voice is strong, as if bracing for a truth she knows will be horrific. And it is. It's so ugly I wake to nightmares of Anna crying beneath the water.

"There was a river, and she was with friends. She wasn't a kayaker, but she went anyway. Her friends gave her basic training, but the run she did was a class four. Her friends told me later that she'd smiled and said she could do it. They admitted afterward that they'd had doubts."

I press my fingers to my eyes, trying to block the visions I've created in my mind of what happened. "Everything was fine at first. Then Anna went around a boulder with a deep whirlpool. Her kayak flipped, lodged under a notch. She couldn't get back up."

I hear Mira's sharp intake of breath, but I press on. "It was a freak situation. Most people would have coasted through that rough spot. Several of her friends already had. They struggled to free her. They"—I swallow, my throat dry, cracking—"they could reach her hand, but they couldn't pull her out. The current was too strong. Her straps tangled. She was under for forty minutes without air."

The images I have of that day, not just the ones I've created from what others have said, still haunt me. "I saw her body in the hospital afterward. The ring I'd selected without thought, still on her hand." The back of my throat burns, along with my eyes, my chest. Damn.

Being in my hometown is supposed to make what happened better. Make this pain and guilt go away. But it hasn't.

I sense Mira's hand rest on my shoulder, feel her crawling onto my lap. She curls around me, and I tuck my head against the crook of her neck, breathing in her scent. Moisture I can't stop from falling from my eyes soaks into her hair.

I don't know if Anna would have gone on that kayak trip if she hadn't been trying to impress me. She might have. Her friends seemed to think so when I worried she'd done it for me. They may have said it to make me feel better. I'll never know. What I know is that Anna died loving someone who didn't love her back. It's that guilt that eats at me.

I wipe my eyes and cup my hands on either side of Mira's face. "I. Am. So. Sorry. For my past in Colorado, without a doubt. But right now, I'm sorry for taking out my guilt on you. I fucked up. I've always wanted you, Mira, and when we had sex the other night and it was so amazing, I didn't think I deserved you. I panicked. I went to a friend's house to get my head straight. I came right back, but you were gone."

I deeply regret the way I handled things with Anna, but it's time I forgive myself. I didn't love her the way I should have, but there's no reason I can't love Mira the way she deserves.

"Did it work?" she asks. "Is your head on straight?"

I puff out a breath. She's teasing me, trying to lighten the mood, and it helps. "Phil told me to leave you. He's pretty much the worst friend to ask for advice about a woman. He's the person who suggested I bring girls home to get you to leave."

Her eyes widen. "Is that why you did it? You were listening to something a stupid guy said?"

This—just this. Mira giving me a hard time, her warm body in my lap—it makes everything better.

I shrug, a small smile returning to my face. "Eh, it was worth a try." She squirms indignantly and attempts to get up. "Calm down." I wrap my arms around her more tightly, holding her close. "I just got you back where I want you. Do you have any idea what I've been going through these last few days? Where the hell have you been?"

"Zach's, but don't change the subject. Did you really bring those women home to piss me off?"

"Yes. Definitely."

"You are such a jackass," she says, but there's humor in her tone. "I totally should have brought a guy home." Her gaze wanders, as if she's reconsidering.

I squeeze her waist. "No, you shouldn't have. That would not have gone over well."

"Why? What would you have done?"

"Thrown him out," I say without hesitation. I lean down and kiss her neck right below her jaw. "I'm not perfect. I've not always done the right thing, but I love you, Mira. You've always had a chunk of my heart nestled in your feisty little hand. Maybe all we needed was that last shove—this forced living situation—for what we have to come together, because over these last few weeks, you've stolen the rest of my heart. It's why you make me crazy. Can you tone down the feist?"

"No," she says automatically, though she blinks several times, as though distracted by my words.

I told her I loved her and I meant it. It's time she knew.

She kisses my forehead, then my nose. "I'm sorry about Anna. It makes sense why you felt you didn't deserve my love if you believed you threw away hers."

Her gaze hardens and she wiggles out of my lap. "But no matter what words you bribe me with, you are not off the hook."

I sigh in frustration. I tell the girl I love her, and she walks away. It would be terrible, if I didn't think she felt the same.

"We are not okay, Tyler Morgan. I may have had trust issues and insecurities when we were younger. I was stupid and didn't tell you how I felt—"

She's going somewhere with this tirade, but I can't help but interrupt. "How do you feel?"

"—but I'm just now dealing with the most destructive

relationship of my life. Being around my mom has messed with my head. I need to know that you're not going to run out, and that we're in the same place emotionally. That we're compatible."

I look beneath my lashes, my gaze raking her body suggestively.

She shakes her head. "In that way we are *too* compatible."

"No such thing as too compatible in *that way*."

She looks to the ceiling in exasperation. "You've changed, Tyler. I'm not saying it's bad. I understand you went through a difficult time in Colorado. Tragedies like that can strengthen a person as much as they can shatter. But I need to know we are compatible enough for a mature relationship. That we can tackle our pasts together. No more running out." She holds her head high. "I'm tired of games. I want something real."

"I do too."

For a moment, we simply stare at each other.

Mira breaks our stare-down when she walks to her bedroom door. She pauses inside the threshold. "You'll need to prove it," she says softly, and closes the door behind her.

Damn, she's going to make me work for it.

What she doesn't know is that I've waited eight years for her, if you count the time when I pined and never did anything.

Mira is the only woman I've ever loved. So deeply, in fact, that my heart was misshapen until I returned to her, molding itself back into the semblance of a human form. I wasn't good for anyone else, but I'm good for this girl.

And if she needs me to prove it, I will.

Chapter Twenty-Seven

Mira

A fter work the next day, Tyler spent the evening cleaning. *Cleaning.* He sorted his books and tucked them into a corner, spines out. He cleared the dining table of his technical journals and scribbled-on papers. And he did the dishes. *The freaking dishes.* I'm seriously considering whether an alien life-form has taken over his body. It could happen. Based on his recent behavior, I rule nothing out.

Tyler told me he loved me last night. Just like that, he laid it all out there. For a moment, I thought I was in some sort of dream state. There's never been any other guy for me but Tyler. To have him tell me he loved me filled me with so much hope, I nearly lost it and told him everything I felt inside. I held on by a thread and remembered what happened the last time I gave Tyler Morgan everything. We have a tendency to run from each other when faced with emotions. And Tyler's still getting over his guilt about his fiancée, for which I can't blame him. But these things combined leave me a little gun-shy.

I don't want to rush into anything. I'm thinking before I act from now on. No more racing to the loan shark in need of funds, no more running into Tyler's arms just because he opens them, even if I think that is where I belong. I want us to ease into this, get to know each other. Be sure.

Tyler stares at the photo on the side of my bed as I pick out a work outfit from my limited selection. We are hanging with each other again, but there is no kissing—my rule, not his. He even took me on a bike ride at the Camp Richardson trail yesterday. This time we rented the easy-does-it comfy cruisers for the two-lane bike path, so I'd have my own ride. The trees smelled so nice, and the air was warm, and Tyler did tricks on his bike to entertain me. It was perfect.

"I think I want to buy a bike," I say, holding up a sleeveless navy blouse. I've been adding to my work wardrobe little by little when I find something nice on sale. "You know, when I've paid everything off."

He looks up. "Yeah?"

"The comfy kind we rode on yesterday."

The sweetest grin spreads across his face, lighting up his eyes. "We can do that. We'll pick out a good one for you. Nice wide seat."

I shoot him a look over my shoulder. "You better not be suggesting I have a big ass."

"Your ass is perfect. I am merely looking out for your comfort."

"In that case, yes, a bike with a wide seat with springs. I want to feel like I'm riding a couch."

He chuckles. "You got it."

It's weird, but I actually feel closer to Tyler than I ever

have. There are no more secrets. He knows what I've gone through since he left, and I know his story.

"You were a baby," Tyler says, as if to himself, a deep V forming between his brows as he studies the picture he grabbed.

It's the framed photo I keep of me and Lewis in front of the Sallees' house, my arms clinging to one of Lewis's long legs. Lewis is a couple of years older than me, but he's always towered above me, especially at that age. I'd not been fed well before I moved in with his family.

"I was three," I say, grabbing beige skinny pants to go with the flowy navy blouse.

Tyler's brow crinkles. "But you're in a diaper."

"I was a toddler," I say defensively. "I wasn't potty trained until I moved in with John and Becky."

He looks up, his expression serious.

I hang my clothes on the hook attached to the closet door. "Don't look at me like that. It's embarrassing."

Tyler carefully places the photo on the nightstand. "This was how old you were when you went to live with Lewis and his parents?"

"Yes."

"Because of your mom?"

I hate it when people ask about that time in my life, but it's important that Tyler knows this part of me. And out of everyone, I want Tyler to understand the connection I have to Lewis. Maybe it will also explain why I'm so protective of the Sallees. "Lewis and his dad found me."

"What do you mean they found you?"

"I was alone—"

He raises his hand. "Hold up. You were alone? At this age?" He points to the photo. "This little baby—toddler, whatever? *Alone*, alone?"

My mouth compresses. "You know I don't have a great mom. My dad didn't last a month after I was born. My mom got word he died of an overdose shortly after. Eventually, my mom stopped coming home some nights."

"When you were three?"

I nod.

Tyler swings his legs off the bed, his forearms resting on his thighs as he stares at me. "What happened, Mira?"

I sit beside him. "One day, John and Lewis were next door helping out a neighbor. I used to sit in the window and watch people pass. John saw me and came over. He introduced himself and asked some questions. I must have told him my mom was gone or something. He asked if I wanted to go with him and Lewis to their house."

I shrug. "That's pretty much how I came to live with them. I don't remember all the details. I'm told Lewis held out his hand and I went straight to him and clung to one of his legs, just like in that photo." I feel my mouth curve into a smile. "I actually remember being a little kid and holding on to Lewis like that. He was so tall. Anyway, that picture was taken around the time I moved in with the Sallees."

Tyler's brow furrows. "Your mom, she didn't..."

I chuckle ruefully. "Try to get me back?" I shake my head. "No, I don't think so. The Sallees diverted my questions as I got older by saying how blessed they were to raise me, but I always knew my mom didn't want me."

"Mira..."

"That sounds harsh. I don't mean it like that. Deep down I think she has affection for me, but the drugs and the drinking, they kind of block it, you know? By the time the Sallees found me, my mom had been bailing for days at a time. I was dehydrated, underfed, dirty. It's a lot of responsibility to raise a small kid. I think my mom was relieved to have the help."

Tyler scratches the side of his jaw. He stares out the window, frowning.

"It's okay, Tyler. It was a long time ago. But you get it now, right? My connection to Lewis, and why his parents are so important to me? They're all I have. And my mom too. She's the only blood family I've ever known. There are no aunts or uncles—no cousins."

He looks over with his cool blue gaze that manages to warm me. "You have us. Me, Cali, Gen, not just Lewis and his parents."

I want to believe his words.

"People leave, Tyler. Sometimes it's for good reasons, like when you went off to college, and sometimes it isn't."

"I won't leave you, Mira."

"You have no idea how many triggers you hit when you walked out after we..."

He sighs and closes his eyes. "I wish I could take that night back."

"I know, and I even understand why you freaked out, but I still need time to feel safe again. And your sister and Gen...They seem like friends. I'd like them to be, but the only friend who's always been there for me is Lewis. Except now Lewis..." I swallow and sink back on the bed, covering my eyes with my hand.

I've been running around trying to not think about it, but it's there. The worry that I've permanently damaged one of the most important relationships in my life.

"Mira?" Tyler stretches out on his side and rests his hand above my heart. "Are you okay?"

"It's nothing." I roll to face him, wiping the tear that

snuck down my cheek. What is up with all the tears? "Sorry. Bad topic."

"What happened with Lewis?"

"He's angry with me for lying about why I owe the money."

"You told him the truth?" I nod. "And you think he's all you have," he says, looking away. He knuckles his forehead. "Mira, you've got to stop believing everyone leaves you."

"I'm working on it, but these things don't change overnight. They're imprinted. If you recall, the people in my life haven't been the most reliable." I glare at him, because like it or not, he's one of them.

"Push people away, and yes, sometimes they go. And sometimes..." He inches closer, the space between us disappearing. His arms come down on either side of me, dipping the mattress and forcing me on my back again. "Sometimes they return because they can't stay away."

It would be so easy to raise my head that last inch to his lips, from which I suddenly can't look away.

I clear my throat and roll out of his reach. The tension between us is the one constant we have. But I want more than attraction.

After an awkward silence, I say, "Are you hungry?"

I look back and he quirks an eyebrow, and I realize with all this electricity zinging between us how that must sound.

My face heats. "I meant food. Are you hungry for food?"

Tyler's gaze drops to my mouth. "Sure." He stands, and I do too.

I sense him walking behind me as I make my way to the kitchen. "Frozen burrito okay?"

"Sounds good." He leans against the counter, watching me.

God, he's unnerving. Does he have to do that? "You can sit at the table. I'll bring it to you."

"I'm good." He smiles. It's sexy and full-blown, brightening his already brilliant eyes.

Oh. God.

I stand there for a moment, staring at that smile. It's the Tyler smile, the one that had me falling in love with him in high school, though the look in his true blue eyes might be a part of it.

My heart races, my face flushing. Tyler doesn't smile at me anymore. Not really. Not the full-blown deal. A quirk of the lips, a grin that might touch his eyes, but this is different. This is unrestrained and glowing. As if I light up his world.

I hadn't realized it until now. Hadn't realized how his not budging an inch when it came to me protected us both. But he's letting down his guard. Pulling out all the stops.

"I have to go." I rush around the counter and snake my purse from the top, gingerly, so as to not brush one hair on his body.

His smile fades. "Where are you going?"

"Out."

I make the mistake of glancing back, not sure what I'm expecting to see. Maybe a smug I-did-that-sexy-smile-on-purpose look. But his expression is one of masked disappointment.

That's worse than smug. If I'm reading it right, it means his smile was genuine. He was happy just being with me. And my reaction—a bone-deep attraction—is totally out of control. If all he has to do before I'm ready to whip off my bra and launch myself on him is smile, we're in the danger zone. Loose cannons everywhere inside our house.

How am I supposed to take things slow when he looks

at me like that? Suddenly, this living together has gone from explosive to downright cataclysmic.

I pull my keys from my purse and walk out the door.

In my socks. Crap.

Too bad. I'm not going back.

Tyler seems serious about his feelings for me, but there's no way I can jump into this. It's not smart after all we've been through.

My feelings for him have grown, and losing him this time might be the one thing in life that finally breaks me.

Chapter Twenty-Eight

I smooth my hand over the new beige upholstery in Tyler's truck on our way into work. Tyler has offered me rides before, but today I gave in. My car wouldn't start. There weren't many other options.

I'd gone by Cali and Jaeger's the other night after I left Tyler—*in my socks*—and hung out until it grew late enough to sneak home and into my room. Tyler was at his dining table office. He looked up when I walked in and shook his head, as if I were a mystery he had no hope of figuring out.

"When did you get this done?" I point to the upholstery. The last time I was in his car, his seats were worn to the padding in some places.

His gaze flickers over. "A week or so ago. It was time. It wasn't safe. You were cutting yourself every time you got in."

I stare at the side of his head. He reupholstered his car for me?

While I'm still puzzling this through, we arrive at the casino parking garage. Tyler sprints around the front of his car and closes the door behind me as I get out. His hand goes to my lower back while we walk to the casino's back entrance, and he opens the door for me. Once inside, Tyler doesn't touch me, but he remains close, as if we are together. *Together,* together.

I said I wanted to take things slow. Wanted to make sure we had a future before rushing into things, but Tyler is already treating me like his girlfriend. It should bother me.

It doesn't.

I realized I was in trouble the other night, and my ability to keep him at arm's length has steadily dropped lower and lower. The funny thing is, I don't think he's doing all this to seduce me, or to convince me of anything. I get the feeling that he's simply not holding himself back anymore.

How does a girl keep to her convictions of going slow when a guy brings his A-game like this?

It's the weekend of the music festival, and both Tyler and I arrived for a later shift in order to work through the evening. We've hung out a bit these last couple of days, but I've also kept busy by visiting Becky and John, Cali and Jaeger, and Nessa. I even swung by to watch more episodes of *GoT* with Zach—anything to keep things from going too far with Tyler, because I can feel the heat.

The longer we live together, hover over each other, the more my defenses break down. I want him. And now, with this business of reupholstering his car so that my arms won't get scratched? He. Is. Killing. Me.

Tyler is still the boy who scared away my bullies in junior high, who made sure I passed algebra in high school, and who sees me like no other human being has before. And now he's a man, self-possessed and confident, and he's showing me in every way possible that I'm important to him. How much longer can I hold myself back? Or do I at all?

In the elevator to the executive floor, I look over and smile. If my smile is filled with love and every other feeling I've ever possessed for Tyler—well, that can't be helped. It's what he brings out in me.

A heated look fills his eyes, sending a spark through my belly.

The elevator doors open and I mumble something resembling "I'll see you later," as I take off toward my office, trying to stifle the lunatic grin on my face.

This tension cannot go on much longer. I will combust.

An hour passes, and I let out a heavy sigh at my desk, forcing my mind off Tyler for the millionth time in the last thirty minutes. I run my finger down the schedule of events and the vendors linked to each. A knock sounds at my office door. And by *office*, I mean *closet*, because my space has no windows and is barely large enough for a desk and chair. But hey, it's an enclosed area and it's all mine, so I'm thrilled.

I glance up. "Hi, Hayden."

Hayden's been pulling fourteen-hour days these last couple of weeks. I'm not far behind her. We're both looking drained, but Hayden seems particularly stressed.

"I have a huge favor to ask. Jessie from hospitality called in sick with appendicitis."

"Jessie?" I say, my voice high-pitched. "As in, Jessie who is saving our asses by running hospitality with minimal help from me while we're short-staffed? That Jessie?"

"Yeahhh."

Oh, no. "What can I do?"

I mean, I'm booked for the night with human resources tasks, but this is an emergency. And I'm Hayden's right-hand woman. I like the little team we've formed. It feels good to be a part of something outside of family and friends.

"We've got people coming in from all over, and every celeb has special requests. I need you to check the suites to make sure they're stocked with the appropriate items. Gummy bears, Roberto Cavalli bath towels in zebra print, rubber duckies—"

"Whoa, seriously?"

She rolls her eyes. "Celebrities. What can you do? Jessie supposedly stocked everything before she left yesterday, but I want to make sure it's all there. She wasn't feeling well."

"Sure, I'll take care of it." I calculate in my head the other items I have left to manage. It's massive, but this is important to Hayden, so it's important to me. "Should I leave now?"

"If you don't mind? Here's the list." She hands me a ten-page document.

I blink, but hold it together. This list will take me hours. "I'm on it. Anything else?"

"No, but maybe just—be careful?"

I frown.

Hayden shifts her feet nervously. "Drake's here."

"*What?*"

"And there's a weird energy among the executives tonight. It's making me nervous."

What the hell? I love my job, but sometimes this place sucks.

"Why did they allow Drake back?" From the rumors I've heard, the CEO is no longer confident of Drake's innocence.

"No idea. My boss has been tight-lipped on the subject."

"Okay," I say, leery. "I'll be careful."

Hayden leaves, and I shoot out one last email before slipping on my heels from under my desk. I exit my closet/office—and stop in the hallway, the hospitality list and other paperwork clutched in my hands.

Male shouts filter down the hall, escalating with each word, as if whoever is yelling is also rapidly approaching.

Drake turns the corner, headed my way. "We had a deal, Joseph," he yells behind him, pacing closer, papers hanging out the unzipped sides of his briefcase. "I sacrificed for you." He stops as if to turn and go back the way he came. But then he catches sight of me.

Drake's eyes narrow and he stalks forward. "You're next, Mira Frasier." His face contorts red with rage. "You think you've come up in the world? I know all about your past. You're like me," he snarls. "Came from the dumps, didn't you? That's where you'll end up. They'll throw you under the bus faster than they did me. You're a *woman*." He grabs my arm. "They're using you. You have less power than any man in this place. You are *nothing*."

I can't move, can't breathe. I shouldn't listen to him, but for some reason his words hit home. I didn't get this job due to merit, and I'm ashamed of some of the things I've done to survive. Pushing people away who didn't deserve it, borrowing from bad men, lying to Lewis. I thought my job at Blue was a step up. But now, with Drake highlighting where I came from—is he right? Am I like that tree root in the woods reaching for the stars, tripping everything in its path, when where I really belong is back in the dirt?

The positive affirmations I've been silently chanting these past months flee my head. My mind is blank.

Tyler and another security guard barrel around the corner. Tyler's gaze darts from me to Drake, his jaw clenching.

He lunges for Drake and wraps a thick arm around his neck. "Let her go, asshole."

Tyler is taller, stronger. Drake grimaces and drops my arm, his briefcase clattering to the ground.

Tyler grabs his handcuffs and restrains Drake's wrists, then shoves him at the other security guard, who's even bigger than Tyler, bald, with a thick mustache that sticks out at the ends.

The other guard grabs Drake in what looks like a bruising grip, but Drake attempts to pull away, his eyes wild. "She's next," he yells, his body shaking as he tries to move toward me. "Mira and that bitch Hayden."

Tyler steps in front of Drake and elbows him in the face, making blood spurt from his nose. Drake stumbles and lets out a piercing cry.

"Get him out of here," Tyler yells.

The guard drags Drake to the end of the hallway, where two policemen round the corner.

Before the policemen can take hold, Drake twists his neck around until our eyes meet, his expression almost calm. "The rings, Mira. Look for the rings." His face contorts into a disdainful, part-mad smile.

And with that cryptic message, he's dragged away by the policemen.

Tyler waits until they're out of sight, then turns and scans my body. "Did he hurt you?" He touches my arm, coming closer, blocking me with his body.

I don't say anything, because the answer is nebulous. Did Drake hurt me physically? Not really. Psychologically? Yes. I'm fighting to negate his words. To positive-affirm the hell out of the stuff he filled my head with.

Tyler's eyes flare at the expression on my face and he guides me into my office a few feet away, closing the door, despite the Blue employees watching us and the spectacle that just occurred.

"Mira?" Tyler touches my face, running his hands down my arms as if to check my pulse. He cups my cheeks gently. "Mira," he says again. "Tell me you're okay before I go back and fuck that guy up. I swear I'll—"

"Fine," I choke out. "I'm fine. He just—got to me."

Tyler pulls me to his chest, his hand running up and down my back, warm and gentle. "He doesn't know anything about you, Mira. Don't listen to a word that asshole said. I know you." He squeezes me close with a little shake. "I. Know. You. You are feisty, and strong, and clever...and you are not your mother. You care about the people in your life. You sacrifice for them, even when they don't deserve it. You protect them, when you're the one that needs protecting—"

"Okay. Stop," I say. Tears build behind my eyes again. This is not the time or place to cry. And damn, Tyler. Why am I always crying around him? "I hear you. I won't listen to him."

Tyler is right. Drake may have had a rough upbringing, but we are not the same. We do not make the same choices. And he doesn't know my heart.

Tyler pulls back and kisses me soundly on the mouth. No tongue, just a *take that and try to stop me* kind of kiss. He grins as if he's proud he got away with it.

"You can't kiss me at work."

"But after...?"

I totally walked into that one. I frown and shake my head in exasperation. "Thank you, Tyler. For what you did out there. And what you said just now." I pull away, putting a little space between our bodies, because this is work. We've already been caught kissing once. No way can I risk losing my job again. "I'm glad Drake is finally gone."

There's no way after that scene the guy will be coming back.

Tyler huffs. "He's going to prison for a long time. I overheard the executives saying Drake is to blame for everything. The assaults. Maybe even money laundering. There could be more—they don't know yet. The security team is going through more footage to make sure they haven't missed anything."

"Good." I take a deep breath and smooth my skirt with a jittery hand, the hospitality list still clutched in the other. I can't deal with thoughts of Drake right now. I have other things to worry about. "I gotta go. Gotta get back to work."

"Mira, take a minute. What happened was crazy. Give yourself time to breathe."

I shake my head. "Can't. This festival has to go off without a hitch. The pressure is on, and I want to help Hayden. I've got suites to check and—"

"What suites?"

"Celebrity suites. I'm making sure they're stocked. Then I've got vendors to touch base with. I also need to make sure the restaurant managers received the last-minute changes to personnel. There's so much. I don't have time to feel sorry for myself."

I walk around him and his hand slips to my waist, circling my stomach. My breath catches and I look up. "Tyler," I say, admonishing.

He doesn't seem to notice what his touch does to me, or he's ignoring it. "I'll go with you."

"Huh? No." I shake my head. "That's unprofessional. You can't tag along. You have a job to do."

"While you and Hayden are understaffed, security was beefed up for this event. There are plenty of guards to go around, especially opening night. I can help you. Four hands are better than two and all that."

"That doesn't apply to what I have to do, but even if it did, really, I'm okay."

I make it to the door and hurry down the hall. I'm twenty minutes behind the schedule I set for myself. People are bustling around me, as if this were the middle of the day. Not even the show Drake put on has slowed the pace for tonight's events. The music festival is one of the major draws to Blue Casino. Everyone is working overtime tonight.

Tyler catches up to my side. "I'll just hang behind. Make sure everything goes okay. It's my job, after all."

"You got this job to torment me, didn't you?"

He winks.

"Don't get in my way, Tyler, I'm serious."

"Would I do that? Pretend I'm your shadow. I won't even say a word."

Somehow I highly doubt that.

I promised Hayden I'd start with the suites, but I've got a meeting with a manager expecting me this very moment. I go there first and make sure everything is set up for the vendors to have access to the kitchens. I also provide the manager with a new list of temporary employees, which changed right up until the last minute. I've assigned badges to offsite vendors, but I'm double-checking everything. Tyler keeps his word and remains silent throughout all this, but I receive odd looks from the manager. It's not every day that hospitality personnel are escorted by security.

I make my way to the penthouse suites elevator bank, inserting a special access key.

Tyler peeks at the list in my hands. "What is this?"

I snatch it away. "Nothing."

He raises his eyebrow. "Doesn't look like nothing. Since when does the hotel provide guests with"—he snoops over my shoulder again—"red satin sheets, extra-large lubricated—"

"Knock it off. These are special guests."

"I'll say." He smirks. "Why are you doing this anyway? You're human resources. This seems a bit outside your job description."

"The girl who's been handling our hospitality shortage is really sick and couldn't come in. That leaves Hayden to make sure there's coverage, hence me. I've been helping out in hospitality anyway, so it's fine."

"Hayden can't hire someone?"

"Will you stop already? Hayden will hire someone when she comes up for air. They've lumped a ton of work on her since she started. There are people around here who want to see her fail. They don't want her in a power position."

"When they give her this much responsibility, they're putting her in a power position."

The elevator doors open and we walk inside. "That's true. Not very smart of them. Anyway, tonight Hayden's responsible for making sure the high-end guests are happy."

"So you're on condom duty."

"Exactly."

Chapter Twenty-Nine

Tyler

This errand Mira's boss has her on is hilarious. Condoms and Pringles? Nice. Then again, I'm in a pretend cop uniform, strutting around like I actually have authority in this place. A walkie-talkie and handcuffs do not a Green Beret make.

Mira stares at her cell phone as we leave the last suite. "Crap. Hayden texted me one more." She slides her finger down the screen of her phone, scrolling. "And they want tons of supplies. Hayden says this suite wasn't on the list, but that she found a file in the hospitality manager's office that had been set aside."

I've already told my boss I'm providing security to the understaffed hospitality department. He's got new recruits for support, so he's good with me assisting where I'm needed. I wasn't lying when I told Mira we've got security covered. We've bulked up to triple our normal personnel for the festival.

I text my boss I've got one more errand and will return in thirty. "Let's do this." I tuck my phone away.

"Tyler," Mira says as she sifts through her plastic key cards and heads down the hall to the last suite. "You should go back. It's all been extremely boring. Only the one room was missing items, and they were probably tack-ons. A phone call took care of it. I've got this. You must have better things to do with your time."

I pretend to consider this for a moment, my lips scrunched in concentration. "Nope. Besides, these special requests are fascinating. They have me thinking of all kinds of...scenarios."

She glances up and huffs out a frustrated sigh that is light and airy and sexy. She had better knock it off, because it's turning me on. Why her frustration is a turn-on, I will never know. Maybe it's because I think she actually likes having me near, and that the constant angst between us is just foreplay.

Her gaze narrows on the cards and she drops her hands to her sides. "Great. Hayden gave me the special code for the keypad, but I hadn't planned on coming here. I don't have the card to enter this room." She stares at the door as though it might magically open.

Lucky I'm here.

"Allow me." I pull out the master key my boss gave me, because I kick ass at my job and he knows what a trustworthy guy I am. Hmm, maybe he can put in a good word for me with Mira?

I slip in the card and Mira types the passcode on the keypad. Which is odd. I've never seen a keypad for Blue hotel rooms.

The door beeps with a green light and I push it open.

Mira walks inside, her eyes scanning the list on her phone. She scrunches her nose. "This is strange."

"More strange than the suite that wanted Uno, Nutter Butters, and lube?"

"Maybe." She scans the large space.

Blue houses several penthouse suites. A view of the lake spans the center of this room, double doors on one side, two separate doors on the other. There's a kitchen, a dining area that seems to be converted into some kind of office with files, two lockboxes, a computer...She's right. This place doesn't look like a normal suite at all.

"Mira, are you sure this one is on the list?"

She stares at her phone. "A dozen robes for each bedroom, ten bottles of kissable massage oil, two hundred condoms—" Her voice breaks off and she looks up. "Okay, that's a lot." She opens the bedroom with the double doors. "Whoa."

I peer over her head. A king-sized bed with a maroon satin comforter takes up half the room, leather wrist and ankle restraints dangling from the head- and footboards. On the wall, a clear case filled with whips, canes, and—I'm not even sure what some of it is.

This *is* post-*Fifty Shades*, but still. Wow.

I walk inside to take a closer look.

"Tyler," Mira hisses. "Get out of there."

"What?" My expression is all innocence. "Let me see that list. We need to make sure they have what they need."

"Get out, get out." She waves at me frantically. "I will take care of this."

"You sure?"

"Yes. Just—leave before you touch something and get me in trouble."

I shake my head. "Where is the trust, Mira?" She snorts as I walk past her, but her lips twist into a small smile.

I stand in the doorway, and she moves toward the bed, glancing at her list warily. Mira gingerly lifts the comforter and drops it quickly, checking off items on her phone.

I'm surprised Blue keeps a place like this around. They cater to all clientele, but this is...elaborate.

I saunter into the main room and pull open a desk drawer. Your basic office supplies, nothing special. The drawer below holds a handful of condoms. Definitely more interesting than the top drawer, but not shocking, considering the supplies in the *Fifty Shades* room. I open the third drawer. Packages of syringes, tubes, light gray powder, pills in locked cases...

"Mira—"

"I'm almost done," she says from somewhere in the second bedroom.

"We should leave." I shut the drawer and walk over to her. "This place isn't right."

"Tell me about it." She slams the nightstand cabinet and shakes her head. "But go ahead if you need to be somewhere. I'm fine." Mira bends over, her head disappearing on the side of the bed as she lifts the comforter. "I just need five more minutes, tops."

"No." I round the bed to where she's standing. "We need to leave. Now. I don't think Hayden was supposed to know about this place."

"What are you talking about?" Her eyes flicker around the room.

This one is toned down, no whipping equipment on display, but there's a sculpture in the corner that looks like a giant dildo, large mirrors on the walls, and I'm pretty sure that's video equipment on the dresser.

"It's unconventional," she says, "but you saw what the other people asked for. That rocker's suite wanted the hot pink two-foot—"

"This isn't the same. This is—"

The door to the suite beeps, indicating someone is about to enter.

I pick up Mira, charge into the main room, and dive behind the couch.

"What the hell, Tyler?" she mouths, brushing hair out of her face.

I jerk my head toward the desk. "There are illegal drugs in here," I say as quietly as I can next to her ear.

Her mouth parts and I push her down until she's practically under me. I scoot us closer to the side of the couch, away from the voices carrying into the room.

"—they want it all removed. New location, same setup. Boss wants it up and running by this evening."

"The entire circuit?"

"All of it. We've got customers arriving in two hours."

"We'll need the rest of the team."

"Already on it."

I peek around the couch.

Two men stand in the middle of the room, both in suits. One guy scratches his jaw, his Blue sapphire ring glinting in the room's designer lighting. The other guy is wearing a Blue ring as well.

How did these grunts get exemplar status? Is this what Drake was talking about? Get a ring and you're on the fast track?

Fuck. There's some sketchy stuff going on around here, and I don't want these guys realizing we know. The worst-case scenarios are flying around in my brain like missiles. If whoever is in charge pinned all of the casino's illegal activities on Drake, who's no longer here, what would they do to Mira? I'll walk away from this place no harm done, but Mira believes she needs this job.

We need to leave without them seeing us. No way am I risking Mira being discovered.

I nudge her to scoot up next to me, holding my finger to my lips.

"If they're here, it can't be wrong that we are. Why don't we just walk out?" she whispers, so only I can hear.

I shake my head fervently and grab her wrist, waiting for the right moment.

The desk is the first place the men box up. A bellman comes to the door and takes the boxes away.

"When are the others arriving?" one of them asks.

"Few minutes," the other guy says. "Team members are already at the new location setting up."

They walk into the sex room, and I pull Mira up with me.

More people will be coming soon and it will be harder to get away unseen. This is our chance. I push her toward the door. She doesn't need much encouragement, and we make it there undetected, but I realize the flaw in my plan.

I lean down, my lips pressed to Mira's ear. "When I open it, they'll hear." The locking mechanism of the hotel doors is loud. "Run to the right as soon as you're out."

Mira nods, her face expressionless, though the base of her throat throbs to the pace of a fast pulse.

Clutching the handle, I open the door as quietly as possible. There's a light click and I shove Mira out, following close behind. I don't bother to silence the door closing. The automatic lock will be loud no matter what I do.

I've been in and out of Blue hotel rooms for one reason

or another often enough these past few weeks to know there's no way to leave a room silently. The weight of the door, the suction of the HVAC system, the locking mechanism—they all combine to make certain the door shuts soundly and, unfortunately, with *lots* of sound.

Once outside, I catch up to Mira. The end of the hall has a housekeeping closet, like most guest floors. It's late in the evening and the majority of the housekeeping staff is gone for the night. I slip my universal key card in the door slot and pull Mira into the closet with me.

My eyes adjust to the dark and her gaze clings to my face. "Why aren't we going somewhere?" she asks. "Shouldn't we make a run for it?"

"Security cameras. In the elevators and emergency stairwells. If we stay here and wait for more people to fill the floor, the bellman, guests, the team members those guys are waiting for, they might assume the sound of the door closing was someone else. It's the best chance we've got. We go out now, and they'll know it was us in there."

"And you think that's dangerous?"

"There were syringes and pills stockpiled in the desk. Whatever went on in there, it wasn't legal. I don't trust those men. They wouldn't lay a hand on you while I'm with you, I'd make damn sure of that, but in the future? When I'm not around? What if they're like Drake? And what about their connections? More idiots like the ones who found you in the woods?" I shake my head. "I don't like it, Mira. I won't risk it. This might make me sound insane, but I'm beginning to agree with Drake. I think whoever is in charge used him as a scapegoat to cover up illegal things at the casino. Drake is guilty for the assaults, but he's not running the *Fifty Shades* suite. Someone else is."

"You're right. They talked about moving the suite, not removing it."

"And the rings. Remember Drake shouting his nonsense about the rings?" She nods. "Both of those men wore them. I think"—my suspicions are stacking, and they're out there, but—"I think they might be covering their tracks now that Drake's in custody."

I scrub my face and press my ear to the door. The sound of another door opening and closing echoes down the hall. Voices drift, growing more distant, as if whoever it was is moving farther away.

"The rings," I say, and turn to her. "What do you know about them?"

"They're for good performance. I overheard people in the break room talking about it one day."

"That's what I've heard too, but do you think they could represent more? Like, if certain people were involved in something illegal at the casino, those rings might be their secret handshake? 'Wear a ring and you're on the inside' sort of thing?"

"Tyler, you're scaring me."

And Mira doesn't scare easily. I grab her hand and pull her into my arms. "Sorry. It'll be okay." I run my palm over her silky hair. "We just have to lie low for a bit."

She looks up, her beautiful eyes searching my face. "What about tonight? The event? I can't let Hayden down."

"We'll only stay in here for a bit. An hour, maybe two. We could exit and pretend we snuck off in here to..." I quirk my brows a couple of times.

"Oh sure, so someone can see us and fire me?"

"Do you really want to work at Blue after what we just witnessed?"

She closes her eyes. "I don't know. I love working with Hayden. I feel needed, valued."

I stare at her lips. "I value you." I run my hands up her neck, cradling her face. "I need you."

"Tyler, we can't—"

I bring my mouth down and kiss her, because this place is more dangerous than I imagined when Mira started working here. And because I don't want to tell her what to do, but I'm afraid of her getting hurt. She's so small, fragile in a way she doesn't show most people. I want to protect her. Care for her.

Whatever protest she was about to give disappears. She runs her hands up my neck and grabs my hair, parting her mouth for me. "Don't do that," she mumbles against my lips.

It takes me a minute to figure out what she's referring to, the hand that's slipping down her top, my tongue teasing her mouth..."What? Kiss you?" I stare into eyes that reflect the beautiful soul I see. "Why not? I love you, Mira."

A wary look crosses her face. "That's what you said the other night."

"You don't believe me?"

Her eyes close tightly.

"Mira, look at me." I lift her chin, and her eyelids flicker open. "Do you love me the way I love you?"

She visibly swallows. "I've always loved you. There's never been anyone else. I've never—I've never been with anyone else." Her shoulders tense as if preparing for a blow.

Does she really believe *that's* going to push me away? Those words are music to a guy's ears, and only solidify what I've always known.

"I think you're the only woman I'm going to love in this lifetime, and you might as well stop fighting this, because I'm the only man for you. I'm going to kiss you and keep kissing you until you realize how much I care, and that I'm never leaving. You can kick me to the curb because you're scared, but whether we're together or not, you'll be inside my heart and head, plaguing me until I'm an old dude who can't get it up anymore. Give in now so we can at least enjoy the constant state of wood you have me in."

"Always classy," she says, but she's smiling. Mira presses her soft chest into my hand that's still resting there, her mouth slamming into my lips in a deep kiss that stops my breath and gets my heart racing.

I grab her waist, guiding her back against the shelves of toilet paper rolls. I reluctantly remove my hand from her beautiful breast, but only to reach down and slide my palms up her thighs, pushing her skirt out of the way so I can lift her and wrap her legs around my waist.

She kisses my cheekbone, nibbles my earlobe. "We can't do this here."

That little nibble shoots straight to my groin. "I beg to differ. I think we can manage."

Some place far off in my mind, there's a distant voice saying that this is the worst timing. But my immediate thoughts are that it's perfect. Never been a better moment.

"This is unprofessional." She rains kisses over my face, her fingers fiddling with the buttons of my collar. "What if those men find us?"

I grab her ass and rock against her. A breathy exhale escapes her lips. "Are you sure you want to stop? If those men haven't found us yet, they're not going to."

Her eyes are dazed for a moment, and then she kisses me hard, her hands working faster at my shirt. Stealthy fingers, pulling the hem from my waistband.

I growl against her mouth. My hands are busy holding her up, and I'm mentally configuring how to get Mira naked without the use of them, or at least partially naked, when the sound of the door opening has me freezing in place.

Shit.

We pull apart slowly, and I gently lower Mira to the ground, helping her tug her skirt in place while blocking the view with my back.

I look over my shoulder to find my boss standing in the doorway, a frown on his face.

"Not cool, man. You've done it now." He points to the small black half-orb—a surveillance camera.

In the closet? Why the hell would they—

"Mandatory. After recent events that involved an employee and a manager in a storage room on the ground floor. Brother, you're in it now."

Mira moves to my side, her head held high.

"Sorry, girly," my boss says, his gaze landing on anything but her. "Think you might need to look for another job too. Tyler, wish I could keep you, man, but this isn't something they'll let me brush under the rug. Come on down to the executive floor. You've both got people who want to see you."

Chapter Thirty

Mira

Tyler and the guy he works with escort me to Hayden's office, and I knock on the door.

"Come in," Hayden says.

I walk inside to find Hayden with her elbows on the desk, her head in her hands. She looks up and waves off Tyler and the other guard.

Tyler gives me a small smile of reassurance before his boss closes the door.

"Really, Mira?" Hayden shakes her head, a lock of dark blonde hair falling over one eye. "What were you thinking?"

"Tyler and I..."

We what? We're a thing? We've known each other for ages, so it's okay for us to hook up in a housekeeping closet? What the hell *was* I thinking?

Haden waves her hand. "I don't want to hear it. I have to let you go, Mira." She run her fingers through her hair and holds her head. "But I don't get it. Couldn't you take it outside, do it on your own time? Why here?"

"We—it's not the way it seems. I mean, it is. I've been trying to take things slow with Tyler, but then those men came into the suite. I was scared and Tyler was comforting me...I'm making it sound worse, aren't I?"

Hayden holds up her hand. "Back up. What men?"

"The last suite you sent me to. The one you tacked on to the list. There are illegal drugs in there, Hayden."

Hayden stands and rounds her desk, plopping into the seat beside me, her face serious. "What are you talking about?"

I take a deep breath to calm my nerves. I've lost my job. Nothing I tell her will change that. Not that I'm responsible for what I saw in the suite. In fact, Tyler made a good point. I don't need this in my life. The things Blue Casino is involved in—the drugs, and who knows what else? What if what goes on in that sex suite isn't consensual?

"Security amped up their personnel for the festival. Tyler's team could spare him, so he joined me on my errands to the suites. I guess he didn't want me going alone after my confrontation with Drake."

"I heard about that." She shakes her head. "I'm so sorry he came after you. That man is insane and he isn't coming back. I received verbal confirmation from the CEO. Even if Drake gets off legally, which I highly doubt he will, Blue Casino already fired him."

That's all well and good, but after what I saw tonight... "Drake is crazy and horrible, but what if there are others? People more powerful than he was who are using the casino as a shield? You told me early on that you didn't trust your coworkers. I'm wondering if the drama around Drake's arrest might also be some kind of smoke and mirrors to hide other things going on at the casino."

Hayden's phone buzzes and she checks the number.

"I'm not sure I understand what you're saying, Mira." She types out a text. "As far as I'm concerned, we had a psychopath in a leadership position who manipulated others and took advantage of young women. He's gone and we can move on now."

Hayden sets her phone down. "I don't like the men Drake worked with, but they haven't caused me more than minor irritation so far. It's baseless for me to assume they are like Drake."

"What about the drugs?"

"If the celebrities in the suites bring in their own—"

"No. This wasn't a celebrity suite. It had a built-in sex room, plus stores of drugs and hypodermic needles. It was a permanent setup. And when the men came in with the Blue Casino signet rings, they talked about relocating it—"

"*What?*" Her body goes completely still.

"Tyler found the drugs and was trying to get me out of there when two men showed up. We hid behind furniture and listened to them talk. They were packing up like crazy, with the intent to relocate everything to another room by this evening. They seemed concerned about a breach. Maybe because of the Drake situation?"

"Fucking hell." Hayden slams her fist on her desk.

Whoa, never heard Hayden swear before. But, yeah, F-bombs are in order.

"Did Jessie know about this place?" Hayden isn't looking at me. She's staring away as if thinking out loud.

Jessie must have known since she had a folder for the suite in her office.

"I'll leave, Hayden." I stand. "You've got a lot to deal with, and I've made this night worse. I'm so embarrassed about the closet. All I can say is that I was freaked out and Tyler was comforting me and, well, we got a little *too* comfortable. I'll fill out whatever forms you need me to and pick up my things another day, when the casino isn't so crazy with the festival. I'm really sorry about tonight."

"No." Hayden shakes her head. "Don't go. Screw this place. So you kissed your boyfriend."

"He's not my—"

"Who hasn't made out in a storage room?"

"Um, o-kay?" That's too much information about my conservative, put-together boss.

"I need you tonight. I'll talk to security. Make sure they keep this between us. And if they don't, I'll talk to management and convince them it's in their best interest not to piss me off."

"Whoa. Like blackmail? Hayden, this is crazy. You could quit. Blue Casino is possibly dangerous, and definitely unhealthy. Believe me when I say I know a thing or two about unhealthy."

She stands and paces the room. "No way. I'm not running this time. I'm going to stay and fight." Hayden stops and faces me. "Are you with me?"

* * *

In a way, Hayden is right. Why let these guys win? I've done nothing wrong. Well, okay, making out in the closet was not cool, but it's nothing compared to the depravity going on at Blue.

I have no idea what Hayden was talking about when she said she wasn't going to run this time. Has she run from this sort of thing before? I don't get her determination to work at Blue Casino and see this thing through, but I love working with her and she asked me to stay. So I did.

The rest of the evening was a blur of errand-running

and schmoozing with vendors, and even some celebrities performing that night. I didn't see Tyler again, but then he doesn't work for Hayden, and I'm pretty sure his boss was serious about letting him go.

It's five in the morning and I'm just getting back. I Ubered it home, since Tyler drove me in to work. I exit the car and wobble up the gravel driveway barefoot. The gravel is hard on my feet, but not as hard as twelve hours in heels. I've lost all feeling in my right big toe.

A smile fills my face as I slide the key quietly into the lock. Tyler and I have traded off fighting this thing between us, and the dam finally burst in a happy-to-be-alive moment in the dark. What he said about me being the only woman he's going to love was so Tyler, and so totally wonderful. I got a little carried away in that closet, but it felt good to let go. Tyler has been showing me in small and large ways he's here for me, and I finally get it.

It's turning light out, but Tyler won't be awake at this hour. I wish I wasn't awake. Better yet, I wish I were curled up next to him. I actually feel like I might be sleepwalking, my head is so fuzzy from exhaustion.

I squeeze the handle to open the door, but the door swings open for me. Tyler is standing on the other side, fully clothed.

"Hey," I say, confused but happy to see him, a smile forming on my face—until I notice the worried look in his eyes. "Is everything okay?"

He doesn't say anything. He grabs my shoes from my hands and closes the door behind me. And then I realize what I glimpsed as I exited the Uber. The old car I've seen my mom drive in was parked on the street in front of our cabin. I was so out of it when the Uber dropped me off, it barely registered.

But it's not my mom sitting on the couch, it's her latest boyfriend. "What's going on?" I ask Tyler. "Where's my mom?"

Billy—Willy? Crap, I don't remember his name, they all run together after a while—stands nervously, setting his beer on the coffee table. Beer at 5 a.m.? Of course. This is my mom's boyfriend, after all. "Hi, Mira. Sorry to catch you so early—uh, late. Been here waitin' for ya. Got some bad news."

Tyler wraps his arm around my waist, his palm warm and a bit clammy on the side of my stomach. His hand is shaking.

I glance up to see worry and tension filling his face.

My heart speeds up and my throat goes dry. The 1970s clock with an orange and yellow rooster ticks loudly above the kitchen table.

My mom isn't here...Where is my mom?

I shake my head. *No.* No, no, no.

"Your mom," Billy/Willy says, "she took a nap and passed in her sleep yesterday."

Chapter Thirty-One

"Was a peaceful way to go," my mother's boyfriend tells me. "Weakened heart, the doctor said." Willy, Billy—*whatever*—shifts his feet. "I'm sorry to bring such sad news. I knew you'd want to know right away. Been keeping Tyler company until you got home."

I swallow, my chest rising on a shaky inhale. "Just tell me one thing. All this time, the money I've been giving her, was it for drugs?"

Did I help put my mother in an early grave?

My mom's boyfriend glances down. "Some, but she was living on scraps. You kept her fed. Wish I had been better about caring for her, but the itch got to me too."

My hands are cold, shaking. I look down and stare at them. "Thank you for coming," I say, going on automatic. "Do you need anything? Food or...?"

"Naw, I'm good. I'll just—" He grabs his beer and walks toward the door. He stops a foot away and pulls out an envelope from his back pocket. It's folded in half, the edges gray from dirt. "Found this in her things. Think she wanted you to have it."

I stare at the envelope that Tyler takes for me, because I can't seem to move my arms.

Tyler mumbles something to the guy and walks him to the door.

A moment later, I'm being wrapped in an afghan. Tyler picks me up and cradles me in his strong arms. He sinks onto the couch, and my body molds to his.

I think I should cry, but my tear ducts aren't working, or my facial muscles. I am frozen.

We sit like that for what seems like hours.

I must fall asleep, because the next thing I know, Tyler is gently setting me aside, re-tucking the blanket around me. He goes to the front door and pulls it from the sticky jamb. Lewis is on the other side. And he looks a mess. His hair is standing on end—which is so not him. Tyler's the one with the messy hair that I love.

"Mira," Lewis says, and crouches beside the couch where I'm curled in the fetal position. "I heard. I'm so sorry. For everything. I should have talked to you sooner. I was worried about your relationship with your mom and I didn't handle it well. I thought it would be you instead of…"

"You thought I'd die first."

He nods.

Deep down, I thought I would die first too. I was supposed to die in those woods, or by the hand of one of my mom's abusive boyfriends. I don't know how to deal with this new reality. It feels no less awful.

Gen and Lewis stay the night in the bedroom, and Tyler and I sleep on the couch because I have no energy to move from where I am. Day turns into night and night day, but my internal clock is off. I am fully awake in the evening and doze during the day while visitors come and go. John and Becky bring food. Nessa and Zach are here, then gone, then back again. I can't keep track. My brain is as cold and slow as my hands. And the whole time, Tyler holds me. When I'm not cradled on his lap, I am tucked next to his side. If anyone notices, they don't say anything.

On day three, or four, I'm not really sure, I take a shower. I stand under the warm stream and the heat loosens the fist that's had a grip on my chest since my mother's boyfriend shared the news. Warmth pools around my heart, my throat goes salty and dry. Tears begin to pour from my eyes. A keening sound pierces my ears. Coming from me?

I can't breathe. I am gasping and choking from the tears and the shower water sluicing down my face.

A loud pop sounds outside the shower curtain. The bathroom door handle being busted off. Tyler walks in and shuts off the water, wrapping me in a towel. He carries me out of the bathroom and up the ladder to the loft, one hand under my knees as I cling to his shoulders and neck. He tucks me under the covers of his bed and curls his body around me, while I weep for a mother who never loved me.

Who left me.

For good.

* * *

THE NEXT MORNING, I wake to light streaming through the small window in Tyler's loft. His face is unshaven, and he looks as if he's gone a good week without a razor. His short beard is red.

I take in the smooth skin above the facial hair, the way his dark lashes fan out above his high cheekbones. He is beautiful.

I kiss his nose.

A thick arm tightens around my waist and his eyes

flicker open. Tyler raises a hand to my forehead, brushing the hair back. "I'm sorry," he says.

I cuddle in closer and Tyler holds me tight. He said I wasn't alone, that I had other people besides my mom and Lewis's family, but it wasn't until I lost my mom that I believed it.

I pull back and look into eyes that hold a touch of shadow beneath, as if he hasn't had much sleep either. "Let's get dressed and take a walk."

Tyler makes me toast and eggs while I change into jeans, flip-flops, and a light sweater. We eat breakfast, then walk into the bright morning light. I touch the envelope I tucked in the back pocket of my jeans as we head for the lake a few blocks away.

Birds chirp, a few cars pass us on their way to places unknown. The world should be a dark place, but it isn't. The sky is bright blue, the crisp scent of the pine and soil cleansing the air. There is laughter as we near a busy intersection. Life goes on, and it seems happier than the one I've lived in.

We cross the boulevard that divides the lake from the strip, and I walk down a flight of stairs to the sand. A portion of an old cement pylon rests at the foot of the stairs and I climb on top, staring out at the lake, mesmerized by its constancy. Tyler stands beside the pylon, picking up rocks and tossing them into the shallow waves.

I pull out the envelope from my mother and open it. Tyler climbs up and sits beside me, close, but not crowding, his gaze on the water.

I unfold lined paper it appears my mother tore from a spiral notepad.

Mira,

This has been gnawing at me, but I never can get it out when you're around, so I'm saying it here. Maybe one day you'll find it. I wish you could have known your daddy. He was a handsome son of a bitch, a charmer. And one day he was mine. I never felt so good as when your daddy was mine. I was happy when you were born, but then your daddy left me. You're not a bad kid, just a reminder of losing him. But you've been there for me, and that's more than I can say for most people in this rotten world. You're different, girl. A good kid.

Mom

My breath hitches. Tyler's arm snakes around my shoulders, holding me up. I fold the note carefully and place it in the envelope.

All these years I thought I wanted my mom's love, and I did, but this means something too. I'm different from her and my father. Even my mother acknowledged it, and for once she didn't seem disappointed.

"Tyler, I think I want to be alone for a couple of days."

He stares down at me, confused. "Why? I don't want to leave you."

I look out at the lake, the pain, the sadness eating at me. At the same time, I am filled with a sense of relief, which frightens me. I don't know what it means.

"You aren't leaving me. I just need to be alone for a little bit."

He leans down and hugs me tight. "If that's what you want."

I'm not sure what's going on in my head, which is why I think I need this. "It is."

Chapter Thirty-Two

As soon as Tyler grabbed his things and moved out of the cabin, I returned to work. I can't say I didn't experience a flash of panic at seeing him leave the house, but it felt right to have this time to myself. I've paid back nearly all the money I owe the loan shark, and the man seems content to let me return the rest in a couple of weeks with my next paycheck.

I agreed to let Lewis make the final cash deliveries, because honestly, he's been a total pain-in-the-ass big brother over the entire thing. Lewis feels helpless and guilty for walking out when I told him the real reason I was in debt. He was hurt that I'd lied to him. Then my mother passed. He felt like he'd taken his frustration too far and wasn't there for me when I needed him. He's being overly protective now. He and Tyler have hounded me to talk to the police about Denim Jacket guy who worked at Blue, so I agreed. I will soon. Right now, I'm seeing my therapist and working, and trying to figure out what it means to not care for or worry over my mother anymore.

It's been almost three days since Tyler moved out. I've

cried, talked to my therapist for hours, and even written down my feelings about losing my mom. SuperMom and I have had poker marathons where we messaged and she comforted me over the loss. What I've learned from all of this? I'm less burdened, and that's why I feel guilty. I'll always wonder if I could have done more for my mom. No matter what she did or didn't do, I miss her. Miss what we could have had if she'd been clean.

I've been slowly building the life I want to lead these past few months, and it's helped me get through this time. Lewis, John, and Becky are my family. Logically, I knew it—but in my heart, I never believed it until now. Most surprising of all, Tyler has been there for me in ways no other person has. Which has me thinking a lot about our relationship and where I want to go from here.

The music festival weekend was a huge success, despite the many obstacles and my absence for a few days, which left Hayden putting out fires. By the time she checked out the sex suite, the place had been cleared. The file she'd found in Jessie's office on the *Fifty Shades* suite also miraculously disappeared. Hayden's been meticulously collecting information ever since on the Blue employees involved in the suite, and keeping what she finds close to her chest. She's waiting until she has enough information to go to the police. Right now, there is no sex suite, no illicit drugs. Nothing on paper, anyway. But knowing how dogged my boss can be, I doubt that will remain true for long.

On the plus side, we've hired a new employee and he starts today. So, yay for me and Hayden. We might get back to something resembling a forty- to fifty-hour workweek if this person pans out.

I walk toward Hayden's office with paperwork for the

new hire. There's a man standing at the door, staring inside, his expression amused, interested.

I walk up to him and peek around the corner.

Hayden is crawling on the ground in a fitted skirt, her cute butt in the air.

So that's what he's staring at.

Before I can rap lightly on the door to warn Hayden she has visitors, the guy beside me clears his throat.

Hayden's tawny head swings around, one silky lock falling across her eye as she looks behind her. "Oh. Excuse me." She climbs to her feet. "I was just, uh, yes, well. I dropped something. My apologies." She smooths her skirt and attempts a professional expression.

I step inside, holding back a smile. I hand Hayden the employment documents. Her eyes flicker behind me and she discreetly mouths, *"Shit,"* which I take to mean she's embarrassed she got caught with her ass in the air.

This is why I love my boss. She's all class and professionalism, but deep down she's a girl's girl.

I scrunch my face and give a subtle head shake to let her know it's probably fine. I don't think the guy minded ogling her ass, considering he stood there staring at it long enough.

Putting on my professional voice, I say, "If you could please sign these by the end of the day, that would be great. They're for the new hospitality assistant we hired."

"And that would be me," the man standing in the doorway says, his deep baritone, cultured and smooth, ringing out.

"Yes." Hayden's voice is a tad high. "Mira, meet Adam Cade. He'll work with Jessie."

Jessie is our hospitality manager who was out for appendectomy surgery. She only just returned, but is in good health. She's also one of the employees Hayden suspects is involved in the drug ring at the casino.

I glance at Adam, this time taking him in. He's tall like Tyler, with wide shoulders. He has on a navy suit and tie, his dark brown hair trimmed short on the sides and slightly longer on top. He's still wearing the smirk he had on while staring at Hayden's ass. And she's still blushing.

Hmmm.

Adam has navy eyes to match his suit and a slightly angular nose. His skin is smooth and he has a chiseled jawline. In short, he's a total babe, and he's looking at Hayden like he wants a piece of that.

He is polished and classy in the way he carries himself. If I had to guess, I would say he should be running the hospitality department, not assisting in it. But what do I know? Hayden hired me for a position I wasn't qualified for.

I greet Adam and take my leave, so Hayden can introduce him to Jessie and his new job duties.

Hayden has completely forgotten the housekeeping closet debacle and tells me I exceeded her expectations as her assistant, which in a way I was forced into with the staffing shortage. The extra workload, however, pushed me beyond my skill set. I'm a quick learner, and Hayden thinks I have upward potential. I'm taking things one step at a time, considering the sketchy crap going on at Blue, but for once, I feel like I'm being challenged at work. I really like that. Plus, I love my boss.

I've needed these last few days to get my head on straight, as Tyler would say, but I miss him so much. I think about him several times a day.

Fine, every hour.

I heard from Gen that Tyler just got offered a job at the community college in town, teaching biology in the fall.

He's been crashing with his friend Phil, who got dumped by his live-in girlfriend. Gen says Tyler seems to be doing fine.

True to his word, Tyler gave me space and hasn't called or stopped by. He didn't seem angry when I asked him to leave, so I have to assume he's staying away for me.

I just hope he still wants to come back.

With my head finally above water these last couple of days since my mother's passing, the thought of losing Tyler makes me incredibly sad. I know now that I'd survive the dreaded "alone," but I want him in my life. If we ended up friends, I would take that, but I want so much more.

This wanting of Tyler is the one constant in my life. It doesn't fade or ebb, it just is.

On my way home from work, I decide to change my clothes and visit. I could call him, but I want to make the extra effort. He was there for me when my mom died. He's been there for me since the beginning when he found me in the woods, if I really think about it. He lived with me despite his misgivings. He got a freaking job at the casino to look out for me when he didn't think it would be a safe environment. In so many ways, his actions have shown how much I mean to him.

I shove open the front door, anxious to change and visit him now that I've made the decision, and freeze on the threshold, my hand on the knob.

Tyler is standing in the middle of the living room, but instead of looking worried the way he did after my mom died, his gaze is steady and intent. "Do you mind? I still have a key. I let myself in."

I glance back. Tyler's car isn't in the driveway, or on the street. "Where's your truck?" I step inside and close the door.

"In the shop. I'm getting new tires. Phil dropped me

off." He absently tugs at his shirt as though it's hot in here, when it's actually cool.

He studies my movements as I set my purse on the counter and kick off my shoes. I'm curious about why he came, but instead I blurt, "I missed you."

Tyler swallows and takes a step toward me.

"I was coming home to change and see you." I clench my hands at my sides, nervous, though I'm not sure why. He wouldn't be here if he didn't care.

"I want to be with you, Tyler, but I'll take whatever you're willing to give. I just don't want you out of my life. I hope you don't think I was pushing you away when I asked for a few days to myself." My face scrunches as I think back. "It didn't feel like that's what I was doing, but it may have come across that way. I was so upset after my mom passed... and relieved, which made me feel like a terrible person. I needed time to figure myself out."

Tyler takes another step closer until we're only a foot apart. "There is no better person than you, Mira."

I look up into his eyes. "How can you say that? I piss you off more than anyone."

He gives me a cocky grin. "But I like it."

"So—we're okay?"

"If you think you can look past it when I'm a dumbass. I promise to make it up to you when I screw up." His brows quirk suggestively.

I press my lips together, holding back the overwhelming happiness filling my heart, but Tyler is having none of it. He wraps his arms around me and touches my hair, my face. His lips are on mine and we're kissing like it's been years instead of a few days since we've seen each other.

And maybe it has been years since we let it all go, the doubts, the fears, and really opened up. I was pushing him away, or he was pushing me away; we've never been on the same page emotionally.

Until now.

Tyler's mouth trails down my neck and I slip my hands under his T-shirt, heat burning beneath my skin. It's terrifying and thrilling all at the same time to realize we are finally together.

Tyler pulls back, his hands slipping to my bottom. "If we're not holding back anymore, then you should know, you're my girlfriend."

"Oh yeah?" I chuckle and he squeezes my ass, returning his lips to the skin at the base of my neck.

"Mm-hmm. Phil knows, ask him."

"Were you going to let me know?"

"Eventually," he mumbles against my skin. His hands slip beneath my slim skirt. "Have I told you how much I like you in these little tight skirts you wear to work?"

"No, but I think I can feel it," I say, and press against the bulge in his jeans.

"As much as I like seeing you in the skirt, I think I'd rather see you without it on."

I lift Tyler's shirt over his head, smiling at his muscled chest and running my hands over it. He attempts to unzip my skirt and pull me toward the couch at the same time.

Something goes wrong. We're kissing, and touching, and tugging at clothing. The next thing I know, I'm falling forward, and Tyler's falling over the end of the couch, his arms cradling me before we land. Hard. On the ground. He lets out a light grunt on impact.

"Oops," he says with a chuckle, and looks up at the couch. "I missed." His hands move back to where they were on my underwear, my skirt hiked up because he got impatient with the zipper.

I'm busy unfastening his pants when I sense a jerk at my hip and hear a tear. "Did you just rip my panties?"

"Shhh," he says, and takes my mouth with his. His hand slips to the place pulsating between my legs, fingers expertly working their magic.

I moan, and start shoving down his jeans with my hands, then with my feet when I get them low enough.

With his jeans around his ankles, boxer briefs out of the way, I grab him and stroke.

Tyler moans, his strong arm lifting me up so I'm hovering above him, that finger never stopping its delicate dance. I lower myself, leaning over to gently bite his lip, because he's hot and the sensation of the tip of him entering me is killing me in all the best ways.

His finger doesn't stop its gentle swirl where we're connected. He's a multitasker, and God, do I appreciate it.

Tyler's head tips back as my pace quickens, my breathing growing ragged. I am *soooo* close. It's been too long, and I missed him. Missed this.

And then I'm there.

Exploding, gasping, moaning. My belly clenching and heaving out of control.

I'm no expert on orgasms, but I'm pretty sure this one is an eleven on a scale of one to ten.

As soon as my senses return to earth, Tyler's tempo increases, his finger shifting from its lovely place at the core of my pleasure to my hip, where he leverages with both hands to drive into me.

My inner walls clench at the sensation of him growing bigger. He feels so good.

Tyler tenses, his grip on my hips tightening, a deep, guttural groan erupting from him.

He stares reverently into my eyes, his breathing heavy.

He runs his hands up my sides, pulling me down until I'm lying flat on his chest, the sound of his heartbeat a rapid drum beneath my ear.

That's when I realize we're halfway on the kitchen vinyl and halfway on the living room rug. Or Tyler is.

I'm on top of my hot boyfriend. And truly happy.

It's Tyler, and it's me in a good place, despite all that's happened. It's both of us.

Together.

* * *

Tyler

"You ruined my panties," Mira says.

I kiss her forehead, tightening my hold on her as she lies on top of me. "Sorry."

She looks up and raises her brow.

"Okay, not really. It was fun tearing them off."

She yawns like she's going to fall asleep. On the living room floor—kitchen—whatever, somewhere that's hard and not at all comfortable. Which I can't seem to care about right now, because I'm still inside her, and there is no better place to be. "Guess we got carried away, huh?"

She rests her head on her hands folded above my chest. "Yeah."

"I should mention, in the heat of things, and because I wasn't expecting this, I sort of forgot..."

Her eyes fill with recognition. "I've been on the pill for years to regulate my period. And I have a clean bill of health, because, you know, you were my one and only."

"Same here. About the healthy part. And as far as me being your one and only sexual experience, I'm not going to lie, it makes my chest swell with pride." I grin cockily, and she starts to protest, because I'm an arrogant bastard. "And we have a lot of making up to do to get you up to speed. So we better"—I waggle my brows—"often. Like a few times a day. To catch you up."

I think she's going to hit me, but her gaze turns serious. "I think I'm going to like having a boyfriend. I love you, Tyler."

Her sweet voice and the sincerity behind her words choke me up. She's the only one who ever reached my heart.

To lighten the mood before I lose it, I counter, "No, *I* love *you*. Long before you loved me."

Her mouth parts. "If there's anyone with a decade of unrequited love, it's me. I loved you before you ever knew my name."

"How do you figure that?"

She tells me the story about the bullies in junior high school. "Huh," I say, as if I don't remember the day I met her. "That was you? I thought you looked familiar. You were so different in junior high. You looked like a small child next to those other girls."

She pushes up on my chest, indignant. "Excuse me?" she says. I love it when she gets riled. I hold her so she can't escape, our bodies still connected. I could go for round two right now. "You were only a year older, and I was small for my age. I've developed since then."

I let out a growl and drag her mouth to mine, kissing her with tongue and teeth. "Tell me about it. Can you feel how much I realize that?"

"You mean, can I feel that rod you've got inside me that's ready to go?" I shift her so she slides up and down, and we both sigh. "Tyler, is this normal for you to be able to..."

"Nah, I just have a lot of pent-up lust for you. Should go away in twenty, forty years."

"What, and then you won't want me anymore?" She picks up her rhythm. Must not be too upset.

I cradle her face, my hand slipping to her breast, because my palm has a mind of its own. "I'll always want you, even when I'm old and can't get it up, remember? It's my curse to love you."

Her hips freeze. "Curse!"

"My curse that I'll love you forever, no matter if you push me away or not." I pull her to my chest, lift her hips at an angle, and drag her back down. Her head tips back on a moan. "So don't push me away, okay? I may make mistakes, but you're the only girl for me. When you push me away it makes me cranky. For like, half a decade."

"Okay," she says dazedly.

And then all conversation stops because my mind goes numb with the pleasure this girl gives me, inside and out.

Chapter Thirty-Three

Mira grabs her torn undies, tucked partway beneath the couch from last night, and holds them up. "These were my favorites."

I hand her the to-go mug of tea I made her (yes, I'm whipped, I freely admit it), and slip on my shoes. We're about to head over to Jaeg's place for a Sunday movie with him and my sister. "I'll buy you another pair. Hey, you know, I don't think I'll mind shopping for your unmentionables. I could go with you into the dressing room and—"

"Stop right there. No way. We're done with closet make-out sessions. And what do you mean, you don't like shopping? You were so good about it when you took me to buy work clothes."

I look over sheepishly. "I hate shopping."

Her expression is blank, and then she smiles. "You did it for me. You are a secret softy, Tyler Morgan."

I tuck her beautiful dark hair behind her ear, bringing her to my chest with my arm. "For you I am. I would do anything for you. Go shopping, hunt down bad guys, stare at algebra equations until I'm cross-eyed. It's a condition I have, but I like it. I think I'll roll with it."

Her face twists in an indignant pout I'd like to take a bite out of. "You make me sound like a disease."

"Mmmm, more like a hot and feisty obsession I don't want to part with. You are the best thing I've ever had in my life, even when I didn't know I had you. And for the record, I did remember you from when we were younger."

She tilts her head, her eyes doubtful as she pulls the strap of her purse across her chest between us without tilting her mug. "In junior high? No, you didn't."

"Yep, had my own crush on the fiery, dark-haired girl with caramel eyes who tried to kick a girl twice her size."

"You did not," she says, but I sense the hesitation in her voice.

"Did."

"If that's the case, then why didn't you say something when we studied together?"

"Didn't want to lay all my cards on the table. Had to make you work for it."

She smacks me in the chest with the flat of her hand, but then stretches up and gives me a scorching kiss.

There is nothing about Mira that has ever been forgettable, not even when we were young. I thought that was my curse, but it's really my fortune.

"Oh, wait," she says, and pulls out of my arms, walking toward the back door. "I told Cali I'd bring a few of the giant pine cones we have in our backyard. She's making some kind of fall centerpiece."

"You mean like for a dining table? I thought Jaeg did the cooking?"

Mira looks up, exasperated. "What does a centerpiece have to do with food?"

I roll my eyes. As if that makes sense. *Girls.* "I'll meet you in the car."

"Okay," she says, and slips out the back door.

My car is still in the shop, so I walk toward Mira's truck, her keys in hand.

A car down the street catches my eye. It's sleek, black, and parked at an odd angle, as if the driver got out in a hurry.

I turn around and stare at the fence to the backyard. There's no sound and Mira has only been gone a minute, but something feels off.

"Mira?" I call. "Everything okay?"

She doesn't answer and my heart begins to race. The hair on the back of my neck stands at attention, my muscles tensing. I run to the gate leading to the backyard and almost bust it down in my attempt to get past the latch.

I hear the sound of feet scuffling, then Mira's whimper. I tear around the side of the house—to find a vision that nearly stops my heart.

The mug I gave Mira is on its side on the ground, and Mira's back is pinned to the chest of the asshole who beat her, his arm locked around her throat. He's leaning over her, his back to me.

I don't consider stealth. I don't think of anything except crippling the bastard.

I sweep up the biggest log within reach on my way to them and swing it at the back of his skull.

His head whips forward and he grunts, but his grip doesn't loosen on my girl. I whack him again, this time nailing him square in the temple.

Asshole goes down, tumbling Mira with him. He doesn't move.

I haul Mira up by the waist and carry her off to the side. I touch her neck, her face. "Are you okay?"

"H-he was angry—said I got him sent out of town." Her face is red and blotchy, her expression confused. "I told him I've been making my payments."

I look over at the guy on the ground and pull out my cell phone. Mira buries her face in my chest. "I paid off the man you owe. This guy has no business being here. And even if he did, he has no right to touch you."

I call 911 and describe the incident.

"What do you mean you paid him off?" she asks when I tuck my phone back.

I glance away, worried how she'll take this. Mira doesn't appreciate me telling her what to do, and this falls in the overbearing category. But I'm not letting anyone hurt her again.

Still, I probably should have mentioned it sooner. "I didn't want you to worry about debt after your mother died. You'd paid most of it off. I paid the last bit. The money you gave Lewis went into a savings account for you."

She stares at me, her face pale, throat red from the clutch hold that asshole had on her. She hasn't cried once during this ordeal, proof she's hard as nails. "Oh."

"*Oh?* You're not angry?" I glance to make sure the guy is still out cold. Just in case, I guide Mira toward the front of the house. I'd feel better waiting for the police out in the open.

"I'm not angry," she says as she walks beside me, her body tucked up close to mine. "You were being thoughtful. And to tell the truth, I'm tired of owing that money. I'll pay you back, of course, but it's nice to not owe that man anymore. Though in a roundabout way, he brought you to me."

Is she referring to the forest? When I found her passed out?

"Yeahhh, how's about we not attract hitmen from now on?"

She huffs out a feisty sigh, her color returning to normal. "Of course not."

I groan. Why do I think this won't be the last time Mira puts herself in the line of fire?

I have my hands full. And I wouldn't have it any other way.

* * *

Mira

TYLER and I never made it to Jaeger's. We spent the afternoon at the police station, where I finally told them about Denim Jacket.

"Ms. Frasier." Sergeant Billings, the officer I spoke to after my attack in the woods, taps his pen on the desk. "You're certain this Ronald Devans is the same man who attacked you weeks ago?"

"Yes. One of them."

"And you've seen him since then? Why didn't you come forward earlier with this information?"

I'd intended to tell the police about Denim Jacket after Lewis and Tyler continued to hound me about it, but apparently not soon enough. I can't believe he staked out my house. All those times I thought I saw him I was probably correct.

I hadn't time to be as terrified as I could have been this afternoon. Because as soon as the man grabbed me, Tyler was there.

"I owed money to a man Ronald Devans worked for. In the beginning, I was worried that telling you I knew who my attacker was would cause me more trouble, but I'd reconsidered. I planned to come in, then this happened."

The officer scribbles down the name of my loan shark.

"And you said Devans was with Drake Peterson at the casino?"

I nod.

"Mr. Peterson is awaiting trial. I don't know what his connection is to Devans, but Devans has a long rap sheet, including drug possession and assault and battery. He's not walking away from this. I'm confident we'll get Devans to give up the name of the other man who attacked you as well. I'll follow up with the loan shark. It sounds like he may be involved."

Once Tyler and I return from the police station, a week passes before he lets me leave the house (i.e., our bed) for anything other than work. The attack freaked him out. It freaked me out. Yes, we had sex. Okay, a lot of sex, but we also spent hours just holding each other, thankful our story ended well.

Because that's what it's been. A long love story involving the boy who caught my eye in junior high and never left my thoughts and heart. I will forever be grateful Tyler found me.

And maybe, just a little, I found him too. The real Tyler, the one he buried all those years ago, but who came back to me.

Again.

Epilogue

Mira
Two months later

Tyler and I stand on the cement stoop of a single-story house in a middle-income Carson City neighborhood.

I am so nervous, I might hyperventilate.

The door creaks open and a pretty, middle-aged woman with bright red hair stands on the other side.

Tyler rests his hand on my lower back. "Hey, Mom." He leans forward and kisses her cheek. "This is Mira."

She lets us in, her eyes never leaving me. I feel bared, buck naked in front of this woman, when I'm wearing my warmest sweater and winter coat.

"Ah." She nods, still eyeing me. She glances at her son. "I see."

Tyler shifts nervously. "Mira's my girlfriend I've been telling you about. We went to school together in Tahoe and recently reconnected. Remember? She's the girl I tutored my junior and senior year."

Madeline Morgan's eyes shift in recognition and she nods. "Well, that explains it." She smiles brightly and gives me a warm hug. "Welcome, Mira. Nice to finally meet you."

I look at Tyler, and he shrugs, shaking his head, as if I shouldn't worry about his mother's strange comment.

"So, how did you two run into each other again?" Mrs. Morgan asks as she leads us to her backyard, where Cali and Jaeger are bundled up and drinking beers on the back patio. There's no snowfall yet, and Mrs. Morgan still has a badminton net set up.

Tyler rubs his jaw. "Yeah, well, you see, Mira was in a bad situation. She's been crashing in Cali's room."

His mom aims an intense look at him. "And where is Cali living?"

Tyler stares like a deer caught in the headlights. "With Jaeg?"

His mother's mouth twists. "Hmm, seems my daughter has some explaining to do. I don't like this, Tyler. This living together before you're married. You know what that leads to?"

She's not going to bring up sex, is she?

I glance desperately at Tyler, but he's staring at his mom, a smirk crossing his face. "Cozy living quarters?"

His mom frowns. "Nice one, son." She shakes her head, exasperated. "Babies. That's what it leads to." She points a finger at the two of us. "Keep that in mind the next time you get cozy."

I cover my face with my hands. Most embarrassing moment ever.

Here I am, meeting Tyler's mom for the first time, *as his girlfriend,* something I've only dreamt of, and it's like I'm sixteen again, getting caught sleeping with my high school crush.

A choking sound erupts from my throat, and I realize I'm laughing. A bit hysterically, to be exact.

Tyler wraps his arms around my shoulders, chuckling in my ear. "She's always like this. You'll get used to it."

I look up and smile. His gaze falters at the loving look I level at him, and he kisses me.

"Babies," his mom calls from her place in front of the barbecue.

I hide my burning face in his chest.

"Hmm," Tyler says. "I wouldn't mind seeing you with my baby in your belly." I look up, my eyes wide. His lips graze my ear. "When we're ready. But we'll be married by then."

I squeeze him around the waist and kiss his lips clumsily, which he doesn't seem to mind as his arms tighten around me.

"Enough PDA, Tyler," Cali calls. "Get over here so I can slam your shuttlecock into next year."

Jaeger rolls his eyes beside her. "Babe, you need to tone down the shit-talking."

"What?" she says. "That's how we do it."

"I know, but—" He leans forward. "You know how you are with balls."

A devilish look crosses her face. "This is a shuttlecock. But how am I with balls, Jaeger?"

He grins, tugging her chair closer to his. "Bad girl."

Cali smiles at her boyfriend, then peers up at us. "Bring it, Tyler. I'm ready for ya."

Tyler huffs out a pained sigh. "Give me a moment to whoop my sister's ass. Should take me two, maybe three minutes."

Tyler picks up a racket and Jaeger tries to give Cali pointers. I'm getting the impression that Cali super sucks and talks out of her ass. Kind of makes me like her even more. Especially when she dishes it to Tyler.

I smile and make my way to his mother. "Can I help you with anything, Mrs. Morgan?"

"Oh, sweetie, you can call me Maddie. I have a feeling we'll be getting to know each other real well. One look at my son with you and I knew you were someone special. You might even be the reason he went from a fun-loving guy to a grump his senior year."

I glance away. "I—I don't know. I mean, maybe. But I didn't mean to."

She waves my words away. "He needed a kick in the butt. That boy can be stubborn. And look how much he appreciates you now."

I smile, unable to hide how happy her words make me. "I care about him." It's a simple statement, and so incomplete when I consider my feelings for Tyler.

She grins, turning the corn on the barbecue. "Oh, I know. He wouldn't be with you if this wasn't something special. Never seen him look at a girl the way he looks at you."

"Mom"—Tyler's voice startles me, and I glance up—"quit giving away my secrets." He approaches from a few feet away.

Behind him, Cali plops onto Jaeger's lap with a frown on her face.

That was a quick ass-whooping.

"She knows you love her," his mother says. "I'm not a blind woman, and neither is she."

Tyler rolls his eyes, sending me a wink.

Maddie is right. I see it now. Tyler's love. We were both blind.

"You know, Tyler," his mother says, "now that those

Jules Barnard

royalty checks will be rolling in, you should think about buying yourself a house. Plant some roots."

"Already on it," Tyler says. "I had my real estate agent contact the owner of Cali's place. It suits me, and it's where I wrote the book." He leans closer. "And where I rediscovered my true love," he whispers in my ear.

Apparently, Tyler wasn't as lazy as everyone thought. While he was "regrouping" and living at Cali's place, he wrote a book. *The Nose Knows* is a popular science book that his agent says will be gobbled up by laypeople and biologists alike. Some professors may even make it assigned reading for students. Apparently, it looks at new research on olfactory senses and attraction and is highly entertaining, which for a biology text is difficult to come by. The students who have seen the manuscript are raving about it.

Tyler returned to our hometown because he needed a place to recover from his loss and guilt over what happened in Colorado, but his intellectual talents haven't been wasted. I should have known Tyler would make something of himself no matter where he landed.

"You're buying the cabin?" I say.

Tyler mentioned he was considering buying a place in Tahoe, and I knew he'd spoken to a realtor. I didn't know he was considering buying Cali's place. Which is really her old place, now that she's permanently residing at Jaeger's.

He nods, his face suddenly serious. "Is that okay? Because I can—"

I beam up at him. "It's perfect. Only"—my mouth twists as I consider the furniture—"can we get a new couch?"

Tyler tucks me close. "Are you kidding? We are buying all new furniture. That place needs to be dragged into this century."

I laugh. "You realize that will involve shopping."

"Yes, but this is for our place. For our life together."
I touch his strong jaw and he leans down to kiss me.
We were meant to be together. And now we finally are.

* * *

Dear Reader,

You may be wondering about Nessa and Zach, since I've more than hinted at a little somethin'-somethin' going on. Grab the next book in the Never Date series, ***Never Date Your Best Friend***, and discover how Nessa finally manages to get out of the friend-zone with Zack.

Xoxo,

Jules

Never Date Your Best Friend

I'm stuck in the friend zone with the hottest guy I've ever known. Oh, and he's my best friend.

Zach pushes me away the moment sparks fly, and sparks have been flying since the day we met. For some aggravating reason, he's intentionally keeping me at a distance.

The way I see it, I have two options. I can leave town and make a fresh start, or I can show Zach how right we are for each other. The problem is, one of those options has the potential to ruin the best friendship I've ever had.

But I'm considering risking it all for love.

EXCERPT

"Nessa." His voice is a strangled growl.

"This shouldn't be a big deal. You said you're not attracted to me," I remind him.

"I didn't say that."

"You said there's nothing to worry about, and that I should make myself comfortable."

"I didn't think you were gonna skinny-dip."

A RITA-nominated friends-to-lovers romance.

Grab *Never Date Your Best Friend* Now!

Also by Jules Barnard
USA Today Bestselling Author

All's Fair

Landlord Wars

Roommate Wars

Never Date Series

Never Date Your Brother's Best Friend (Book 1)

Never Date A Player (Book 2)

Never Date Your Ex (Book 3)

Never Date Your Best Friend (Book 4)

Never Date Your Enemy (Book 5)

Cade Brothers Series

Tempting Levi (Book 1)

Daring Wes (Book 2)

Seducing Bran (Book 3)

Reforming Hunt (Book 4)

About the Author

Jules Barnard is a *USA Today* bestselling author of romantic comedy and romantic fantasy. Her romantic comedies include the All's Fair, Never Date, and Cade Brothers series. She also writes romantic fantasy under J. Barnard in the Halven Rising series *Library Journal* calls "...an exciting new fantasy adventure." Whether she's writing about steamy men in Lake Tahoe or a Fae world embedded in a college campus, Jules spins addictive stories filled with heart and humor.

When she isn't in her sweatpants writing and rewarding herself with chocolate, Jules spends her time with her husband and two children in their small hometown in the Pacific Northwest. She credits herself with the ability to read while running on the treadmill or burning dinner.

Stay informed! Join Jules's newsletter for writing updates and bonus scenes: